Journal of the Alamire Foundation

■

Journal of the Alamire Foundation

∎

Volume 6 - Number 1, Spring 2014

∎

General editors:
David Burn
Katelijne Schiltz

Journal of the Alamire Foundation

■

Volume 6 - Number 1, Spring 2014

BREPOLS

The *Journal of the Alamire Foundation* is published twice a year (spring and autumn)

- **General editors:**
  David Burn
  Katelijne Schiltz
- **Editorial board:**
  Barbara Haggh
  Christian Thomas Leitmeir
  Pedro Memelsdorff
  Klaus Pietschmann
  Dorit Tanay
  Giovanni Zanovello
- **Advisory board:**
  Bonnie J. Blackburn
  M. Jennifer Bloxam
  Anna Maria Busse-Berger
  Fabrice Fitch
  Sean Gallagher
  David Hiley
  Andrew Kirkman
  Karl Kügle
  John Milsom
  Emilio Ros-Fabregas
  Rudolf Rasch
  Thomas Schmidt-Beste
  Eugeen Schreurs
  Reinhard Strohm
  Philippe Vendrix
  Rob Wegman

- **Coordinator:**
  Stratton Bull
- **Music examples:**
  Vincent Besson
- **Music font:**
  Theodor Dumitrescu (CMME)

- **Subscriptions:**
  Brepols Publishers
  Begijnhof 67
  B-2300 Turnhout (Belgium)
  Tel.: +32 14448020
  Fax: +32 14428919
  periodicals@brepols.net

- **Submissions:**
  Journal of the Alamire Foundation
  c/o Prof. Dr. David Burn
  KU Leuven – Onderzoekseenheid
  Musicologie
  Mgr. Ladeuzeplein 21, bus 5591
  B-3000 Leuven (Belgium)
  jaf@alamirefoundation.be

  Submissions to the Journal can be sent
  at any time to the address listed above.
  For further information, including the
  Journal's style-sheet, see: http://www.
  alamirefoundation.org/en/publications/
  journal-alamire-foundation.

The Alamire Foundation was founded in 1991 as a collaborative venture between the Musicology Research Unit of the University of Leuven and Musica, Impulse Centre for Music. The organization is named after Petrus Alamire, one of the most important sixteenth-century music calligraphers. The Foundation aims to create an international platform for promoting research on music in or connected to the Low Countries from the earliest documents to the end of the Ancien Regime. The Foundation hopes especially to promote dialogue between the worlds of scholarship and performance. For more information, see: http://www.alamirefoundation.org/.

ISBN: 978-2-503-55077-0
ISSN: 2032-5371
D/2014/0095/84

Table of Contents

■

Theme

■

The Alamire Complex

Guest Editor: Zoe Saunders

Introduction

■

ZOE SAUNDERS

It is fitting that the theme of this tenth issue of the *Journal of the Alamire Foundation* should focus on Petrus Alamire and the manuscripts that emanated from his 'scribal workshop(s)'. Among surviving sources of Renaissance music, the Alamire manuscripts are perhaps the most astonishing.[1] Certainly the largest coherent group of sources from the time, they comprise a complex of more than sixty choirbooks and partbooks prepared between about 1498 and 1534. The earliest group of manuscripts included under the heading 'Alamire complex' consists of manuscripts prepared between about 1498 and 1508 under the supervision of a copyist that Herbert Kellman and others call Scribe B, who has sometimes been associated with one Martin Bourgeois.[2] The Scribe B manuscripts are similar to those produced by Alamire and his colleagues and are certainly related to the later Alamire manuscripts, but they are generally of smaller dimensions and contain more compositions. Each Scribe B manuscript was copied by Scribe B or his associate (called Scribe B'), both of whom had fine handwriting. Their uniformity and decoration are sure indicators that they were prepared as presentation manuscripts. Although the Scribe B and Alamire manuscripts are grouped together as one complex based on similarities in visual appearance and repertoire, the degree of continuity between the workshops of Scribe B and Alamire remains unclear.[3]

The beautiful products of the 'scribal workshops' of Petrus Alamire and Scribe B were prepared at or around the Habsburg-Burgundian courts of Maximilian I of Austria, Philip the Fair, Margaret of Austria, Charles V, and, briefly, Mary of Hungary. The Alamire codices contain over 600 polyphonic works, with a strong emphasis on liturgical or devotional music, by three generations of leading Renaissance composers. Alamire was not only a well known music scribe, but also a composer, an instrument dealer, a diplomat, and a spy.[4] Alamire is a pseudonym derived from the solmization of the note A in different hexachords. He was born Petrus Imhoff to an important merchant family in Nuremburg, and had relocated to the Low Countries (where his family had connections) by the 1490s. He was paid for producing music manuscripts by the

---

[1] The best overview of the Alamire manuscripts is still Herbert Kellman (ed.), *The Treasury of Petrus Alamire: Music and Art in Flemish Court Manuscripts 1500-1535* (Ghent-Amsterdam, 1999). See also Bruno Bouckaert and Eugeen Schreurs (eds.), *The Burgundian-Habsburg Court Complex of Music Manuscripts (1500-1535) and the Workshop of Petrus Alamire*, Yearbook of the Alamire Foundation 5 (Leuven-Neerpelt, 2003).

[2] Herbert Kellman, 'The Origins of the Chigi Codex: The Date, Provenance, and Original Ownership of Rome, Biblioteca Vaticana, Chigiana C VIII 234', in *Journal of the American Musicological Society* 11 (1958), 6-19; and idem, 'Josquin and the Courts of the Netherlands and France: The Evidence of the Sources', in *Josquin des Prez: Proceedings of the International Josquin Festival-Conference: New York, 21-25 June 1971*, ed. Edward E. Lowinsky and Bonnie Blackburn (London, 1976), 181-216. Kellman later commented that neither of the two hands that appear in the Scribe B manuscripts can be identified as that of Bourgeois. See Kellman, 'Production, Distribution, and Symbolism of the Manuscripts – A Synopsis', in *Treasury*, 11.

[3] Fabrice Fitch has questioned the continuity of Scribe B's enterprise with that of Alamire. See his 'Agricola versus Alamire: The Lie of the Sources', in *The Burgundian-Habsburg Court Complex*, 299-308; and idem, 'Agricola and the Rhizome: An Aesthetic of the Late Cantus-Firmus Mass', in *Revue Belge de musicologie* 59 (2005), 65-92.

[4] For Alamire's biography, including payment records, see Eugeen Schreurs, 'Petrus Alamire: Music Calligrapher, Musician, Composer, Spy', in *The Treasury*, ed. Kellman, 15-27; and Herbert Kellman, 'Alamire, Pierre', in *Grove Music Online. Oxford Music Online*, <http://www.oxfordmusiconline.com/subscriber/article/grove/music/00399>.

Habsburg-Burgundian court, as well as other institutions, including the Church of Our Lady in Antwerp and the Confraternity of Our Lady in 's-Hertogenbosch, over a period of about thirty years. Though Alamire was paid for copying books of music and his hand can be identified in several manuscripts in the complex, he seems to have played the role of editor or supervisor of a workshop of copyists, who sometimes copied manuscripts even in Alamire's absence.[5]

The significance of the Alamire complex has been long appreciated—a number of the Alamire manuscripts were first noticed and discussed by scholars in the early nineteenth century.[6] The manuscripts have been the subject of many studies since.[7] The repertoire they transmit, including Franco-Flemish polyphony by composers such as Josquin des Prez, Pierre de la Rue, Johannes Ockeghem, Jean Mouton, and others, was composed during the cultural shift from manuscript to print as the primary medium by which music was transmitted; the transition to fully imitative counterpoint; and the rise of the imitation mass, which would remain the standard compositional technique applied to masses up to the end of the sixteenth century, for example. This unique complex of music manuscripts that Alamire and his associates produced is thus vital to any understanding of the polyphony composed around the turn of the sixteenth century. Nevertheless, much mystery still surrounds the man, the manuscripts, Alamire's methods, the various repertories transmitted, and the patrons who commissioned or received the manuscripts as gifts. Deplorably little is known about the precise circumstances in which the manuscripts were conceived, produced, and utilized.

The three articles that appear in this volume deal with sources that, when considered closely, reveal more differences than commonalities. Honey Meconi focuses on the Alamire portion of VienNB 9814, a manuscript made up of separate paper folios or small fascicles ranging in date from Alamire's time to the later sixteenth and early seventeenth centuries. Meconi suggests that the repertoire that the Alamire leaves transmit—five motets and the anonymous chanson *Plus Oultre*—was copied for use by the Imperial chapel of Charles V. Meconi also considers the non-Alamire sections of the manuscript to provide valuable insights into the purpose and provenance of a compilation

<hr>

5 For a more detailed explanation of Alamire's enterprise, see Zoe Saunders, 'Anonymity and Ascription in the Alamire Manuscripts: Toward a New Understanding of a Repertoire, an *Atelier*, and a Renaissance Court' (Ph.D. diss., University of Maryland, College Park, 2010), 290-313; and eadem, 'Anonymity and Ascription in the Alamire Manuscripts', in *Revue belge de musicologie* 57 (2013), 247-81.

6 Some of the earliest studies on Alamire include John Sherren Brewer (ed.), *Letters and Papers, Foreign and Domestic, of the Reign of Henry VIII*, vol. 2, pts. 1 and 2 (London, 1864); Edmond vander Straeten, *La musique aux Pays-Bas avant le XIXᵉ siècle: documents inédits et annotés, compositeurs, virtuoses, théoriciens, luthiers, opéras, motets, airs nationaux, académies, maîtrises, livres, portraits, etc., avec planches de musiques et table alphabétique*, 8 vols. (Brussels, 1867-88); Alexandre Pinchart (ed.), *Archives des arts, sciences et lettres: documents inédits* (Ghent, 1860-81); Henri Michelant, *Inventaire des vaisselles, joyaux, tapisseries, peintures, manuscrits, etc., de Marguérite d'Autriche, régente et gouvernante des Pays-Bas, dressé en son palais de Malines, le 9 juillet 1523* (Brussels, 1871); Chrétien Dehaisnes, *Inventaire sommaire des archives départementales antérieures à 1790. Nord. Archives civiles, Série B. Chambre des comptes de Lille. Nos. 1842-2338*, vol. 4 (Lille, 1881); Jules Finot, *Inventaire sommaire des archives départementales antérieures à 1790. Nord. Archives civiles, Série B. Chambre des comptes de Lille*, vols. 5 and 7 (Lille, 1885 and 1892); Léon De Burbure, 'Étude sur un manuscrit du XVIᵉ siècle, contenant des chants à quatre et à trois voix', in *Mémoires couronnés et autres mémoires publiés par L'Académie Royale des Sciences, des Lettres, et des Beaux-Arts de Belgique* 33 (1882), 1-44.

7 The first studies to examine the Alamire manuscripts as a cohesive group are Kellman, 'The Origins of the Chigi Codex'; idem, 'Illuminated Choirbooks and the Manuscript Tradition in Flanders in the Early 16th Century', paper read at the Annual Meeting of the American Musicological Society, Columbus, 1962; idem, 'The Role of the Empire in the Radiation of the Northern Repertoire, 1500-1530', paper read at the Annual Meeting of the American Musicological Society, Ann Arbor, 1965; idem, 'Musical Links between France and the Empire, 1500-1530', paper read at the Annual Meeting of the American Musicological Society, Toronto, 1970; and 'Josquin and the Courts of the Netherlands and France'.

that has hitherto been assumed to have been assembled out of unrelated parts. Her close reading of the text and music of the anonymous chanson *Plus oultre* examines the possibility that Pierre de la Rue composed it, but shows convincingly that he is not likely the composer, even though the chanson contains several quotations from other works by La Rue. In his study of MunBS 34, Aaron James emphasizes the unique nature of this manuscript in the Alamire complex, containing as it does twenty-nine polyphonic settings of the *Salve regina*. In this respect, MunBS 34 is also unique among sixteenth-century sources as a whole. This unusual repertoire poses questions that James addresses through an analysis of the source, an overview of the history of the antiphon and contexts for performance of polyphonic settings of it, and musical and stylistic analyses of its repertoire. Pointing out that despite its seemingly uniform contents, MunBS 34 transmits a repertoire that varies greatly both in musical style and theological matter, James thus achieves not only a better understanding of the polyphonic *Salve regina* as a distinct genre, but also of MunBS 34 as a vehicle through which a prestigious repertory was communicated. Hannah Mowrey examines the theological implications raised by the miniature that accompanies Obrecht's *Missa Sicut spina rosam* in JenaU 22, a manuscript attributed to Scribe B. Theological themes that are prominent in the rather early manuscript JenaU 22 are shown to prefigure similar messages that appear in later Alamire manuscripts as well. Both collectively and individually, these three studies highlight some of the ways in which each Alamire manuscript is a unique source that calls for detailed analyses of its various aspects including repertoire, decoration, codicological and paleographic features, patronage, and provenance. In so doing, they open a new phase of research on the Alamire complex, and bring us closer to understanding the Alamire manuscripts as a group.

Finally, I would like to express my gratitude to Katelijne Schiltz and David Burn for inviting me to guest edit this volume, and to them as well as Stratton Bull for the time and patience that all three devoted to editing and proofreading. The experience has been much more pleasure than work.

Plus oultre, Pierre de la Rue, and the Emperor's Music[*]

■

HONEY MECONI

The manuscript Vienna, Österreichische Nationalbibliothek, Handschriftensammlung, Ms. 9814 (hereafter VienNB 9814), is anomalous within the Alamire manuscripts[1] in its physical format, consisting as it does not of fascicles but rather of a series of separate paper folios included within a much larger collection of purportedly unrelated musical material. It is unusual, too, though not unique, in containing Alamire's signature. Table 1 lists the contents of the Alamire portion of the collection.[2] Five of the works are motets by Agricola, Ghiselin, Mouton, La Rue, and Richafort; the sixth work is an anonymous chanson, *Plus oultre pretens parvenir*, which takes as its opening words the motto adopted in 1516 by future Holy Roman Emperor Charles V.

The text and translation of the chanson, an old-fashioned rondeau quatrain, are given below.[3] The language is that of the *rhétoriqueurs*, difficult to capture in modern English, with the final two lines being especially opaque.

Plus oultre pretens parvenir	Even further I intend to reach
Et venir ou mon eur tiendra	And come where I am destined.
Mon cueur son propos maintiendra	My heart will sustain its purpose
Adviengne ce q[u]'en doibt venir	Whatever may come of it.
Par vertuz Je voeil subvenir	Through virtue I mean to provide,
e[n] paix ou guerre *Qui vouldra*	In peace or war, whoever wishes it.
Plus oultre	Even further...
Jay empris Mesure tenir	I have undertaken to observe moderation
En toute choze quand viendra	In all things, whatever will come
Tant vault q[ue] fait [est] mieulx viendra	The goal is worth all the more
Pour ung jamais les obtenir	Even if never achieved.
Plus oultre pretens parvenir	Even further I intend to reach...

> *Plus oultre* = motto of Charles V
> *Adviengne ce qu'en* ≈ motto of Margaret of York, 'Bien en aviegne'
> *Qui vouldra* = motto of Philip the Fair
> *Jay empris* ≈ motto of Charles the Bold, 'Je l'ay empris'
> *Mesure tenir* = motto of Maximilian, 'Halt Maß'
> *Pour ung jamais* = incipit of poem by Margaret of Austria

[*] A version of this essay was presented at the University of Leuven on 26 March 2013. I would like to thank David Burn for his invitation to speak there, as well as Bonnie Blackburn, Naomi Gregory, Yannick Godts, and an anonymous reader for this *Journal* for assistance in preparation of this essay. Manuscript sigla are taken from *Census-Catalogue of Manuscript Sources of Polyphonic Music 1400-1550*, 5 vols., ed. Herbert Kellman and Charles Hamm, Renaissance Manuscript Studies 1 (Neuhausen-Stuttgart, 1979-88), hereafter *CC*.

[1] This term refers to the more than sixty manuscripts described in the basic reference work for the collection, Herbert Kellman (ed.), *The Treasury of Petrus Alamire: Music and Art in Flemish Court Manuscripts 1500-1535* (Ghent-Amsterdam, 1999; hereafter *Treasury*), which includes even those manuscripts prepared before Alamire formally joined the court of Habsburg-Burgundy. Alamire's continued relationship with the court after leaving its chapel is discussed in Honey Meconi, 'Alamire, Pierre de la Rue, and Manuscript Production in the Time of Charles V', in *"Qui musicam in se habet"*: *Essays in Honor of Alejandro Planchart*, ed. Stanley Boorman and Anna Zayaruznaya (Münster-Middleton, in press).

 10.1484/J.JAF.1.103835

In writing about this work, Juri Giannini and Herbert Kellman noted that the complete poem included references to the motto of Philip the Fair, 'Qui vouldra', as well as to Margaret of Austria via the phrase 'Pour ung jamais', which refers to one of her poems that noted court composer Pierre de la Rue set to music.[4] Nicole Schwindt has identified further dynastic connections: 'J'ay empris' recalls the motto of Charles the Bold, 'Je l'ay empris', while the line 'Adviengne ce qu'en est doibt venir' brings to mind the motto of his third wife, Margaret of York, 'Bien en aviegne'. 'Mesure tenir' is the French equivalent of Maximilian's 'Halt Maß'.[5]

On the basis of the poem's promises and interwoven references, Giannini and Kellman characterized the song as 'a dynastic statement, indeed a state chanson'.[6] And although the song is transmitted anonymously, one composer leaps to mind in connection with the court's chansons, their transmission anonymously in court sources, and, in fact, compositions that serve the court's rulers in one form or another: Pierre de la Rue, longtime composer of the court and the leading individual to work for almost all of the rulers alluded to in the song's text. The anonymous chanson also follows the La Rue motet in VienNB 9814—a tantalizing placement, given the frequent proximity of La Rue's compositions to one another in court sources. Pierre de la Rue is thus the first composer to consider when attempting an attribution for this special composition.

Charles's Motto

To begin with Charles's motto: 'Plus oultre' was the brainchild of the Milanese humanist Luigi Marliano, who served as court physician to, successively, Maximilian, Philip the Fair, Margaret of Austria, and Charles, the last from at least 1512.[7] Marliano's reward for creating Charles's motto was evidently the bishopric of Tuy in Galicia, an appointment being written about by 31 July 1516, making that the *terminus ante quem* for the invention of the motto if the motto was the impetus for the bishopric.[8] Earlier, Charles had used 'Nondum in Auge' ('Not yet at my zenith'). It is likely that the new motto made its first public appearance at the meeting of the Order of the Golden Fleece held at St. Gudule

---

[2] A second foliation, used in Table 1, was added after the various leaves of the entire collection were rearranged.

[3] All translations are my own unless otherwise indicated. A modern edition of the work appears in Nicole Schwindt, 'Habsburgische Kulturpolitik im Spiegel des Liedrepertoires: französisch-flämisch-deutsch', in *Die Habsburger und die Niederlande. Musik und Politik um 1500*, ed. Jürgen Heidrich, Trossinger Jahrbuch für Renaissancemusik 8 (Kassel, 2008/2009), 27-67 at 37-39.

[4] Juri Giannini and Herbert Kellman, 'Vienna, Österreichische Nationalbibliothek, Handschriftensammlung, MS 9814, fols. 132-52', in *Treasury*, 146. The poem's author may have wanted to avoid Margaret's motto, 'Fortune infortune fort une', with its emphasis on Fortune. Any intimation that Charles's position was owing to luck would have been undesirable.

[5] Schwindt, 'Habsburgische Kulturpolitik', 35-36. The poet's choice of individuals to be represented was hardly haphazard. His father, grandfather, and great-grandfather all represented major components of Charles's inheritance. Philip's marriage to Juana of Spain eventually made Charles King of Spain; Maximilian's marriage to Mary of Burgundy added Habsburg lands to the dynasty; and Charles the Bold was the last duke of Burgundy proper and the person after whom Charles himself was named. Margaret of York (wife of Charles the Bold, and representative of the off-and-on alliance with England against France) was one of Charles's two godmothers; the other was Margaret of Austria, who had essentially reared Charles after his father's death.

[6] Giannini and Kellman, 'Vienna, Österreichische Nationalbibliothek, Handschriftensammlung, MS 9814', 146.

[7] On Charles's motto, see Earl E. Rosenthal, 'The Invention of the Columnar Device of Emperor Charles V at the Court of Burgundy in Flanders in 1516', in *Journal of the Warburg and Courtauld Institutes* 36 (1973), 198-230; and idem, 'Plus ultra, Non plus ultra, and the Columnar Device of Emperor Charles V', in *Journal of the Warburg and Courtauld Institutes* 34 (1971), 204-38.

[8] Rosenthal, 'The Invention of the Columnar Device', 200.

Table 1. Contents of Alamire portion of VienNB 9814

Folder[a]	Folio[b]	Rubric[c]	Composition/Observations
20	132r	*Alexander*	Ave domina sancta maria [superius]
	132v	Verbonnet	Ave domina sancta maria [superius] + Alamire signature
	133r	*Tenor*	[= Agricola]
	133v	Verbonnet	[= tenor; teardrop notes first two staves only[d]]
	134r	*Tenor* Contra[ten]or	[= Agricola]
	134v	Con[traten]or	[= Verbonnet; teardrop notes first staff only]
	135r	*Bassus*	[= Agricola]
	135v	Verbonnett[e]	[= bassus; teardrop notes first staff only]
21	136r	*Mouton*	Tua est potentia [superius; almost all teardrop notes]
	136v		blank
	137r	*Sequere me In subdyatessaron*	[= Mouton canonic tenor; almost all teardrop notes]
	137v		blank
	138r	*Contratenor*	[= Mouton; teardrop notes end of staff 5 only]
	138v		blank
	139r	*Bassus*	[= Mouton]
	139v		blank
22	140r	Rue	O domine Jhesu [Christ]e
	140v		blank
	141r	Tenor	[= La Rue]
	141v		blank
	142r	Contratenor	[= La Rue]
	142v		blank
	143r	Bassus	[= La Rue]
	143v		blank

	Folio		
23	144r	[anonymous]	Plus oultre pretens parvenir
			[= altus; concludes with proofreading mark]
	144v		blank
	145r		[= superius]
	145v		blank
	146r		[= tenor; concludes with proofreading mark]
	146v		remainder of rondeau quatrain text
	147r		[= bassus; concludes with proofreading mark]
	147v		blank
24	148r	Richafort *Prima pars*	Ia[m] non dica[m] [= superius]
	148v	*Secunda pars*	
	149r	Altus *Prima pars*	[teardrop notes first staff only]
	149v	*Secunda pars*	
	150r	Tenor *Prima pars*	[teardrop notes first staff only]
	150v	*Secunda pars*	
	151r	2[us] Tenor *Prima pars*	[teardrop notes first staff only]
	151v	*Secunda p[ar]s*	
	152r	Bassus *Prima pars*	[teardrop notes "end" of first staff only]
	152v	*Secunda pars*	

a   All folders are modern.
b   Modern foliation; all folios are loose sheets.
c   Italics = red ink.
d   Teardrop notes = Alamire.
e   The second 't' (if that is what it is) appears to be an addition to the ascription. If it is another proofreading mark, it does not match those that appear in *Plus oultre*.

in Brussels at the end of October 1516, the first meeting over which Charles presided as sovereign.[9]

Charles's motto was incorporated into numerous artistic works in tandem with his device of two columns representing the pillars of Hercules, but it inspired relatively few musical compositions. Including the chanson of VienNB 9814,[10] a mere seven pieces are known to refer to the motto.[11] These include an anonymous textless setting in the Pernner Codex [RegB C120],[12] the chanson *Plus oultre j'ay voulu marcher* by Nicolas Gombert,[13] who worked for Charles, and three now-lost works: a six-voice piece supposedly by Josquin, a five-voice work by Gregor Peschin, and a composition by Costanzo Festa, evidently written for Charles's triumphal entry into Rome in 1536. The final composition, a mass by Lupi, is titled *Missa Plus oultre* in the manuscript MontsM 771. That collection was compiled at the court of Mary of Hungary, Charles's sister, and is one of the manuscripts designated by Jacobijn Kiel as 'post-Alamire', containing as it does the scribal hand of one of Alamire's collaborators.[14] The scribe in question, Scribe K, appears to be following the long-standing court tradition of altering mass titles to flatter a manuscript's patron, for Lupi's supposed *Missa Plus oultre* is known in its other, probably earlier, sources as *Missa Mijn vriendinne*.[15] Certainly no one has yet traced any musical reference to any *Plus oultre* composition in the mass. For whatever reason, then, composers apparently did not leap to incorporate Charles's motto with the same eagerness that visual artists did.

La Rue as Composer of *Plus oultre*

As noted, Charles is thought to have adopted his new motto in the summer of 1516, with its public debut taking place at the Golden Fleece meeting of October 1516. This timing

[9] Rosenthal, 'The Invention of the Columnar Device', 201 ff.

[10] The piece is also found, with textual incipits only, in the partbooks MunU 328-31 and VienNB Mus. 18810, both likely copied in Augsburg and both likely later than VienNB 9814. The readings of all versions are close. For recent thoughts on these collections, see David Fallows, 'The Copyist Formerly Known as Wagenrieder: Bernhart Rem and His Circle', in *Die Münchener Hofkapelle des 16. Jahrhunderts im europäischen Kontext: Bericht über das internationale Symposion der Musikhistorischen Kommission der Bayerischen Akademie der Wissenschaften in Verbindung mit der Gesellschaft für Bayerische Musikgeschichte München, 2.-4. August 2004*, ed. Theodor Göllner and Bernhold Schmid with Severin Putz, Bayerisch Akademie der Wissenschaften Philosophisch-Historische Klasse Abhandlungen, Neue Folge, Heft 128 (Munich, 2006), 212-23. On the owner of MunU 328-31, see Honey Meconi, 'The Ghost of Perfection: The Munich Partbooks and Some Thoughts on Renaissance Manuscripts', in *The Sounds and Sights of Performance in Early Music: Essays in Honour of Timothy J. McGee*, ed. Maureen Epp and Brian E. Power (Aldershot, 2009), 85-101 and Plate 1.

[11] See Schwindt, 'Habsburgische Kulturpolitik', 33-48, and Mary Tiffany Ferer, *Music and Ceremony at the Court of Charles V: The Capilla Flamenca and the Art of Political Promotion*, Studies in Medieval and Renaissance Music 12 (Woodbridge-Rochester, 2012), 7-9.

[12] This appears in the second part of the codex, possibly from Augsburg. Rainer Birkendorf, *Der Codex Pernner: Quellenkundliche Studien zu einer Musikhandschrift des frühen 16. Jahrhunderts (Regensburg, Bischöfliche Zentralbibliothek, Sammlung Proske, Ms. C 120)*, 3 vols., Collectanea musicologica 6 (Augsburg, 1994), vol. 1, 233, suggested that La Rue was the composer, but this idea was dismissed on stylistic grounds in Honey Meconi, *Pierre de la Rue and Musical Life at the Habsburg-Burgundian Court* (Oxford, 2003), 164-67.

[13] Ferer, *Music and Ceremony*, 7, notes the (less likely) attribution to Lupi in one printed source.

[14] See Jacobijn Kiel, 'Terminus post Alamire? On Some Later Scribes', in *The Burgundian-Habsburg Court Complex of Music Manuscripts (1500-1535) and the Workshop of Petrus Alamire: Colloquium Proceedings Leuven, 25-28 November 1999*, ed. Bruno Bouckaert and Eugeen Schreurs, Yearbook of the Alamire Foundation 5 (Leuven-Neerpelt, 2003; hereafter *BHCC*), 97-105. Interestingly, Scribe K (the specific scribe) was also one of the scribes for VienNB 9814.

[15] On the Lupi mass see Bonnie J. Blackburn, 'The Lupus Problem' (Ph.D. diss., University of Chicago, 1970), 134-37 and 398.

immediately creates problems with La Rue as hypothetical composer of the dynastic chanson, for he retired from court employment in the spring of 1516, and moved permanently to Kortrijk by 16 June at the latest.[16] Conceivably La Rue, as a sort of composer emeritus for the court, could have been called on for one last piece, a kind of farewell gift to the place where he spent at least two dozen years. Another possibility, since we do not know the exact date that the phrase 'Plus oultre' became Charles's byword, is that Charles adopted the motto shortly before La Rue's retirement. The phrase is one thing, though, the poem another; the latter was not necessarily created immediately after Charles switched to his new motto. Further, the full text of the rondeau, with its combination of six different mottos or motto references, seems to imply some sort of state-inspired occasion rather than casual entertainment.

As such, the song occupies a strange position generically, and one that sits uneasily next to La Rue's other works that refer to court individuals. Several of his motets are linked with his patrons: *Salve mater salvatoris* makes reference to Margaret of Austria in her position as governor of the Low Countries; *Delicta iuventutis*, *Considera Israel*, and possibly *Absalon fili mi* reflect the death of Philip the Fair. The *Missa O gloriosa domina* served as a mass for Margaret. Of La Rue's secular works, those connected with courtiers or rulers include *De l'oeil de la fille du roy*, with Margaret as the implied subject; *Tous les regrets* and *Tous nobles cueurs*, which both come from the poem of Octavien de Saint-Gelais in honor of Margaret; *A vous non autre* with a text reworked to speak directly to Margaret; *Dedans bouton* with its reference to the Bouton family of courtiers; and *Cueurs desolez/Dies illa* as a motet-chanson for the death of Jean de Luxembourg. Except for the last, though, the texts for these pieces all fall in the realm of courtly love.

That the text is a rondeau is not a problem regarding La Rue's potential authorship; he was one of the last major composers to set this form, with sixteen of his secular works—more than a third—using rondeau texts, though only four of these are rondeaux quatrains.[17] The use of such an old-fashioned poetic structure as late as 1516 (or even later) suggests that the poet—possibly Jean Lemaire de Belges, according to Nicole Schwindt[18]—wanted the venerable tradition of the form to underscore the venerable tradition of which Charles himself was now part, with the rondeau form in its heyday during the time of his great-grandfather Charles the Bold.

Both text and timing, then, might work with La Rue as composer for *Plus oultre pretens parvenir*. Alas, the music itself does not cooperate especially well with this possibility. To begin with, the composition is for four essentially equal voices. Table 2 includes the cleffing and the range for *Plus oultre*, with two C3 and two C4 clefs, the top two voices with exactly the same range and the bottom two going a mere step below the top two.[19] Voice crossing is constant. In La Rue's attributed chansons, voice crossing occurs frequently between interior voices, and sometimes between other voice parts as well. And of course, voice-crossing is to be expected in any piece written with equal voices, but that choice is not La Rue's norm.

[16] On the date of La Rue's retirement, see Meconi, *Pierre de la Rue*, 44.
[17] The relevant pieces are indicated in Meconi, *Pierre de la Rue*, 136-37.
[18] Schwindt, 'Habsburgische Kulturpolitik', 36.
[19] As the parts are without voice indication in VienNB 9814, I have arranged them so that the final cadence follows the standard vocal layout for the time.

Table 2. Cleffing and ranges in VienNB 9814, Alamire portion

Composition	Clefs				Ranges
Agricola, *Ave domina*	c2	c4	c4	f4	
Ghiselin, *Ave domina*	c4	c4	c4	f4	
Mouton, *Tua est potentia*, 5 vv.	g2	c2	c3	X f3	
La Rue, *O domine Jhesu Christe*	g2	c2	c3	f3	
Anonymous, *Plus oultre*	c3	c3	c4	c4	
Richafort, *Iam non dicam*, 5 vv.	g2	c2	c3	c3 c4	

Example 1. Contrasting use of melodic phrase
a. Pierre de la Rue, *De l'oeil de la fille du roy*, bb. 1-11

b. Anonymous, *Plus oultre pretens parvenir*, bb. 25-39

A second very striking aspect of *Plus oultre* is its borrowing of a melodic phrase from an unquestioned La Rue chanson, *De l'oeil de la fille du roy*. Example 1a shows the beginning of La Rue's chanson, where the opening motive appears in strict imitation in all voices. Example 1b shows how this motive—very slightly changed—appears in all four voices of *Plus oultre*. But the two compositions treat this material very differently. In *Plus oultre*, after all four voices present the motive on D, superius, altus, and bassus repeat it sequentially, moving up by thirds through F, A, and finally C, in a clear example of direct text-painting. In *De l'oeil de la fille du roy*, La Rue also employs motivic repetition, but very differently: the superius, altus, and tenor repeat the motive, but not the full motive—the beginning has been lopped off. Altus has a long extension (bb. 3-4) of the original motive before bringing back its truncated form. Superius repeats the motive on A and adds a little filip on the end, while altus and tenor bring it back on C, a seventh away from the original gesture. The first extended appearance in the altus ends with the motive's turn. This is classic La Rue, variety within unity, and this melodic writing presents a strong contrast to the more automatic sequencing going on in *Plus oultre*.

Another discrepancy with La Rue's usual style involves the harmonic structure of *Plus oultre*. The work opens and closes clearly in D; that is not a problem. But the lack of cadential variety is. Even in his shortest chansons La Rue strives for a significant amount of variety in his cadences in terms of their structure and especially in terms of the tonal areas (to use an anachronistic term) that they mark. With a single exception, the cadences of *Plus oultre* are all on D or A. Such harmonic predictability is not the norm for La Rue. The final cadence, shown in Example 2, is also not to be found in any unquestioned La Rue chanson. The norm for a final cadence in a four-voice La Rue chanson is for superius, tenor, and bassus to share an octave or a unison, with the bassus pitch approached by a falling fifth, and for the altus to supply the fifth. In the rare four-voice chansons that do not follow this pattern,[20] the altus has a third. Final triads, like the one we see in *Plus oultre*, simply are not found in La Rue's chansons. The bassus in *Plus oultre*, moreover, approaches its closing pitch by step rather than by leap, moves in parallel fourths with the superius, and closes above the tenor. It is true that in VienNB 9814 the voice parts are not indicated (see Table 1), and that in the concordant sources VienNB Mus. 18810 and MunU 328-31 the voice I have placed in the superius position appears in the altus partbook while the voice I have put in the tenor slot appears in the bassus partbook. But if VienNB Mus. 18810's and MunU 328-31's voice designations reflect the original intention of the composer, they create a final cadence generated by altus and bassus voices—again, something La Rue never does.

Other details in *Plus oultre* are problematic in terms of La Rue's authorship, but the idea is clear. Obviously it is not normally the presence or absence of a single characteristic that proves or disproves a composer's authorship of a given composition. Rather, it is a combination of factors that points to the probability (or not) of identification with a specific composer. While it is true that La Rue's style evolved over the decades of his compositional activity, it is unlikely that, even in what would have been a farewell composition, he moved so far away from his stylistic preferences to generate the music of *Plus oultre*. The reference to one of La Rue's chansons shown in Example 1b should be seen, then, as a gesture by the anonymous composer that holds a double meaning. It

---

[20] *Il est bien heureux* and *Aprez regretz*.

Example 2. Anonymous, *Plus oultre pretens parvenir*, bb. 70-71

calls forth the composer most closely associated with the young Charles, and it also refers to the woman who raised the new ruler, Margaret of Austria, for the text of the original chanson refers to 'the eye of the daughter of the king': Margaret.[21]

VienNB 9814 as Performing Parts

VienNB 9814, as noted earlier, is unique within the Alamire complex in its format. Based on this format, Giannini and Kellman hypothesized that the various loose sheets making up the collection could have been used for performance.[22] Students of the Alamire manuscripts know that the 'performability' of the surviving manuscripts remains problematic, with some manuscripts showing clear signs of use and others not. Further, the accuracy of the readings of individual pieces across the complex varies greatly, as does the character of the text underlay. VienNB 9814 thus presents a promising test case for performability.

In the most general terms, VienNB 9814 seems as if it would work for performance. The folios are an adequate dimension, about the size of A4 paper, and Giannini and Kellman have noted that they are, in fact, larger than those of the largest partbooks in the court complex, VienNB Mus. 15941.[23] All notes are clearly written (see Figure 1). An individual singer would have no trouble reading the music; for that matter, even three could have shared a part without difficulty.[24] Indeed, to realize the canon in the Mouton motet, which was written on a single folio, at least two would have to share a part. The works are laid out so that the Ghiselin voice parts are on the verso side of the Agricola voice parts, superius for superius, etc. Both motets, of course, set the same text (see Table 1 for the layout).

For *Plus oultre*, and for the manuscript in general, text underlay is by phrase, giving the performer guidance but much freedom. General alignment of text among the different voice parts is relatively good, i.e., the same text usually appears in different voice parts at the same time. Yet what if more than one voice is singing an individual line, as might have happened? Would the lack of precision in underlay have made this

[21] Though king of no country *per se*, Margaret's father Maximilian was elected King of the Romans, a title he valued very highly, on 16 February 1486.
[22] Giannini and Kellman, 'Vienna, Österreichische Nationalbibliothek, Handschriftensammlung, MS 9814', 146.
[23] Giannini and Kellman, 'Vienna, Österreichische Nationalbibliothek, Handschriftensammlung, MS 9814', 146.
[24] See Ferer, *Music and Ceremony*, 92, on three to a part as the norm for Charles's chapel in the 1520s.

Figure 1. Pierre de la Rue, *O domine Jhesu Christe*, tenor. VienNB 9814, fol. 141r. Copyright Österreichische Nationalbibliothek. Reproduced with permission

manuscript problematic for performance? This perennial question of coordination among multiple voices on the same part is hardly limited to VienNB 9814, though; most manuscripts (including those clearly used for performance) present the same problem.[25]

More pressing issues do arise with *Plus oultre*. First, the chanson is a rondeau quatrain, but the B section is not marked by any sign of congruence: in Example 1b see b. 38, which is where the B section begins. In contrast, the folio for the canonic voice part in Mouton's *Tua est potentia* provides both instructions and the appropriate signs of congruence for both the beginning and the end of the canon.

Second, Table 1 shows that although the full rondeau text of *Plus oultre* is given, it appears in a single place, somewhat inconveniently on the back of the tenor voice part. The singers would thus have had to memorize the text—admittedly a not especially difficult task for professionals.

Figure 1, which shows the tenor part of La Rue's motet *O domine Ihesu Christe*, shows another potential difficulty. Here the scribe left out a breve's worth of music not quite halfway through the work; the missing notes were then added at the bottom of the page.[26] Would that present a stumbling block for the performer?

As it turns, out, VienNB 9814 presents no real problems for performance. On 26 March 2013, in a workshop at the Alamire Foundation's House of Polyphony in Leuven, five professional early music singers tested the performability of the manuscript; they encountered no serious roadblocks to its use as a performing medium for any of the works, not even with the inserted tenor correction.[27] An added bonus to this experiment was demonstrating that these parts could be used for 'rehearsal', for learning the music as well as for performance. No piece was done faultlessly on an initial reading, but—with amazing consistency—singers who faltered and had to drop out temporarily all re-entered once they 'found their place' again aurally. For every piece, the third read-through generated an accurate rendition of the work. Quite possibly, more singers to a part would have resulted in an even more rapid mastery of the composition. With three singers to a part, for example, the odds increase that at least one of them will 'get it right' and provide an example for the others.

Imperial Connections

The traditional interpretation of VienNB 9814's provenance is that it was owned by the Fugger family, even if not originally intended for them.[28] The assumption is

[25] A discussion of texting matters that includes precisely this problem is Edward Wickham, 'Realization and Recreation: Texting Issues in Early Renaissance Polyphony', in this *Journal* 3 (2011), 147-66.

[26] This sort of insertion is not unusual in the Alamire manuscripts.

[27] I would like to thank Emily Thelen for inviting me to present a workshop, and I especially wish to thank Stratton Bull, Tore Denys, Matthew Gouldstone, Paul Kolb, and Pieter de Moor for their fine singing and extremely perceptive comments.

[28] On the Fugger connection, see Leopold Nowak, 'Die Musikhandschriften aus Fuggerschem Besitz in der Österreichischen Nationalbibliothek', in *Die Österreichische Nationalbibliothek Festschrift herausgegeben zum 25 jährigen Dienstjubiläum des Generaldirektors Univ.-Prof. Dr. Josef Bick*, ed. Josef Stummvoll (Vienna, 1948), 505-15. Nowak (506-7) acknowledges that VienNB 9814 cannot be clearly identified in the inventory of the Fugger library prepared by Mattheus Mauchter in 1655. On the deficiencies of that inventory (Vienna, Österreichische Nationalbibliothek, Ms. 12579), see Paul Lehmann, *Eine Geschichte der alten Fuggerbibliotheken*, 2 vols., Schwäbische Forschungsgemeinschaft

reasonable: the Fuggers were closely connected to Charles, who would not have been elected Holy Roman Emperor without their money.[29] They were music lovers based in Augsburg, site of the election and, just as importantly, a city where Alamire lingered and apparently helped in the campaign towards Charles's election.[30] More specifically, the Österreichische Nationalbibliothek, where VienNB 9814 now resides, includes the huge library of Philipp Eduard Fugger, grandson of Raimund Fugger the Elder, who owned the Alamire motet collection VienNB Mus. 15941 and likely the other Alamire manuscripts with the Fugger coat of arms (VienNB 4809, VienNB Mus. 18825, and VienNB Mus. 18832). But Flynn Warmington has proposed that, rather than the Fuggers, the Empire itself was involved:

> VienNB Mus. 18832[31] and VienNB 9814, which...were linked with the Fuggers in an early study...in fact have no arms or other identifying marks of the Fuggers and are not precisely mentioned in any Fugger inventory. I would suggest that they are more likely to have come down to us through imperial channels, and the library of Emperor Matthias II is a very likely route...the Alamire folios in VienNB 9814 are part of a collection associated with Matthias II, portions of which he may have inherited.[32]

Following Warmington's lead generates fascinating results. The Alamire section of VienNB 9814 is not the only court-related manuscript to appear as part of another collection; the earlier fragment OxfBA 831 does so as well. But in contrast to OxfBA 831, where a single bifolium of what was originally a larger manuscript is simply tacked on at the end of a huge and unrelated nonmusical miscellany, VienNB 9814's Alamire folios are surrounded by other musical compositions, and it is here that the Matthias connection is evident.

Table 3 shows the composition of the entire manuscript.[33] As Herbert Kellman has noted, the contents consist of either individual folios or small fascicles, all organized by voice part.[34] The collection opens with a series of unaccompanied polychoral works, starting with a parody mass and followed by four motets; the mass and three of the motets evidently date from the early years of the seventeenth century.

---

bei der Kommission für Bayerische Landesgeschichte, Reihe 4, Bande 3 and 5; Studien zur Fuggergeschichte, Bande 12 and 15 (Tübingen, 1956-60), vol. 1, 229. Lehmann, vol. 2, 552, gives the date of the inventory as 1654.

[29] On the Fuggers and their influence, see Mark Häberlein, *The Fuggers of Augsburg: Pursuing Wealth and Honor in Renaissance Germany* (Charlottesville-London, 2012), esp. 64-67.

[30] See Eugeen Schreurs, 'Petrus Alamire: Music Calligrapher, Musician, Composer, Spy', in *Treasury*, 15-27, at 20, where Margaret of Austria's secretary Jean Marnix writes her that he has 'urged Alamire, who was then in Augsburg with nothing to do, to visit the duke of Saxony [one of the Electors] and find out who his guests were'.

[31] The reference to VienNB 18832 is surely a slip of the pen for VienNB 11883, as the former contains the Fugger arms while the latter does not.

[32] Flynn Warmington, 'A Survey of Scribal Hands in the Manuscripts', in *Treasury*, 41-52 at 46 n. 62.

[33] Table 3 uses the second set of modern foliation, which organizes each polychoral work by chorus (chorus primus, chorus secundus, etc.) and typically by descending clefs within each chorus. The earlier modern foliation indicates that the collection, although presenting the pieces in the same order, followed a more random organization within each piece. In the earlier foliation the Alamire section arranged the voice parts thus: Agricola/Ghiselin = BTSA; Mouton = BTAS; La Rue = ABTS; Plus oultre = BSAT; Richafort = T1T2BAS. The earlier foliation also did not include two voices of the first piece: one of the C1 voices of Chorus Primus (currently fols. 7-12) and the F4 voice of Chorus Tertius (currently fols. 67-72); it is not clear why they were not numbered, unless they had been misplaced. Two other folios elsewhere were left unnumbered: current fol. 131, with the lowest voice of the chorus tertius, and current fol. 76, with the C1 part of the chorus primus in the second work.

[34] See *CC*, vol. 4, 90. The contents are currently gathered in individual folders, with folders 20-24 containing the Alamire pieces.

Table 3. Contents of VienNB 9814

No.	Composer	Title	Scoring	Folios
1	Johann Stadlmair	*Missa Hor che nel suo bel seno*	12 vv. in 3 choirs	1r-72r
2	Alexander Utendal	*Angelus domini descendit de coelo*	23 vv. in 4 choirs	73r-96r
3	Thomas Bodenstein	*Dicite o caelites*	9 vv. in 2 choirs	97r-106r
4	Thomas Bodenstein	*Magi et pastores*	12 vv. in 3 choirs	108r-119r
5	Thomas Bodenstein	*Benedictus Deus*	11 vv. in 3 choirs	120r-131r
6	Alexander Agricola	*Ave domina sancta maria*	4 vv.	rectos of fols. 132-135
7	Johannes Ghiselin	*Ave domina sancta maria*	4 vv.	versos of fols. 132-135
8	Johannes Mouton	*Tua est potentia*	5 vv.	136r-139r
9	Pierre de la Rue	*O domine Jhesu Christe*	4 vv.	140r-143r
10	Anonymous	*Plus oultre pretens parvenir*	4 vv.	144r-147r
11	Jean Richafort	*Iam non dicam*	5 vv.	148r-152v
12	Anonymous	*Exaudiat dominus*	4 vv.	153r-v / 157r-v / 161r-v / 165r-v
		[secunda pars]: *Ne vos deserat in tempore*		153v-154r / 157v-158v / 161v-162r / 165v-166r
13	Costanzo Festa	*Vidi speciosam / Assumpta est Maria*	6 vv. (incomplete)	154r-v / 158v-159r / 162r / 166v-167r
		[secunda pars]: *Quae est ista quae precessit* [sic]		155r-v / 159r-v / 162r / 167r-v

The Alamire group follows. The collection concludes with the *prima* and *secunda pars* of two sixteenth-century motets on biblical texts, the former composition an anonymous work setting 2 Maccabees 1:5.[35] The latter is Costanzo Festa's six-voice motet from the Song of Songs, here incompletely preserved.[36] The motets are copied by voice part, that is, altus parts for both motets together, tenor parts together, and so on.[37]

Four of the five opening compositions are connected to Matthias II (1557-1619), who was Holy Roman Emperor from 1612 to 1619.[38] *Dicite o caelites*, *Magi et pastores*, and *Benedictus Deus* were all composed by Thomas Bodenstein (Podenstain), organist for Matthias's chapel and chamber. *Dicite o caelites* and *Benedictus Deus* were specifically dedicated to Matthias, the latter for his sixtieth birthday on 24 February 1617.[39] *Benedictus Deus* is also indicated in the manuscript as being for Saint Matthias.[40] *Dicite o caelites* was possibly for a birthday as well; it is designated as a 'musical gift' ('Xenium hoc musicale').[41] *Magi et pastores* was presumably for the use of Matthias's chapel during the Christmas season.

In addition to the three Bodenstein motets, *Angelus domini descendit de coelo*, with its spectacular use of twenty-three voices in four choirs, was also a birthday 'gift' for Matthias's sixtieth birthday, as its own title page indicates.[42] In this case the motet was not specifically created for Matthias's birthday, as the composer, Alexander Utendal, died in 1581. Rather, a performance of this gargantuan work marked the birthday.[43] Utendal had his own strong Habsburg connection, though, with service for both Mary of Hungary and the Archduke Ferdinand (son of Holy Roman Emperor Ferdinand, Charles's brother and immediate successor), working for the latter in the important imperial city of Innsbruck. The Archduke Ferdinand, in fact, inherited his father's library.[44]

One striking feature of this motet is the fact that three of its voices are written in F5 clef. In two of these parts the vocal line extends to C below the staff; in a third, the melodic line goes to the B♭' below that. This exploration of extreme ranges

---

[35] Bonnie Blackburn (private communication) notes that the *prima pars* of the motet paraphrases the relevant chant melody, the Magnificat antiphon for the Saturday before the fourth Sunday in October; see *The Liber Usualis* (Tournai, 1962), 995.

[36] My thanks to Bonnie Blackburn for this identification. VienNB 9814 is missing the highest and lowest voices of this six-voice work.

[37] The exception is the first set of voice parts, where the superius of the anonymous motet is followed by the tenor secundus part of the Festa motet. The motets are copied in a casual but clear music script distinctly different from that used by any Alamire scribe; the text appears to be in a sixteenth-century Italian hand.

[38] Matthias was the first Holy Roman Emperor of that name; his title Matthias II refers to his being the second King of Hungary so named. No full study of music under Matthias exists; overviews appear in Robert Lindell, 'Music at the Court of Emperor Matthias', in *Hudební věda* 27 (1990), 291-98; and Horst Link, 'Die matthianische Regenschaft in ihrem geschichtlichen Rahmen und musikhistorischen Kontext', in *Gedenkschrift für Walter Pass*, ed. Martin Czernin (Tutzing, 2002), 341-52.

[39] As indicated on fol. 120r.

[40] On fol. 131r.

[41] As indicated on fol. 97r.

[42] On fol. 73r.

[43] On this motet and its copyist at the imperial court, see Ignace Bossuyt, *De Componist Alexander Utendal (ca. 1543/1545-1581): Een bijdrage tot de studie van de Nederlandse polyfonie in de tweede helft van de zestiende eeuw*, Verhandelingen van de Koninklijke Academie voor Wetenschappen, Letteren en Schone Kunsten van België, Klasse der Schone Kunsten, Jaargang 45, Nr. 36 (Brussels, 1983), 120-22. Bossuyt shows that the copyist, Georgius Khnes, likely acquired the composition from Utendal himself when the two were colleagues in Innsbruck.

[44] See Eric Jas, 'Vienna, Österreichische Nationalbibliothek, Musiksammlung, MS Mus. 15495', in *Treasury*, 153.

immediately calls to mind the Habsburg-Burgundian court of the early sixteenth century, where Pierre de la Rue regularly wrote for voices that sank below the traditional gamut and where manuscripts emanating from the court's scriptorium included bottom-scraping works by other composers as well.[45] In fact, the only other works from this time that use low Bb' are linked with La Rue himself: his chanson *Pourquoy non*, his Requiem mass, and the striking motet that is potentially his as well, *Absalon fili mi*.

The opening mass, based on Andrea Gabrieli's eight-voice motet, is by another composer with a Habsburg connection. From 1607 Johann Stadlmayr was Kapellmeister at the court of Archduke Maximilian II, again in Innsbruck. As for the final two motets of VienNB 9814, the Festa motet is by one of the very few composers ever to set Charles V's motto to music. It is tempting to think that Festa's VienNB 9814 motet entered Habsburg possession around the time of Charles's Roman entry in 1536, the presumed occasion for the Italian composer's setting of the motto. For the remaining motet, no Habsburg connection is currently known, but this may be simply because the composer has not yet been determined. Examples 3a and 3b give the incipits of the *prima* and *secunda pars* respectively to facilitate identification.

Example 3. Anonymous motet incipits, VienNB 9814

a. Prima pars, *Exaudiat dominus* b. Secunda pars, *Ne vos deserat in tempore*

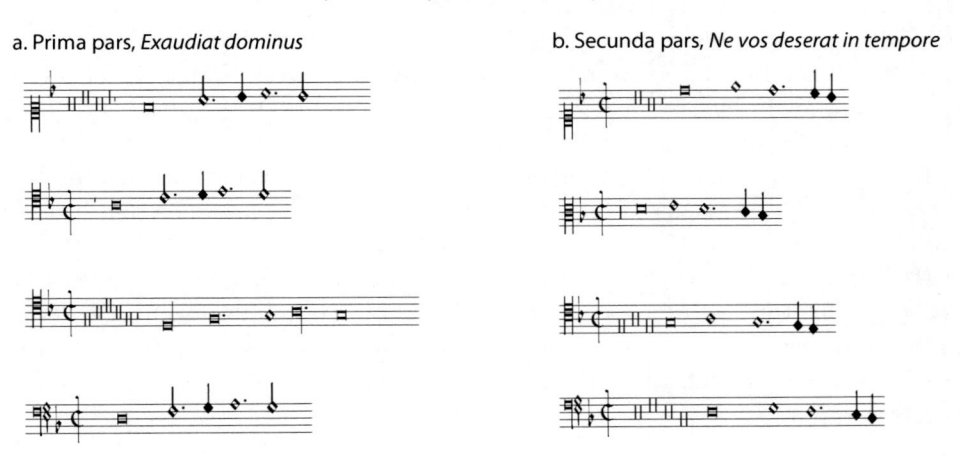

The Alamire collection within VienNB 9814, with its imperial chanson, is thus contained within surroundings that make considerable sense: it is preceded by five compositions that all have direct links to the Habsburgs themselves. Four of these pieces have their own imperial connections. Of the two motets that currently follow the Alamire portion of the manuscript, one is by a composer who set Charles's motto to music, providing yet one more imperial connection. As noted above, it was previously assumed that VienNB 9814—at least the Alamire part—was one of the more than 15,000 volumes owned by Philipp Eduard Fugger. But it was not the Österreichische Nationalbibliothek,

45 See Honey Meconi, 'The Range of Mourning: Nine Questions and Some Answers', in *Tod in Musik und Kultur. Zum 500. Todestag Philipps des Schönen*, ed. Stefan Gasch and Birgit Lodes, Wiener Forum für ältere Musikgeschichte 2 (Tutzing, 2007), 141-59.

of course, that purchased Fugger's library in 1655, for the Österreichische Nationalbibliothek did not then exist. It was the imperial court library. VienNB 9814 was very likely there all along.

Imperial Celebrations

The correction of the tenor part in La Rue's motet confirms that the Alamire portion of VienNB 9814 was proofread, which we would assume anyway from both the presence of the scribe's signature—a surprisingly rare event—as well as small marks that occur at the end of certain voices.[46] There was thus some concern to 'get it right', and an evident interest in accuracy over appearance.[47]

When we return to *Plus oultre*, the question of performance has an added dimension. Giannini and Kellman have suggested performance at court in connection with Charles's election as Holy Roman Emperor in 1519—a plausible hypothesis, though not the only possibility.[48] One thinks immediately of Charles's coronation in Aachen the following year (October 1520) or his assumption of duties as head of the order of the Golden Fleece in October 1516, either an occasion to generate both public and private celebration.[49] For that matter, almost any landmark in Charles's political life might merit the highlighting of both his motto and those of his illustrious relatives. But we should consider the connection of *Plus oultre* to the other pieces in the Alamire section of the manuscript, all motets.

First, the collection appears to have been carried out as an entity. The same hands appear throughout[50] and the staff size is consistent for five of the six pieces. The Ghiselin motet has a slightly larger staff size, but Alamire's signature at the end of the superius of that motet shows that he considered even this slightly later stage in compilation part of the whole. Three of the pieces are rubricated similarly. In several instances Alamire has begun a voice part with the other scribe, Scribe K, taking over almost immediately (in Table 1, this is indicated by the use of teardrop notes), strongly suggesting that Alamire was 'marking' the sheets, showing what was supposed to be the subject of that page for Scribe K to complete.

---

[46] On fols. 144r, 146r, and 147r, all for *Plus oultre*. These are different from the marks in other court manuscripts that Michael Friebel has suggested served as aids to copying; see idem, 'Die Handschriften Wien, Österreichische Nationalbibliothek, MS 11883 und Vatikan, Biblioteca Apostolica Vaticana, MS Chigi C VIII 234 als Vorlagen am Burgundisch-Habsburgischen Hof', in *BHCC*, 59-96. The marks in VienNB 9814 are at the ends of voices, not within, and look somewhat like a monogram or other form of joined initials.

[47] Evidence of proofreading is not unique to VienNB 9814 but is found in numerous Alamire manuscripts.

[48] Giannini and Kellman, 'Vienna, Österreichische Nationalbibliothek, Handschriftensammlung, MS 9814', 146.

[49] Schwindt, 'Habsburgische Kulturpolitik', 33 notes the use of music in connection with the new devise during the ceremonies.

[50] Music scribes K and Alamire; text scribes F and Y. See Warmington, 'A Survey of Scribal Hands', 52 for this identification; samples of music and text hands throughout the complex are given on 47-51. A clear example of Alamire's music hand can be seen in Karen Dalton and Herbert Kellman, 'Vienna, Österreichische Nationalbibliothek, Musiksammlung, MS Mus. 18825', in *Treasury*, 163; his hand appears as well in VatP 1976-79, VienNB 11778, VienNB 11883, and VienNB Mus. 18832, and possibly in BrusBR 228, BrusBR IV.922, JenaU 8, JenaU 21, MunBS 7, MunBS 34, VienNB Mus. 15941, and VienNB Mus. 18746. VienNB 9814 cannot be dated precisely, but the combination of scribes places it in the later part of Alamire's activity.

A second thing to note are the relative ranges of the compositions in VienNB 9814, given in Table 2. In contrast to many manuscripts in the court complex, nothing goes very low—or very high, either.[51] Any four singers who can perform the Ghiselin should be able to perform the Agricola. Any five singers who can perform the Mouton should be able to perform the Richafort, or, for that matter, the La Rue. *Plus oultre* is an outlier here, but in this case our knowledge of Charles's specific singers comes in handy. During La Rue's time at the court we know the voice parts of very few singers, though we know that La Rue sang superius (*dessus*), and we can surmise that he worked with a splendid batch of extremely low basses. Not long after La Rue's death, though, the famous chapel paylist of 1522[52] breaks down its singers into specific voice parts: four *dessus*, four *haultcontres*, five *haulteneurs*, four *basscontres*. At least two of the *haultcontres* and three of the *haulteneurs* on the 1522 list were almost certainly with Charles in October 1520 when he was crowned Holy Roman Emperor.[53]

Although Alamire and his team did not explore the motet repertoire to the extent that they did the mass repertoire, his motet collections nonetheless frequently demonstrate a kind of internal coherence—at least for much of an individual collection.[54] We should therefore examine the possibility that the Alamire portion of VienNB 9814 has its own unity, with the hypothesis that the pieces in this section—not just the imperial chanson *Plus oultre*—represent music used to honor and celebrate Charles in his imperial duties.[55]

The five motets set four texts. Two of these are prayers that do not use standard texts: *Ave domina sancta maria* and *O domine Jhesu Christe*, of which the former is an indulgenced prayer said to be by Pope Sixtus IV.[56] Let us consider their meanings. First, *Ave domina sancta maria*:

Ave domina sancta Maria,	Hail, holy Lady, Mary,
Regina caeli, porta paradisi,	Queen of heaven, gate of paradise,
Domina mundi, tu es virgo.	Lady of the world, you are a virgin.
Tu concepisti Jesum sine peccato,	Without sin, you conceived Jesus,
Salvatorem huius mundi,	Saviour of this world,
In quo non dubito.	In whom I do not doubt.
Libera nos ab omnibus malis.	Deliver us from all evil.
Et ora pro peccatis nostris.	And pray for our sins.
Amen	Amen.

---

[51] Although fixed pitch did not exist in the sixteenth century, the Habsburg-Burgundian court, which traveled everywhere with a *positiv* organ, seems to have been aware of the implications of notation at different pitch levels. See Meconi, 'The Range of Mourning'.

[52] Published most recently in Ferer, *Music and Ceremony*, 77.

[53] Although no chapel paylist survives from Charles's coronation, paylists before and after that date enable one to surmise which singers were in his service at that time. See Ferer, *Music and Ceremony*, 68-77 for paylists from that period.

[54] For example, the Paschaltide motets in VienNB Mus. 18825, the *Salve regina* collection of MunBS 34, the symbolically charged repertoire of LonBLR 8 G. vii.

[55] Both the Agricola and the Mouton motets appear elsewhere in the Alamire manuscripts, in VatP 1976-79 and 's-HerAB 72C respectively; the La Rue motet is unique to VienNB 9814. From the surviving sources, it seems that neither the Agricola nor Ghiselin pieces circulated widely (three and two sources respectively), but Mouton's work (eight sources) and especially the Richafort motet (nineteen sources) were popular. Although the repertoire of the Alamire portion of VienNB 9814 may seem somewhat old-fashioned, with probably at least half of the composers already deceased at the time of its production, Alamire continued to draw on older music through his scribal career; see Meconi, 'Alamire, Pierre de la Rue, and Manuscript Production'.

[56] On this text, also known as 'Ave sanctissima Maria', see Bonnie J. Blackburn, 'The Virgin in the Sun: Music and Image for a Prayer Attributed to Sixtus IV', in *Journal of the Royal Musical Association* 124 (1999), 157-95.

And *O domine Jhesu Christe*:

O domine Jhesu Christe, fili Dei vivi,	O Lord Jesus Christ, son of the living God,
Qui dignatus es pro me nasci pro me pati,	Who didst deign to be born for me, to suffer,
Mori et resurgere a mortuis,	To die, and to be raised again from the dead,
Sicut sis et vis, miserere nobis,	As thou livest and art willing, have mercy upon us,
Et sanctissima Maria, mater tua,	And may thy mother, most holy Mary,
Sit advocata nostra dum mortis venerit hora.	Be our advocate when the hour of death comes.
Amen.	Amen.[57]

The two are complementary in various ways. Each invokes a leading intercessor, mother and son, but each also mentions the other: the prayer to Mary refers to her son; the call to Christ asks for Mary's help as well. Each uses phrases reminiscent of better-known prayers: 'queen of heaven', 'deliver us from all evil', 'be our advocate when the hour of death comes'. Each closes with an 'amen'. Any ceremonial occasion using these motets would show Charles's piety, his desire for divine blessing and care, his support of traditional (as opposed to Reformational) Christianity, and his Habsburg belief in the Immaculate Conception: all worthwhile sentiments for the person who became Holy Roman Emperor.

The other motets have a rather different flavor. Here is *Tua est potentia*:

Tua est potentia tuum regnum, Domine.	Yours is the power, yours the kingdom, Lord.
Tu es super omnes gentes.	You are above all nations.
Da pacem, Domine, in diebus nostris.	Give peace in our time, o Lord.[58]

Though the text is about the Lord, the ideas are surely those that Charles thought about himself upon his ascent to the position of Holy Roman Emperor: his was now the power, he was now above all nations, and he wished to be the bringer of peace. As for *Iam non dicam*:[59]

---

[57] Translation from Pierre de la Rue, *The Motets*, ed. Nigel St. John Davidson, Corpus Mensurabilis Musicae 97 (Neuhausen, 1996), vol. 9, lv.

[58] Translation after Edward E. Lowinsky (ed.), *The Medici Codex of 1518: A Choirbook of Motets Dedicated to Lorenzo de' Medici, Duke of Urbino,* 3 vols., Monuments of Renaissance Music 3-5 (Chicago-London, 1968), vol. 1, 186.

[59] During the workshop it was pointed out that a brief motive in the Richafort (tenor 2 bb. 17-19, superius bb. 22-24) is that of the opening imitative gesture of *Plus oultre*. David Burn noted that this rising fifth followed by a rising third is often found in chants that use the so-called German dialect.

Iam non dicam vos servos sed amicos meos,	I will not now call you servants, but my friends,
Quia omnia cognovistis	Because you have known all the things
Quae operatus sum in medio vestri, alleluia.	That I have done in the midst of you, alleluia.
Accipite spiritum sanctum:	Receive the Holy Spirit:
Quorum remiseritis peccata,	Whose sins you shall forgive,
Remittuntur eis, alleluia.	They are forgiven them, alleluia.
Cum venerit ille spiritus veritatis,	When he, the spirit of truth, shall come,
Ille docebit vos omnem veritatem, alleluia	He will teach you all truth, alleluia
Et quae ventura sunt	And those things that are to come,
Annunciabit vobis alleluia	He shall tell you, alleluia.[60]

This text is superficially more modest, but if we read Charles as the implied protagonist, it casts him as magnanimous, a team player, first among equals, and a vanguard of the future. Perhaps most interesting, it serves as a foil to *Tua est potentia*, and the two motets together reflect the main sentiments of *Plus oultre*: the powerful ruler destined for greatness who nonetheless leads by virtue and follows the virtue of moderation above all.

This interpretation of these texts is prompted by the presence of *Plus oultre*, the solitary non-religious work among five motets, all of which were obviously copied in close proximity. The uniqueness of *Plus oultre*'s text and the fact that this small circle of compositions travelled together suggests a unified purpose. Other factors support this interpretation. First, though it may appear to be stretching a point to read Charles into texts about divine beings, this is precisely what Charles—or rather, his publicity machine—did. In 1515, when he made his triumphal entry into Bruges, three angels sang the 'Fecit potentiam' verse from the Magnificat: 'He hath shown strength with his arm'.[61] Identification of the court's rulers with the divine was not limited to Charles; his grandfather (and predecessor as Holy Roman Emperor) Maximilian employed various analogies with Christ as well.[62] In addition, when Charles made his triumphal entry into Barcelona in 1519, he was greeted by four people singing 'Domine tua est potentia'.[63] This could not have been Mouton's motet unless the chronicler muddled the text slightly and miscounted performers (both errors possible, of course). But this reference does confirm the practice of conflating sacred and secular dominion, and it provides a specific association of the 'Tua est potentia' text with Charles and ceremonial display. And then there is the likely provenance of VienNB 9814 as a whole within imperial collections.

We see a pattern here, and it is one of the empire's music. For whatever reason, the six pieces in VienNB 9814 that originated under Alamire's scrutiny were kept together as an entity and passed down in conjunction with music from imperial courts and imperial centers. *Plus oultre* was the composition in Alamire's half dozen with the most

---

[60] Translation after Johannes Richafort, *Opera omnia*, ed. Harry Elzinga, Corpus Mensurabilis Musicae 81 (Holzegerlingen, 1999), vol. 2, xiv.

[61] Ferer, *Music and Ceremony*, 226.

[62] See Larry Silver, *Marketing Maximilian: The Visual Ideology of a Holy Roman Emperor* (Princeton-Oxford, 2008), especially 136 ff. I suspect a systematic search would reveal similar tactics by other rulers.

[63] Emilio Ros-Fábregas, 'Music and Ceremony during Charles V's 1519 Visit to Barcelona', in *Early Music* 23 (1995), 375-91 at 376.

obvious and direct connection to Charles, but its companions in preservation were works that just as readily, if more subtly, called to mind the young Charles, his dreams, his aspirations, and his hopes for the future as he embarked on his reign as Holy Roman Emperor.

Abstract

The manuscript Vienna, Österreichische Nationalbibliothek, Handschriftensammlung, Ms. 9814 includes a section compiled under the supervision of Petrus Alamire that contains five motets and one anonymous chanson, *Plus oultre*. The works are anomalous within Alamire's output, copied as they are on a series of separate paper folios. The essay demonstrates that the anonymous chanson, inspired by the motto adopted by Archduke Charles at the age of sixteen, is unlikely to be by the recently retired court composer Pierre de la Rue. It further documents how most of the non-Alamire works included in the manuscript are directly connected to later members of the Habsburg dynasty, strengthening the likelihood that the Alamire portions of the manuscript were not transmitted through the Fugger family, as usually assumed, but via imperial channels. The texts of the Alamire motets are shown to reflect the image of the young Charles and to mirror the sentiments of the *Plus oultre* chanson, thereby unifying the collection.

The Apotheosis of the *Salve regina* and the Purpose of Munich, Bayerische Staatsbibliothek, Mus.ms. 34[*]

A a r o n J a m e s

The collection of the Bayerische Staatsbibliothek in Munich contains four musical manuscripts prepared in the illustrious workshop of the Burgundian court copyist Petrus Alamire.[1] Although the precise circumstances of their copying are not known, three of these were almost certainly destined for the duke of Bavaria, Wilhelm IV (r. 1508-50), as they are decorated with the ducal arms and entered the Bayerische Staatsbibliothek collection through the ducal court library.[2] Two of the three manuscripts in this group, MunBS 6 and 7, contain masses by composers such as Bauldeweyn, Champion, Févin, and Gascongne—the characteristic mixture of Burgundian and French court composers whose works often feature in Habsburg-Burgundian court manuscripts.[3] The most exceptional manuscript of the group, however, is MunBS 34, a source likewise containing music by northern composers but consisting entirely of vocal polyphonic settings of the Marian antiphon *Salve regina*.[4] For a complete list of the contents of MunBS 34, see Table 1.[5] Its twenty-nine settings of the text make this manuscript one of the largest and most significant sources for the polyphonic *Salve regina*, and the only known surviving manuscript of the early sixteenth century dedicated exclusively to this genre.

[*] Portions of this article were read at the annual meeting of the Renaissance Society of America, New York City, 27-29 March, 2014, at the conference 'Sources of Identity: Makers, Owners and Users of Music Sources before 1600', University of Sheffield, 4-6 October, 2013 and at the McGill University Music Graduate Symposium, 15-17 March 2013. This study has benefited from suggestions by Jack Blaszkiewicz, Julie Cumming, Roger Freitas, Naomi Gregory, Jacobijn Kiel, Eric Lubarsky, and Thomas Schmidt. I would especially like to thank Michael Anderson, Patrick Macey, Honey Meconi, and the two anonymous readers for this Journal for their detailed and helpful comments on this article.

[1] On the significance of Alamire, see Herbert Kellman, 'Production, Distribution, and Symbolism of the Manuscripts - A Synopsis' and Eugeen Schreurs, 'Petrus Alamire: Music Calligrapher, Musician, Composer, Spy', both in *The Treasury of Petrus Alamire*, ed. Herbert Kellman (Ghent-Amsterdam, 1999), 10-14 and 15-27 (henceforth abbreviated as *Treasury*); and Hannah Hutchens Mowrey, 'The Alamire Manuscripts of Frederick the Wise: Intersections of Music, Art, and Theology' (Ph.D. diss., Eastman School of Music, University of Rochester, 2010), 1-17.

[2] MunBS 6, 7, and 34. See Eric Jas, 'Munich, Bayerische Staatsbibliothek, Musiksammlung, Musica MS 34', in *Treasury*, 118. A fourth Alamire manuscript not part of this group, Mus.ms. F is now housed in the Bayerische Staatsbibliothek but was not prepared for the Bavarian court.

[3] Abbreviations for Renaissance manuscripts follow Herbert Kellman and Charles Hamm (eds.), *Census-Catalogue of Manuscript Sources of Polyphonic Music 1400-1550*, 5 vols., Renaissance Manuscript Studies 1 (Neuhausen-Stuttgart, 1979-88).

[4] The one German composer represented in MunBS 34—Adam Rener, a chapel musician at the electoral chapel in Saxony—was born in Liège and trained in Burgundy, and his *Salve regina* setting is in a northern style.

[5] This table is adapted from that in Sonja Stafford Ingram, 'The Polyphonic *Salve Regina*, 1425-1550' (Ph.D. diss, University of North Carolina at Chapel Hill, 1973), 133-37. Ingram identifies five patterns of sectional division in *Salve regina* settings: *alternatim*, tripartite, nine-sectioned, bipartite, and continuous; see her 'Polyphonic *Salve Regina*', 91-102. I have simplified her schema to a three-part model (*alternatim*, motet-like, nine-sectioned), to emphasize that these structures also correspond to distinct traditions of performance practice. The spelling of Molinet's name adopted here is taken from the court chapel's records rather than from the unique spelling "Molunet" in MunBS 34: see Honey Meconi, *Pierre de la Rue and Musical Life at the Habsburg-Burgundian Court* (Oxford, 2003), 76.

Table 1. Musical contents of MunBS 34

No.	Fols.	Composer	Voices	Key	Text setting	Added secular melody
1	1v-7r	Josquin	5	♭	Motet-like (three *partes*)	None
2	7v-8r	La Rue I	4		Motet-like (two *partes*)	None
3	8v-11r	Divitis	5	♭	Motet-like (one *pars*)	*Adieu, mes amours* (anon., polyphonic setting by Josquin)
4	11v-20r	Richafort	5	♭	Motet-like (three *partes*)	None
5	20v-25r	Rener	5	♭	*Alternatim* (even verses)	None
6	25v-29r	Pipelare	5		*Alternatim* (even verses)	None
7	29v-33r	Molinet	5		*Alternatim* (even verses)	*O werde mont* (anon.)
8	33v-37r	Vinders I	5		*Alternatim* (even verses)	*Ghy syt de lefte* (Ghiselin)
9	38v-43r	Bauldeweyn	6		*Alternatim* (even verses)	*Je n'ay deuil* (Ockeghem)
10	43v-49r	Obrecht	6	♭	*Alternatim* (even verses)	None
11	50v-54r	Anonymous	4		*Alternatim* (even verses)	None
12	54v-57r	Lebrun	4	♭	*Alternatim* (even verses)	None
13	58v-64r	La Rue II	4		Motet-like (three *partes*)	None
14	64v-68r	La Rue III	4		Motet-like (two *partes*)	None
15	68v-72r	Reingot	4		Motet-like (three *partes*)	None
16	72v-81r	Anonymous	4	♭	Nine sections	None
17	82v-86r	La Rue IV	4		*Alternatim* (even verses)	*Par le regart* (Du Fay) *Je ne vis oncques* (Du Fay/ Binchois)
18	86v-90r	La Rue V	4		*Alternatim* (even verses)	None
19	90v-96r	De Vourda I	4		*Alternatim* (even verses)	None
20	96v-99r	De Vourda II	4		*Alternatim* (even verses)	None
21	99v-103r	Anonymous	4		*Alternatim* (even verses)	*Myn hert heeft altijt* (La Rue)
22	104v-108r	Craen	4		*Alternatim* (even verses)	None
23	108v-112r	Anonymous	4		*Alternatim* (even verses)	*O werde mont* (anon.)
24	112v-115r	Anonymous	4		*Alternatim* (even verses)	None
25	115v-118r	Anonymous	4		*Alternatim* (even verses)	*Myns liefkens bruyn ooghen* (anon.)
26	118v-122r	Anonymous	4		*Alternatim* (even verses)	None
27	122v-124r	Ghiselin	4		*Alternatim* (even verses)	*Je ne vis oncques* (Du Fay/ Binchois)
28	124v-127r	Vinders II	4		*Alternatim* (even verses)	None
29	127v-131r	Vinders III	4		*Alternatim* (even verses)	None

Despite the unique contents of MunBS 34, few scholars have examined it in detail. The most extended discussion remains that of Sonja Stafford Ingram in her 1973 dissertation; however, Ingram's survey of *Salve regina* settings over a 125-year period necessarily limits any discussion of specific sources.[6] Several scholars have discussed

---

[6] Ingram, 'The Polyphonic *Salve Regina*'. Ingram discusses MunBS 34 from pp. 131-38, but her discussion is brief and has in places been superseded by more recent scholarship; for example, she writes that MunBS 34 belonged to Raimond

individual *Salve regina* settings in this manuscript, particularly those by well-known composers such as Pierre de la Rue.[7] To date, however, no extended study of the manuscript as a whole has been published.[8]

In general, previous commentators on MunBS 34 have assumed that its repertory was 'meant to be used in daily *Salve* or *lof* services',[9] laic paraliturgical services at which performances of the *Salve regina* were prominently featured. Indeed, it seems more than likely that most of the settings in MunBS 34 were composed for performance at such services. If the repertoire was intended for use in such services, however, it does not follow that the manuscript was itself used for that purpose. For example, the recent catalogue of the Bayerische Staatsbibliothek choirbooks notes that this manuscript shows no sign of being used in performance, or, for that matter, of having been present at the ducal chapel.[10] I will further describe several notational features that make it unlikely that MunBS 34 was designed for use as a performing source. If the manuscript did not play an immediate practical role in performance, however, it could still impress its owners with the magnificence and stylistic variety of its contents, showing how a familiar devotional text could become a vehicle for compositional virtuosity and polytextual expression.

The polyphonic *Salve regina* is thus of interest not only for its intrinsic cultural significance but for the light it sheds on concepts of musical genre in the early sixteenth century. It is now customary for scholars to distinguish between the relatively simple polyphony used within the liturgy itself and the more musically elevated genre of the motet, whose most typical performance contexts were paraliturgical or devotional.[11] Since the *Salve regina* is a well-known text that was used in numerous liturgical and devotional contexts, it is not surprising to discover that musical settings of the text varied from simple sectional chant harmonizations to elaborately constructed through-composed settings. This stylistic flexibility allowed composers of *Salve regina* settings to stake out a higher or lower place on the generic continuum, depending on the level of symbolic and musical elaboration that was brought to bear on the text. I will argue, then, that the compilation of MunBS 34 demonstrates a concept of the polyphonic *Salve regina* as a prestige genre in a similar sense to the mass, in which a familiar text could

---

Fugger the Younger rather than Wilhelm IV.

[7] See, for example, Julie Cumming and Peter Schubert, 'Text and Motif c. 1500: A New Approach to Text Underlay', in *Early Music* 40 (2012), 3-13, which discusses La Rue's *Salve regina* II; Martin Just, 'Das *Salve-Regina*-Repertoire von Pierre de la Rue in den Handschriften Brüssel, Bibliothèque Royale de Belgique, Ms. 9126 und München, Bayerische Staatsbibliothek, Musiksammlung, Musica MS 34', in *The Burgundian-Habsburg Court Complex of Music Manuscripts (1500-1535) and the Workshop of Petrus Alamire: Colloquium Proceedings Leuven, 25-28 November 1999*, ed. Bruno Bouckaert and Eugeen Schreurs, Yearbook of the Alamire Foundation 5 (Leuven-Neerpelt, 2003), 337-348 (henceforth abbreviated as *BHCC*); Jacobijn Kiel, 'Songs and Salves: The Case of *Vita Par le Regart* by Pierre de la Rue', in *Die Tonkunst* 5 (2011), 44-50; and Meconi, *Pierre de la Rue*, 116-20.

[8] A detailed codicological study is in preparation by Jacobijn Kiel, to whom I am indebted for sharing some of her transcriptions and an unpublished paper drawn from her research.

[9] Jas, 'Munich 34', 118.

[10] Martin Bente et al., *Bayerische Staatsbibliothek: Katalog der Musikhandschriften 1: Chorbücher und Handschriften in Chorbüchartiger Notierung*, Kataloge Bayerische Musiksammlungen 5 (Munich, 1989), 12.

[11] Such simpler polyphonic genres would include *falsobordone* settings of office hymns and psalmody. The classic formulation of this view is Anthony Cummings, 'Toward an Interpretation of the Sixteenth-Century Motet', in *Journal of the American Musicological Society* 34 (1981). 43-59. Cummings's findings are revisited and further nuanced in John Brobeck, 'Some "Liturgical Motets" for the French Royal Court: A Reconsideration of Genre in the Sixteenth-Century Motet', in *Musica Disciplina* 47 (1993), 123-57. For a more extended study of genre, see Julie E. Cumming, *The Motet in the Age of Dufay* (Cambridge, 1999), esp. ch. 2.

accumulate a variety of possible meanings, serving not only as a practical piece of liturgical music but also as a platform for the compositional ingenuity of Franco-Flemish composers.

The antiphon *Salve regina*, first attested in the mid-twelfth century, is a product of the Marian theology of its time, in which both official church pronouncements and popular piety placed increased emphasis on Mary's role as a mediator and conduit of divine grace.[12] Example 1 gives one version of the melody and text of the *Salve regina*.[13] Although the liturgical use of the antiphon was first promoted by monastic orders, the quick absorption of the *Salve regina* into popular culture is demonstrated by references to the antiphon in literary and poetic sources and by the establishment of *lof* or *Salve* services, which were instituted and financed by lay confraternities.[14] Although such services were popular throughout Europe, they had a particularly high standing in the thriving market towns of the Low Countries, where confraternity members often included wealthy tradesmen who could afford to provide opulent music for these services. Among the first such organizations to sponsor a daily *lof* was the Marian confraternity at St. Gudule in Brussels, which instituted the service beginning in 1362.[15] At the Church of Our Lady in Antwerp, perhaps the most famous foundation for lay Marian devotion, a polyphonic *Salve regina* was normally sung at a daily *lof* sponsored by the Confraternity of Our Lady, a service requiring a priest, an organist, the choirboys of the parish, and four adult professional singers.[16]

Despite the existence of this rich devotional context, MunBS 34 was created in a very different milieu: it was destined not for a confraternity, but for a ducal court.[17] The attractive appearance of this choirbook seems to point to a function as a presentation manuscript; the music of MunBS 34 is copied on parchment, decorated with the ducal coat of arms, and introduced by elaborate initials with grotesques.[18] What might the value of such a manuscript have been to the duke of Bavaria, its intended recipient?

---

[12] Its earliest known appearance may be the Cistercian antiphoner Paris, Bibliothèque nationale, n.a. 1412 (c. 1150-60); see Jeannine S. Ingram and Keith Falconer, 'Salve regina', in *Grove Music Online. Oxford Music Online*. Oxford University Press, <http://www.oxfordmusiconline.com/subscriber/article/grove/music/24431> (accessed 12 December 2012). On the Marian theology of the twelfth century, see Eva de Visscher, 'Marian Devotion in the Latin West', in *Mary: The Complete Resource*, ed. Sarah Jane Boss (Oxford, 2007), 181.

[13] Hypothetical reconstruction of plainchant in the form it was used by Josquin, from John Milsom, 'Analysing Josquin', in *The Josquin Companion*, ed. Richard Sherr (Oxford, 2001), 431-84 at 442, based on Josquin's *Salve regina à 5* (MunBS 34, No. 1). This version contains melodic variants used in the other settings in MunBS 34.

[14] The *Salve* is mentioned, for example, in Dante's *La Divina Commedia* (Purgatorio VII: 79-84) and in the *In promptuarium discipuli de miraculis de Beata Virginis* of Johannes Herolt, a collection of one hundred miracles of Our Lady of which six cite the particular power of the *Salve regina*. See Ingram, 'The Polyphonic *Salve Regina*', 22-31.

[15] Kristine K. Forney, 'Music, Ritual and Patronage at the Church of Our Lady, Antwerp', in *Early Music History* 7 (1987), 1. Robert Nosow has recently presented documents from the Confraternity of Our Lady of the Snow in Bruges, which established their own *lof* in 1428; see his *Ritual Meaning in the Fifteenth-Century Motet* (Cambridge, 2012), 128-31. Nosow's book provides a written outline of the structure of a *Salve* service in Bruges, which could include Marian hymns, motets, and the *Ave Maria* in addition to the *Salve regina* itself.

[16] Forney, 'Music, Ritual and Patronage', 9-11.

[17] Alamire was familiar with both contexts, having been commissioned to create manuscripts for famous confraternities in Antwerp and 's-Hertogenbosch. His manuscripts for the Confraternity of Our Lady in Antwerp include two 'Virgo books' in 1514 and 1519, presumably collections of Marian motets or *Salve regina* settings; see Forney, 'Music, Ritual, and Patronage', 30-33.

[18] The manuscript's size (480 × 275 millimetres) is also impressive, although it is not as large as some other Alamire manuscripts (MunBS 6 and 7, for example, are both approximately 560 × 390 millimetres).

Example 1. *Salve regina* chant

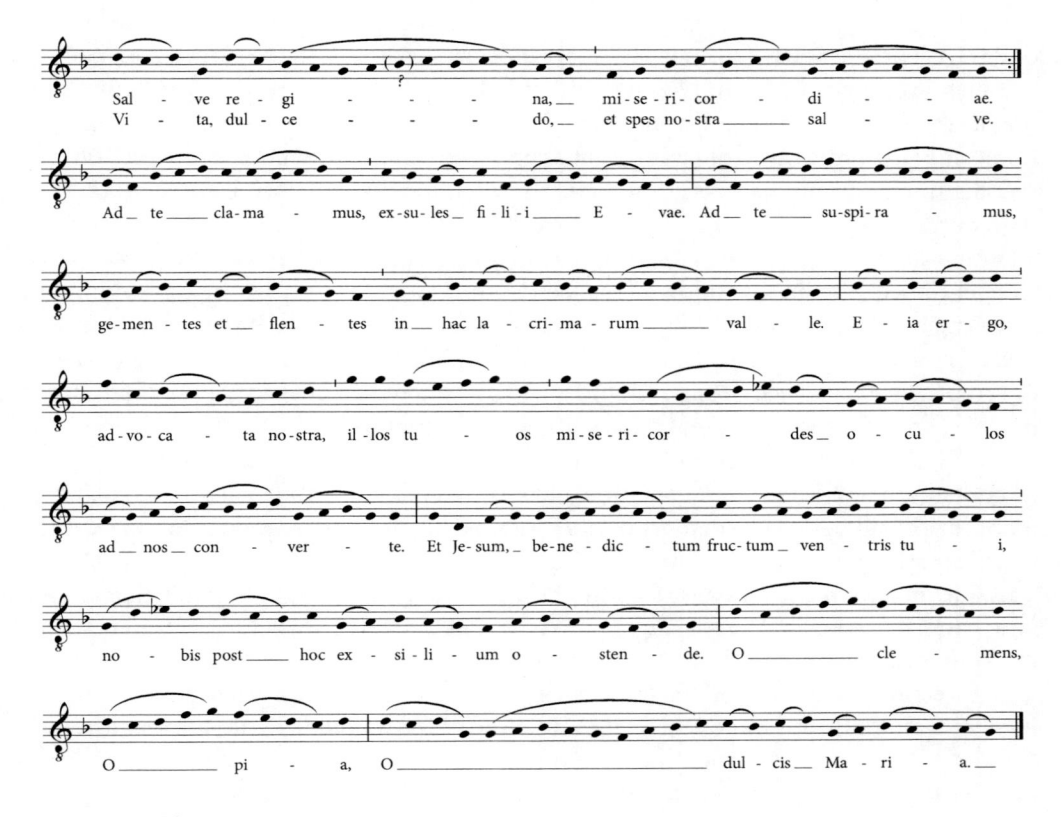

Translation:

Hail, Queen, mother of mercy, our life, sweetness, and hope, hail. To you we cry, exiled children of Eve, to you we sigh, mourning and weeping in this vale of tears. Ah then, our advocate, turn your merciful eyes upon us, and show to us Jesus, the blessed fruit of our womb, after this exile. O merciful, O loving, O sweet virgin Mary.[19]

The Purpose of the Manuscript: Politics and Performance

Scholars have identified various possible purposes, not mutually exclusive, for the manuscripts produced in Alamire's workshop.[20] Some, like the choirbook prepared as a gift for Henry VIII,[21] were intended to flatter or curry favour with a foreign ruler. Honey

---

[19] Translation mine.

[20] Relatively little is known about the conditions under which Alamire and his scribes produced their manuscripts; the makeup of the organization and its relationship to the Burgundian court varied considerably between 1508 and 1534. Although I use the term 'workshop' and occasionally 'scriptorium' for this organization, these terms should not be taken to suggest that the workshop had a fixed membership or single physical location. On the institutional context for Alamire manuscript production, see Zoe Saunders, 'Anonymous Masses in the Alamire Manuscripts: Toward a New Understanding of a Repertoire, an *Atelier*, and a Renaissance Court' (Ph.D. diss., University of Maryland, College Park, 2010), 309-13.

[21] London, British Library, Royal 8 G.vii; on this manuscript, see Honey Meconi, 'Another Look at Absalon', in *Tijdschrift van de Koninklijke Vereniging voor Nederlandse Muziekgeschiedenis* 48 (1998), 3-29.

Meconi has proposed such a diplomatic purpose for Alamire's three Bavarian manuscripts, MunBS 6, 7, and 34, which seem to stem from a period of goodwill between Wilhelm IV of Bavaria and the newly crowned Habsburg emperor Charles V in the early 1520s.[22] Since disputes over land ownership led to conflict between the two rulers in 1526, this date provides a presumptive *terminus ante quem* for all three manuscripts.[23] As Herbert Kellman points out, the production of lavish manuscripts also served to symbolize the prestige of the Habsburg-Burgundian court, particularly when the manuscripts featured works by the court's famous house composer, Pierre de la Rue.[24] Stanley Boorman has drawn attention to a third possibility, that some manuscripts in the Burgundian court complex were designed primarily with performance in mind, as 'gifts of repertoire for use in the recipients' performing institutions'.[25] Boorman points to the care taken by the scribes of several manuscripts to clarify text underlay, to provide cautionary accidentals, and to add or remove ligatures; such details point to an artistic interest in questions of performance practice, and an expectation that the resulting manuscript would be used by singers.[26]

Evaluating these possibilities in detail will require a closer look at MunBS 34 and its contents, beginning with its notation and layout. Following Boorman's criteria, if the manuscript had been intended primarily for practical performance, one should expect to see notational features designed to aid performers in singing the piece easily at sight. This does not seem to be the case for MunBS 34; instead, the details of notational practice and patterns of scribal error suggest that the manuscript was not compiled with performance as a primary purpose.

Reconstructions of Alamire's scribal practice posit a multi-stage process often involving multiple music and text scribes; after the music was copied into the manuscript and texted, the book was proofread for errors and decorations were added.[27] This scribal process allowed errors introduced at one stage of copying to be corrected in another, as seen in Figure 1: here, a music scribe inadvertently copied the same line of music twice, and a later scribe crossed out the excess music. Since the text of the music has been added around the crossed-off passage, this correction was presumably made by a proofreader at the Alamire workshop either before or during the copying of the text. However, this division of labour could also result in errors and omissions in the finished product. In the *Salve regina* setting by Ghiselin, the added melody *Je ne vis oncques* has not been labelled by the text scribe. The omission of an indication here is unusual: every other secular song used in MunBS 34 is labelled correctly, and it is possible that the text scribe simply did not know this chanson.[28]

[22] Honey Meconi, 'The Function of the Habsburg-Burgundian Court Manuscripts', in *BHCC*, 121-22. Meconi cites the codex Wolfenbüttel, Herzog August Bibliothek, Cod. Guelf. A Aug. 2° [WolfA A], a lavishly decorated choirbook prepared at the Bavarian court in 1519-20, which may have initiated the exchange of gifts between the two rulers. See also Saunders on MunBS 6 in 'Anonymous Masses', 146-48 and 180-83.

[23] Meconi, 'The Function of the Habsburg-Burgundian Court Manuscripts', 122.

[24] Herbert Kellman, 'Production, Distribution, and Symbolism of the Manuscripts - A Synopsis', in *Treasury*, 14. Two manuscripts that display this prestige particularly clearly are Mechelen, Archief en Stadsbibliotheek, Ms. s. s. and Vienna, Österreichische Nationalbibliothek, Mus. Ms. 15946 [VienNB 15946], both decorated with symbols of imperial power and consisting almost entirely of masses by La Rue.

[25] Stanley Boorman, 'The Purpose of the Gift: For Display or Performance?', in *BHCC*, 108.

[26] Boorman, 'The Purpose of the Gift', 109.

[27] Warmington, 'A Survey of Scribal Hands in the Manuscripts', in *Treasury*, 41-43; and Saunders, 'Anonymous Masses', 290-98.

[28] On the Alamire scriptorium's approach to borrowed material, see Honey Meconi, 'Habsburg-Burgundian Manuscripts, Borrowed Material, and the Practice of Naming', in *Early Musical Borrowing*, ed. Honey Meconi (New York, 2004),

Figure 1. Excerpt from anonymous *Salve regina*, No. 26 (MunBS 34, fol. 121v), showing a line of music copied twice, struck out and marked with *signa congruentiae*. Reproduced with permission

The first *Salve regina* setting by Vinders (setting No. 8 in the manuscript; see the Appendix for a transcription) contains some particularly revealing irregularities in text underlay. In the 'Et Jesum' verse of this setting, the scribe has supplied incomplete text for the tenor and discantus voices, which are texted only for the first half of the verse ('Et Jesum…fructum ventris tui'). The remainder of the text ('nobis post hoc exilium ostende') has been omitted, presumably in error. This error has been duplicated in the bassus voice, which is divided between the bottom of the recto and verso pages in order to fit five voices on a single opening. Rather than continuing the text begun by the bassus on the facing recto page, the scribe copied the text from the tenor line above. The result is shown in Figures 2 and 3: after the bassus sings the phrase 'post hoc', the setting continues not with the words 'exilium ostende' that should follow, but with the word 'tui', found in the tenor part on the line immediately above.[29]

Figure 2. Bottom of fol. 36r in MunBS 34, showing bassus part in Vinders, 'Et Jesum' section (corresponds to b. 79 in modern edition). Reproduced with permission

Figure 3. Bottom of fol. 35v in MunBS 34, showing continuation of bassus part from Figure 2 with incorrect text copied from tenor (bassus part corresponds to b. 92 in modern edition). Reproduced with permission

86-95. *Je ne vis oncques* is also not labelled in its other appearance in this manuscript (in the 'Et Jesum' section of the fourth *Salve regina* by La Rue, No. 17).

[29] As Flynn Warmington notes, these 'voice completions' were typically added in the last stages of copying; see her 'A Survey of Scribal Hands', 41.

Instances of impractical or incomplete text underlay are not necessarily significant; vague underlay is typical of this source and of sixteenth-century manuscripts in general.[30] With a text as familiar as the *Salve regina*, moreover, it would not be difficult for singers to correct the text underlay in performance, filling in the antiphon text based on their experience of singing other *Salve regina* settings. Although this is far from a unique example of incomplete text underlay,[31] this particular pattern of error suggests that the text scribe's attention was on the physical appearance of the score rather than on the syntactical correctness of the text; the text phrases are carefully aligned to create a symmetrical appearance. A comparison to Figure 4 is instructive, showing a similar instance in which a single line of the bassus part is copied below the bottom of the tenor part. Here again the word 'valle' is carefully aligned vertically so that the two parts match, even though the text in the tenor part would presumably begin with the musical phrase at the left side of the line.[32] In both cases, text is underlaid in such a way as to create a symmetrical and visually attractive layout.

Figure 4. Bottom of fol. 34v in MunBS 34, showing vertical alignment of text at cadence on the text 'lacrimarum valle'. Reproduced with permission

The instances of missing or misplaced text which account for many of the errors in MunBS 34 can be attributed to Scribe Z, identified by Flynn Warmington as the sole text scribe for this manuscript.[33] The patterns of error in this manuscript suggest that Scribe Z was not the most careful of copyists, occasionally omitting phrases of text or performance directions; similar error patterns occur in MunBS 6, where he left out large

---

[30] On text underlay, see Honey Meconi, 'Is Underlay Necessary?', in *Companion to Medieval and Renaissance Music*, ed. Tess Knighton and David Fallows (London, 1992), 284-91; and Cumming and Schubert, 'Text and Motif c. 1500'.

[31] Other infelicities in texting in this source can more easily be attributed to simple oversight, such as the omission of two words of the antiphon text ('et flentes') in the discantus part of the anonymous setting No. 21 (fol. 100v). Such an error pattern suggests that the scribe simply skipped ahead to the next phrase of the familiar antiphon text. Here, again, a skilled performer could correct the error by supplying the missing text from memory and underlaying it to an untexted phrase of the music. Other texting errors are more perplexing, such as the text phrase 'O Salve' (instead of 'O pia') in the bassus voice of the first setting by Vinders (fol. 37r).

[32] The word 'lacrimarum' cannot be aligned precisely between the two parts because there is a rest in the bassus part below the word 'lacrimarum' in the tenor part.

[33] Warmington, 'Overview of the Scribes', 52. Scribe Z was also solely responsible for copying the text of MunBS 6 and Brussels, Bibliothèque royale Albert I, Ms. 15075 [BrusBR 15075], both presentation manuscripts. In addition to the text hand Z, Warmington identifies three music hands (C2, H2, and I). Of these four music and text hands, all except C1 are associated with the later stages of the Alamire scriptorium; Warmington suggests that the hand C1, present only here and in VienNB 18746, might belong to Alamire himself.

portions of text for the tenor part of Champion's *Missa Sing ich nit wol*,[34] and also neglected to include instructions for the tenor canon in the anonymous *Missa Du bon du cueur*, leaving the mass unrealizable as written.[35] Despite the sometimes striking errors in his work, Scribe Z seems to have had some experience as a performer: repeated motives, such as the repetition of 'nobis' in Figure 2, are often re-texted, and individual syllables are frequently underlaid rather than entire words—details that suggest attention to the practical needs of performers. Nonetheless, the significant mistakes in texting here and in the other manuscripts texted by Scribe Z suggest that he did not possess the eye for detail of a more experienced scribe.

A final pattern of scribal error can be seen in the placement of line endings, which do not always correspond to Alamire's usual practice. As a general rule, Alamire's scribes aimed to end each line with a complete perfection—a practice that aided performers in negotiating the rhythms of the piece, since they could expect that each new line would correspond to the beginning of a new metrical unit.[36] This general notational practice was relaxed only if the music contained syncopated rhythms that crossed the perfection boundary, making it impossible for the scribe to notate the music according to the preferred practice. MunBS 34, however, contains several instances where the line endings are placed in the middle of a perfection, even though the music does not contain syncopations and there is no lack of space on the manuscript line.

Figure 5, taken from the opening of the first *Salve regina* setting by Laurentius de Vourda (No. 17), shows one such instance. Throughout this section of music, notated in perfect tempus, the line endings fail to correspond to complete perfections. If the music is read in imperfect tempus, however, each line ending corresponds precisely to a perfection boundary, matching Alamire's normal scribal practice. Since duple mensurations had become the norm by the 1520s, it is not difficult to reconstruct how such an error might have taken place; a scribe accustomed to the repertoire of the 1520s, in which imperfect tempus predominates, was unused to the conventions for notating perfect tempus and slipped into the more familiar notational patterns of imperfect tempus. This error is thus a barometer of stylistic change, demonstrating the increased prevalence of imperfect tempus after 1500, but it could also point to a somewhat hurried compilation for MunBS 34, in which the scribe copied according to a default pattern rather than following the mensuration of the piece being copied.

Various explanations are possible for the error patterns in MunBS 34, either singly or in combination; the manuscript could have been copied in haste, or have been copied by scribes with limited training and expertise. Previous scholars have noted that the Habsburg-Burgundian manuscripts of the 1520s and 1530s contain a higher frequency of errors than the earlier manuscripts of the complex. Zoe Saunders has shown that the

---

[34] See fol. 126v and subsequent openings in MunBS 6. A later (non-Alamire) hand has added the missing text in the tenor part, as well as numerous additional text repetitions (primarily in the Sanctus and Agnus Dei) and several *signa congruentiae*. These patterns of correction illustrate specific ways that the Alamire codices might have been found wanting by performers.

[35] On this mass, see Saunders, 'Anonymous Masses,' 148. BrusBR 15075 does not contain the striking errors of MunBS 6 or 34, although its page layout shows the same preference for symmetrical text layout noted earlier; see also Bernadette Nelson, 'The *Missa Du bon du cuer*. An Unknown Mass by Noel Bauldeweyn?', in *Tijdschrift van de Koninklijke Vereniging voor Muziekgeschiedenis* 51 (2001), 103-30. The mass also survives in Munich 5 and Toledo 33.

[36] The PRoMS project (Production and Reading of Music Sources), under the direction of Thomas Schmidt, has shown that this is true of sixteenth-century sources in general.

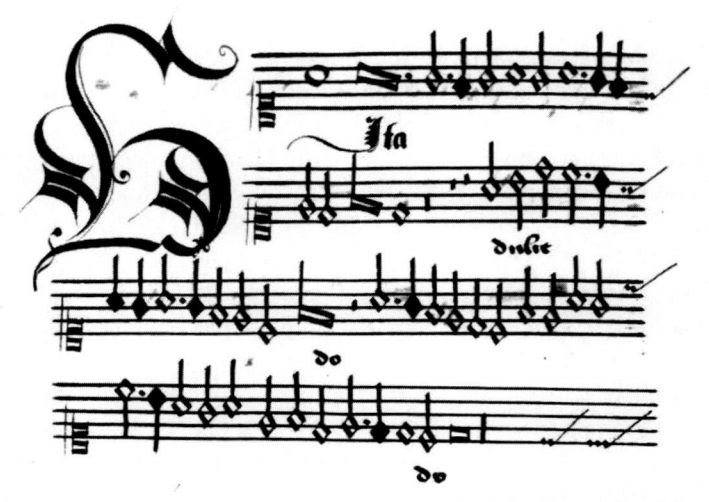

Figure 5. Opening of discantus voice in Laurentius de Vourda, *Salve regina* I (MunBS 34, fol. 90v). Reproduced with permission

process of proofreading became less rigorous in the later stages of Alamire's manuscript production, with later manuscripts showing a significantly larger number of uncorrected errors.[37] Honey Meconi has linked this later period of manuscript production to the departure of Charles V for Spain on 8 September 1517, arguing that the severing of direct links to the Habsburg court chapel took away Alamire's established stable of copyists and forced him to 'build up a new cadre of scribes', perhaps employing musicians from the retinue of Margaret of Austria or from one of the other performing institutions in Mechelen. This group of newly-hired musicians might well have included Scribe Z.[38]

Although a more careful proofreader might have corrected some of the notational infelicities in MunBS 34, the manuscript's untouched condition does not suggest that the errors were of great concern to its Bavarian recipients: if the Munich court musicians sang the *Salve regina* settings in this manuscript, they may well have done so by copying them out of MunBS 34 into a more user-friendly format.[39] The purpose of the manuscript is instead signalled by its attractive appearance, including elaborately decorated initials with grotesques, aligning the choirbook with other presentation manuscripts created in the Alamire workshop.[40] The function of MunBS 34 as a presentation manuscript points to the importance of the *Salve regina* settings it contains, suggesting that the symbolic significance of this repertory could outweigh the practical needs of performance.

---

[37] Saunders, 'Anonymous Masses', 295.

[38] Honey Meconi, 'Alamire, Pierre de la Rue, and Manuscript Production in the Time of Charles V', in '*Qui musicum in se habet*': *Essays in Honor of Alejandro Planchart*, ed. Stanley Boorman and Anna Zayaruznaya (Münster-Middleton, forthcoming). I am grateful to Prof. Meconi for allowing me to see a version of this article prior to publication.

[39] I am grateful to Patrick Macey for suggesting this possibility.

[40] Many Alamire presentation manuscripts also contain errors that make them less satisfactory as performing sources: this group includes the two other manuscripts texted by Scribe Z, MunBS 6 (prepared for Wilhelm IV) and BrusBR 15075 (bearing portraits of John of Portugal and Catherine of Austria, who married in 1523).

The Contents of the Manuscript: Repertory and Style

The compilers of MunBS 34 carefully chose the opening pieces of the collection with the goal of immediately impressing the book's recipient. The manuscript opens with a particularly impressive setting, the five-voice *Salve regina* by Josquin, with its recurring ostinato taken from the opening notes of the chant.[41] Following the occasional practice of the Alamire workshop, a small cross next to the composer's name indicates that Josquin had recently died.[42] Second in the collection is a setting by Pierre de la Rue,[43] the leading composer of the Habsburg-Burgundian court complex; his setting of the *Salve regina* is a strict canon, with four voices derived from a single notated part. The third setting—*Salve regina/Adieu mes amours* by Antonius Divitis[44]—is notable for the skill with which the chanson tenor *Adieu mes amours* is woven into the contrapuntal structure of the other four voices. As David Fallows notes, the reference here is not simply to the monophonic song by that title, but to the setting by Josquin, since the tenor line from Josquin's piece is transferred literally into the *Salve regina* as a cantus firmus, with rests exactly as they appear in the context of that chanson.[45]

These three compositions set a high standard of compositional virtuosity for the *Salve regina* settings that follow. Opening the manuscript with Josquin's *Salve regina* was a logical choice, beginning the manuscript with a work whose ostinato repetition of the word 'Salve' foregrounds the motto of the entire collection. The use of Josquin's music may also have been designed to exploit the popularity of Josquin's music in Bavaria, a particularly appropriate gesture in the immediate aftermath of his death.[46] Indeed, the compilation of MunBS 34 is roughly contemporary with the collecting activities of the Fugger family, wealthy bankers in nearby Augsburg with close ties to the Bavarian court who commissioned at least two Alamire manuscripts dedicated entirely to masses by Josquin.[47] The Bavarian court would acquire a significant repertory of Josquin's music after the arrival of Ludwig Senfl in 1523; the Munich choirbooks prepared under his

[41] In addition to the ostinato repetition of the chant motive in the tenor, the chant melody is paraphrased extensively in the other voices, especially the discantus; the melody appears in the bassus at 'Et Jesum'. A modern edition of the work is in *New Josquin Edition: The Collected Works of Josquin des Prez*, ed. Willem Elders (Utrecht, 2009), vol. 25, 24-35 (subsequently abbreviated to *NJE* 25.5). This setting is analyzed by John Milsom in his 'Analysing Josquin', and by Cristle Collins Judd in 'Josquin: Salve regina (à 5)', in *Models of Analysis: Music Before 1600*, ed. Mark Everist (Oxford, 1992), 114-53.

[42] This practice is used in various Alamire manuscripts to indicate the deaths of composers: e.g., Robert and Antoine de Févin in MunBS 7 and Mattheus Pipelare in BrusBR 215-216. It is not entirely consistent, however; one composer whose death is never indicated in this manner is Pierre de la Rue.

[43] Modern edition in Pierre de la Rue, *Opera Omnia*, ed. Nigel Davison, Corpus Mensurabilis Musicae 97 (Rome, 1996), vol. 9, 122-29.

[44] Modern edition in Antonius Divitis, *Collected Works*, ed. B. A. Nugent, Recent Researches in the Music of the Renaissance 94 (Madison, 1993), 216-20.

[45] David Fallows, 'Afterword: Thoughts for the Future', in *The Josquin Companion*, ed. Sherr, 575.

[46] Four Habsburg-Burgundian manuscripts open with works attributed to Josquin: Jena, Universitätsbibliothek, Ms. 3 [JenaU 3], VienNB 4809, VienNB 11778, and VienNB 15941. With the possible exception of VienNB 11778, which was acquired by the Fugger family but may not have been commissioned by them, all of these manuscripts were sent to recipients in Germany or Austria, and with the possible exception of JenaU 3 (compiled sometime after the death of Compère in 1518), all were copied after 1521. A strong case can thus be made that Alamire's manuscripts played an important role in the posthumous 'German Josquin Renaissance' usually connected with the distribution of prints by Hans Ott and others. See Stephanie P. Schlagel, 'The *Liber selectarum cantionum* and the "German Josquin Renaissance"', in *Journal of Musicology* 19 (2002), 564-615.

[47] VienNB 4809 and VienNB 11778.

direction include numerous motets by Josquin alongside those of Senfl.[48] La Rue's music was also familiar in Munich, where Wilhelm IV likely owned manuscript copies of La Rue's *Requiem* and two of his other masses by the time he received the five La Rue *Salve regina* settings in MunBS 34.[49] Besides the established familiarity of their composers, the opening pieces of the manuscript would also have impressed Bavarian musicians through their ingenious compositional construction, including the structural ostinato of Josquin's setting, Divitis's clever incorporation of a Josquin song tenor, and La Rue's strict canon with four voices in one.[50] From the beginning of the collection, the compositional variety of MunBS 34 demonstrates that the *Salve regina* offers rich and varied compositional possibilities to a skilled composer.

An examination of the complete contents of the manuscript reveals some large-scale patterns in voicing, text setting, and general musical approaches to the *Salve regina* text. Many of these differences are summarized in Table 1. As the titles of the pieces show, the *Salve regina* settings vary in scoring (between four and six voices) and some make use of borrowed material from secular songs.[51] The settings are carefully arranged according to scoring, with five-voice settings at the beginning of the manuscript, two six-voice settings immediately following, and four-voice settings in the remainder of the book.[52]

The differing patterns of scoring in MunBS 34 are complicated, however, by the existence of different dispositions of voices within the manuscript, which suggest that the repertory in the manuscript might have been intended to be sung by ensembles of different makeups. Surviving records from such organizations as the Confraternity of Our Lady in Antwerp suggest that boys participated in the *Salve* service in addition to (or instead of) male falsettists; the presence or absence of boys might explain the high clefs used in such settings as La Rue's fourth *Salve regina*, with a discantus part notated in treble clef (G2) and ranging up to notated *g″*. In the anonymous setting No. 23, on the other hand, the discantus ascends only to *a′* and could be sung by male falsettists. Although some of the settings notated at different pitches could in fact have been

---

[48] The manuscript MunBS 10, for example, consists entirely of Josquin and Senfl motets, with a combination of repertory that invites comparison between the two composers, particularly the combination of Josquin's famous *Miserere mei, Deus* with the setting of the same psalm by Senfl. Besides his activities in the Munich court chapel, Senfl played an important role in Josquin reception as the editor of the *Liber selectarum cantionum* (RISM 1520⁴).

[49] MunBS 65, with La Rue's *Requiem* and *Missa Cum iucunditate*, and WolfA A, with another copy of the *Requiem* and the *Missa Incessament*, both of which are presentation manuscripts presumably copied by 1520. On La Rue's reception in Munich, see Meconi, *Pierre de la Rue*, 192.

[50] La Rue's canonic *Salve regina* may also be linked to Josquin, since Josquin's four-voice *Salve regina* setting (*NJE* 25.4) is also a strict canon, with four voices derived from two notated voices; to my knowledge, this is the only other *Salve regina* setting of the period written completely in canon. If La Rue knew this setting, he could have written his setting either as a tribute to Josquin or as an attempt to go the master one better by constructing a canon from a single notated voice rather than Josquin's two voices. There is no direct evidence that La Rue would have come into contact with this piece, but his position at the Habsburg-Burgundian court gave him the opportunity to come into contact with a wide range of international repertoire. Honey Meconi discusses Josquin's influence on La Rue in her *Pierre de la Rue*, 172-80.

[51] Table 1 does not include changes in scoring within a piece caused by the addition or subtraction of a voice for a single *pars*, although this phenomenon will be discussed below.

[52] The single exception to this organizational scheme is La Rue's four-voice canonic *Salve regina*, the lone four-voice setting among a group of five-voice settings. As Jacobijn Kiel has suggested, this piece might have been added at a late stage of copying to fill blank pages between pieces already copied; its ingeniously concise canonic layout allows a piece of substantial length to fit on a single opening. See Kiel, 'Songs and Salves', 45. If Kiel's suggestion is correct, and La Rue's setting is a later addition, the scribe nonetheless chose a piece that reinforced the impressions of prestige and compositional virtuosity set by the opening works.

performed at the same pitch level,[53] this is not the case for all the settings in MunBS 34. In the *Salve regina* setting by Adam Rener, for example (No. 5), a discantus part in high clef (G2) sits above four parts in lower clefs (C3, C4, F3, F4), so that a transposition either up or down would put the music outside the range of the gamut. In other cases, the presence or absence of a flat in the key signature of an *alternatim* setting can indicate that the *Salve regina* chant should be sung at a higher or lower pitch level. Thus, although the setting by Lebrun (No. 12) is notated in 'normal' clefs (C1, C3, C4 and F4), the flat in its signature indicates that the chant would have to be sung at a pitch either a fifth lower or a fourth higher than in the other *alternatim* settings, with a final on G rather than D. While a fixed pitch standard did not exist in the sixteenth century, such striking contrasts in vocal scoring suggest an attention by composers to the different musical possibilities of tessitura and vocal timbre.[54]

As a result of these complexities in performance practice, the systematic ordering of MunBS 34 does not always accord with the needs of a particular performing group. The settings at different pitch levels are scattered throughout the manuscript, and settings that appear next to each other in the manuscript do not always call for the same performing forces. For example, the adjacent settings by Molinet and Vinders (Nos. 7 and 8) are both five-voice *alternatim* settings based on secular songs, but would presumably be sung by quite different ensembles; the setting by Molinet has two discantus parts with low ranges (notated in C1 and C2 clefs), which could be sung by male altos, while the Vinders setting has a high-pitched discantus part (G2 clef) which would be suitable for boys. Even if sung at the same pitch level, such settings have a very different effect in performance because of the different dispositions of voices: the high-pitched discantus line of Vinders's setting moves in a range well above the four lower voices, in distinct contrast to the more closely-packed effect of Molinet's setting. The different voicings of the settings by Molinet and Vinders can presumably be related to the different institutions for which they wrote their music: Molinet's only known place of employment was at the Burgundian court from 1509-17, while Vinders served at St. John's church in Ghent from 1525-26. The different voicings of the settings in MunBS 34 thus likely reflect the rich variety of performing traditions at the numerous performing institutions of the Low Countries.

The greatest variety of approaches to the *Salve regina* in MunBS 34 can be seen in the different methods of text setting. Only one composer, Antonius Divitis, sets the *Salve regina* text in a single continuous section; all the other composers represented in the manuscript divide the antiphon text in order to create a multi-sectional piece of music. One possibility, used in the anonymous setting No. 16, is to divide the text into nine

---

[53] The anonymous setting No. 21, for example, is notated in high clefs (G2, C2, C4, F3) in MunBS 34, but is sung by an all-male ensemble in the recording by Capilla Flamenca (Naxos 8.554744)—in modern terms, the music is performed down a fourth from its notated pitch. Such transposed performances are practical possibilities for many of the settings in MunBS 34.

[54] In foundations where the *Salve regina* was sung in *alternatim* with organ, of course, the organ pitch could provide a pitch standard. On the implications of notated vocal range for Renaissance music, see Kenneth Kreitner, 'Very Low Ranges in the Sacred Music of Ockeghem and Tinctoris', in *Early Music* 14 (1986), 467-79; and Honey Meconi, 'The Range of Mourning: Nine Questions and Some Answers', in *Tod in Musik und Kultur: Zum 500. Todestag Philipps der Schönen*, ed. Stephen Gasch and Birgit Lodes, Wiener Forum für ältere Musikgeschichte 2 (Tutzing, 2007), 141-56. The *Salve regina* settings in MunBS 34 exceed the limitations of the gamut both in the upper range (with the notated high G called for by Vinders and Bauldeweyn) and in the lower range (with the notated low D called for by Molinet, in La Rue's first setting, and in the anonymous setting No. 11).

sections corresponding to the nine phrases of the chant. Other settings divide the *Salve regina* text into two or three substantial *partes*, in the manner of a motet. The remaining twenty-one settings in the manuscript are set in *alternatim* fashion, with only the even-numbered verses of the text set polyphonically. A complete performance of these *Salve regina* settings would include the written polyphony in alternation with chant or with improvised organ versets.

The differing approaches to text setting have been noted by previous scholars,[55] and their placement in the manuscript suggests that the scribe also attempted to distinguish between them: as Table 1 shows, the groups of five- and four-voice *Salves* each begin with motet-like settings and end with *alternatim* settings.[56] Previous writers have not noted, however, that these approaches to text setting are closely tied to geographical origin. Surveying the extant sources of sixteenth-century *Salve regina* settings, a general pattern emerges: nine-sectioned settings of the text are most commonly seen in sources of German provenance,[57] motet-like settings are typical of sources from Rome and from the orbit of the French court,[58] and *alternatim* settings are most typical of sources from the Low Countries.[59] The contents of MunBS 34 confirm this impression; the vast majority of its *Salve regina* settings are in the *alternatim* style, far outnumbering those using any other style of text setting. All of the settings by foreign musicians, including Josquin as well as the French court composers Richafort and Divitis, are of the motet-like type, although the existence of motet-like settings by La Rue and the Burgundian court musician Gilles Reingot shows that this structure was occasionally cultivated in the Low Countries as well.[60] With the possible exception of Jean Lebrun, every one of the named composers of *alternatim* settings had close connections to the Low Countries or to the Habsburg-Burgundian court.[61] Included among the composers of *alternatim* settings are several Burgundian chapel musicians who are otherwise little known as composers: MunBS 34 contains the only known work by Johannes Molinet (No. 7), one of two known compositions by Gilles Reingot and two of three known complete compositions by Laurentius de Vourda.[62] The presence of so many works by relatively obscure Netherlandish musicians reinforces the impression that *alternatim* vocal settings are a phenomenon particularly associated with the Low Countries.

[55] Ingram, 'Polyphonic *Salve Regina*', 91-102.

[56] This pattern does not apply to the two six-voice settings, since both are *alternatim*.

[57] For example the settings by Finck and Isaac, and the anonymous settings in Berlin, Staatsbibliothek, Preußischer Kulturbesitz, Mus. Ms. 40021 [BerlS 40021], MunBS 3154, and Regensburg, Bischöfliche Zentralbibliothek, Ms. C98 [RegB C98].

[58] For example the settings in Vatican City, Bibliotheca Apostolica, Ms. Capella Sistina [VatS] 15, 19, 42, and 49, and those published by Attaingnant in RISM 1535⁴.

[59] For example the settings in Leiden, Stedelijk Museum in de Lakenhal, Ms. 1440 [LeidSM 1440], and Leiden, Gemeentearchief, Archieven van de Kerken, Ms. 1442 [LeidGA 1442], in addition to those in MunBS 34 itself.

[60] Josquin is classed as a foreigner because his primary places of employment were outside the Low Countries, in Italy and France.

[61] Not enough is known about Lebrun's biography to verify whether or not he had any connections to the Low Countries, or whether he was employed by the French court as claimed by Fétis. See John T. Brobeck, 'Jean Le Brung', in *Grove Music Online, Oxford Music Online*, <http://www.oxfordmusiconline.com/subscriber/article/grove/music/16213> (accessed 12 December 2013).

[62] On Molinet, see note 5 above; despite the tantalizing similarity with the name of the French court poet Jean Molinet, this composer can be identified with a chapel musician active at the Burgundian court during the time of Pierre de la Rue. Reingot's only other known composition is a setting of *Fors seulement* in RISM 1504³. Besides his *Salve Regina* setting, De Vourda also composed a *Kyrie Paschale* which is transmitted in two Habsburg-Burgundian court manuscripts: BrusBR IV.922 and VatS 160. A fourth work by De Vourda, the motet *O florens rosa*, exists in an incomplete form in the three surviving partbooks of VienNB 15941.

The *Alternatim Salve*: Style and Substance

The *Salve regina* chant does not initially seem a promising candidate for *alternatim* setting, a mode of musical setting that is most familiar from polyphonic Magnificat and hymn settings. Hymns and canticles are always divided into verses in liturgical books, making *alternatim* performance a logical possibility. The liturgical function of the *Salve regina*, by contrast, does not suggest that it should be divided into verses, nor do the earliest sources for the chant indicate sectional divisions within the text or music of the antiphon.[63]

Despite the apparent unlikelihood of this chant for *alternatim* treatment, by the time of the compilation of MunBS 34 this had become a prevalent method of setting the *Salve*.[64] In contrast to the older tradition of *alternatim* hymn and Magnificat settings, vocal polyphonic settings of the *Salve regina* in *alternatim* style seem to have been a comparatively late development, and one particularly associated with the Low Countries;[65] *alternatim* settings account for nearly three-quarters of the settings in MunBS 34. These settings relied upon a conventionalized method of dividing the *Salve regina* chant into nine sections, shown in Table 2.[66] As the table shows, this division exploits clear musical and structural parallelisms within the chant, and each of the nine phrases ends on a clear cadence to either the chant's final of D or its tenor of A.[67] In three cases, pairs of adjacent phrases share a distinctive opening melodic motive: a descending fifth in sections 1 and 2, an ascending triad in section 3 (intensified in section 4 by the expansion to a seventh), and an ascending third in sections 7 and 8. Indeed, the melodies of sections 1 and 2 are so similar that the second might be considered a varied restatement of the first.[68] In the remaining two cases, the musical parallelism is enhanced by a similar parallelism in the text ('Ad te clamamus'/'Ad te suspiramus' and 'O clemens'/'O pia'). Phrases 5 and 6 are not so much parallel as complementary, the first invoking Mary

[63] See, for example, Klosterneuburg, Augustiner-Chorherrenstift-Bibliothek, 1012, a twelfth-century antiphoner that contains an early version of the *Salve regina* chant; there is no punctuation in the text nor are there any markings in the musical notation that would indicate that a pause or division was anticipated in performance.

[64] The extant sources of fifteenth- and sixteenth-century liturgical organ music provide evidence for the prevalence of *alternatim* performance of the *Salve regina*, showing that similar alternation schemes were used at a variety of different performing institutions. Indeed, all of the earliest surviving settings of the *Salve regina* for organ consist of *alternatim* versets for the odd verses of the chant, including settings in the Buxheim tablature (MunBS 3725), the Lublin tablature (Kraków, Biblioteka Polskiej Akademii Nauk, Ms. 1716), and the Sicher organ book (St. Gallen, Stiftsbibliothek, Handschriftenabteilung, Ms. 530), as well as the manuscripts Basel, Universitatsbibliothek, Ms. F.VI.26c, Basel, Universitätsbibliothek, Ms. F.IX.22, BerlS 40613, and Arnolt Schlick's 1512 print *Tabulaturen etlicher lobgesang*.

[65] Vocal polyphonic *alternatim* settings of the *Salve regina* likely did not originate in the Low Countries, but settings by early sixteenth-century Flemish composers provide the first evidence of the *alternatim Salve regina* as a prevalent practice with consistent musical features. Of the numerous surviving settings of the polyphonic *Salve regina*, only five *alternatim* settings of southern European provenance exist that may date from earlier than MunBS 34. All are anonymous: one in Milan, Archivio della Veneranda Fabbrica del Duomo, Sezione Musicale, Librone 1 (fols. 117v-118r), one in MunBS 3154 (fols. 410r-v), one in Trent, Museo Provinciale d'Arte, Castello del Buonconsiglio, Ms. 89 (fols. 146v-148r), and two in Wrocław, Biblioteka Uniwersytecka, Ms. 428 (fols. 200v-202r and 236v-239r). Two other anonymous settings, in Prague, Strahov Monastery Library, D.G.IV.47, and Copenhagen, Kongelige Bibliotek, Ms. 1848, employ an alternation scheme opposite from that in MunBS 34, in which the odd verses of the antiphon are set in polyphony. These settings, however, are too stylistically dissimilar to constitute a distinct compositional tradition.

[66] This tradition of verse division is reflected in the modern Solemnes edition of the *Salve regina* by double bar lines, even though the chant was no longer typically performed in an *alternatim* fashion in the nineteenth and twentieth centuries. See *Liber Usualis*, ed. the Benedictines of Solemnes (Tournai, 1962), 276.

[67] In Example 1, the pitch of the antiphon is transposed up a fourth to match the pitch of Josquin's five-voice *Salve regina*, so that the final and tenor become G and D.

[68] In polyphonic settings, particularly those of the nine-sectioned type, the music of *Salve regina* is sometimes repeated to serve as the second phrase *Vita dulcedo*.

('advocata nostra') and ascending to the highest note of the antiphon, and the second invoking Christ ('Jesum, benedictum fructum ventris tui') and descending to the lowest note of the chant. These four pairs of closely related phrases are rounded off by a ninth phrase, which revisits the distinctive descending-fifth motive that opened the chant. The choice to divide the *Salve regina* chant into nine verses is thus not merely a matter of performance expediency, but a response to real musical features of the antiphon's text and pre-existing chant melody.

Table 2. Phrase structure of the *Salve regina* chant

Phrase No.	Text incipit	Cadence	Melodic characteristics
1	Salve Regina	D	Falling fifth motive (A-D)
2	Vita dulcedo	D	Falling fifth motive (A-D) Parallels phrase 1
3	Ad te clamamus	D	Rising triad motive (D-F-A)
4	Ad te suspiramus	D	Rising triad motive expanded to seventh (D-F-A-C) Parallels phrase 3
5	Eia ergo advocata	D	Ascent to highest note of chant ('Illos tuos')
6	Et Jesum	D	Descent to lowest note of chant ('Et Jesum')
7	O clemens	A	Rising third motive (A-C)
8	O pia	A	Rising third motive (A-C) Parallels phrase 7
9	O dulcis virgo	D	Falling fifth motive (A-D) Parallels phrases 1 and 2

An examination of the *alternatim* settings in MunBS 34 yields several recurring patterns in compositional treatment; particular verses of text are often set in similar ways, and the treatment of added secular melodies also displays a consistent pattern. A piece that demonstrates many standard features of the genre is the five-voice setting by Vinders, an *alternatim* setting based on Ghiselin's song *Ghy syt de liefte* ('You are the dearest').[69] As is typical of Habsburg-Burgundian scribal practice, the opening words of the song are indicated in the manuscript, although the music is texted with the words of the *Salve regina*. (See Figure 6 for the opening of the discantus as it appears in the manuscript, and Example 2 for Ghiselin's complete song melody.) Because the sections of the *Salve regina* vary in length, the song melody is abbreviated as necessary to fit the length and tonal structure of each polyphonic section; this means that Ghiselin's tune is drastically shortened to fit the shortest section, 'O pia'. These alterations to the song, however, do not affect its melodic contour, which is identical in each of the four sections: a phrase from the end of the song may be omitted, but the tune is never changed. This strict treatment is in distinct contrast to the loose paraphrase of the chant melody in the lower voices; if the chant melody conflicts with the secular song in the upper voice, it is

---

[69] For an edition of Ghiselin's song, see Johannes Ghiselin, *Opera Omnia*, ed. Clytus Gottwald, Corpus Mensurabilis Musicae 23 (Rome, 1968), vol. 4, 30-31. This edition titles the song *Ghy syt die wertste*, following the song's only complete source, a 1551 print by Tylman Susato; it is possible that the title given in MunBS 34 preserves an earlier version of this text, now lost.

the chant melody that is altered to compensate. This strictness in setting ensures that, while the *Salve regina* chant is often still recognizable in the lower voices, it is the secular song that is most clearly audible, highlighted by its fourfold repetition, unambiguous phrase structure, and placement in the uppermost voice of the musical texture.

Figure 6. Opening of Vinders, *Salve regina/Ghy syt de liefte.* MunBS 34, fol. 33v. Reproduced with permission

Example 2. Top voice of Ghiselin, *Ghy syt de liefte*

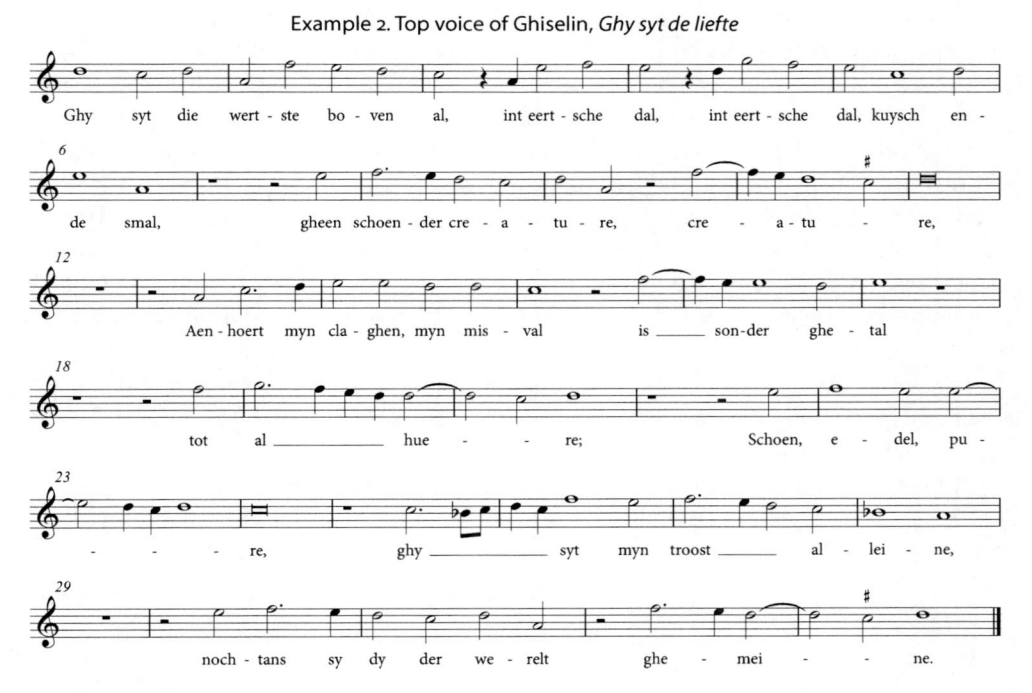

Translation:

You are the worthiest of all in this earthly valley, chaste and slender: there is no fairer creature. Hear my plea: my misfortune is beyond measure at every hour. Beautiful, noble, pure, you alone are my comfort, yet you are here for the whole world.[70]

[70] Translation in Timothy McTaggart (ed.), *Musyck Boexken, books 1 and 2: Dutch Songs for Four Voices,* Recent Researches in the Music of the Renaissance 108 (Madison, 1997), xxxvi.

The opening verse of Vinders's setting ('Vita dulcedo') begins with a prominent point of imitation on the opening motive of the *Salve regina* chant, with its familiar descending-fifth melody. A clear statement of this opening melody is a consistent feature of *alternatim* settings, with rare exceptions; it is this distinctive melodic motive, after all, that identifies the music as a *Salve regina* setting.[71] Thus, Vinders allows the *Salve regina* melody to be heard in three lower voices before the song melody enters in the discantus; withholding the song melody until the chant melody has been heard is a typical feature of the song settings in MunBS 34.[72] Once the song melody enters, however, it dominates the musical texture, and after the opening word 'Vita', there are no clear references to the plainchant melody.

The second verse ('Ad te suspiramus') is often taken as an opportunity for a thinner musical texture; many settings in MunBS 34 set this verse with a reduced number of voices. Although Vinders does not reduce the number of voices for this verse, the texture is noticeably sparser than before; instead of all five voices singing throughout, three or four voices are usually sounding at any given time. This greater textural clarity enables the listener to hear two simultaneous melodies: the song melody in the discantus as well as the chant melody in the contratenor, which appears here in a relatively unadorned and clearly stated form.

The opening of the third verse ('Et Jesum') provides Vinders with the opportunity to exploit a clever melodic connection: the first notes of the chant melody (D-A-C-D) are the same as the opening notes of *Ghy syt de liefte*. Vinders's setting features another point of imitation, with three entries on 'Et Jesum' preparing a fourth entry using the song melody. This style of text setting is not typical, however: most of the *alternatim* settings in MunBS 34 separate the words 'Et Jesum' from the remainder of the verse, often setting the words in long-note texture, as in Example 3, from Lebrun. This texture, reminiscent of the elevation motet or the 'Et incarnatus' section of the Credo, separates the address to Christ in the *Salve regina* as a turning point of the text; it also helps to give shape to the verse of the *Salve* with the longest text. As in the previous verse, Vinders paraphrases the chant melody accurately in the contratenor against the song melody in the discantus, but here he places particular emphasis on the chant motive 'nobis', which is paraphrased in all four lower voices. This emphasis is typical of the settings in MunBS 34, in which the chant motive on 'nobis' is almost always used as the basis of a new point of imitation, providing a formal landmark in this polyphonic verse.

---

[71] The chant motive 'Vita' is usually set either as a point of imitation, as here, or as a long-note tenor with faster-moving counterpoint in the outer voices, as, for example, in the setting by Lebrun (No. 12). The most important exception to this pattern is the setting by Ghiselin, mentioned above, which is based on the song *Je ne vis oncques* and does not include audible references to the *Salve* melody.

[72] In two cases, the song melody begins at the opening of the piece but is not immediately recognizable. The songs *Par le regart* and *O werde mont* both begin with long repeated notes, so that the melody only emerges as a recognizable tune after the opening chant motive has been stated.

Example 3. Opening of verse 'Et Jesum' in Lebrun, *Salve regina*, showing distinctive long-note texture

Vinders did not use long-note texture for the verse 'Et Jesum', but he does use this texture for the final verse of polyphony ('O pia'). The use of long-note texture here, a standard feature of the *alternatim* settings, emphasizes the importance of this verse as a final supplicatory address to Mary. To match the slow-moving texture of the other voices, the song melody is also reduced in speed, with all note values doubled, and the texture is thickened further by the addition of a sixth voice. This treatment ensures that a verse of polyphony that could easily have been anticlimactic, setting only two words of text, provides a fitting conclusion to the cycle with its full texture and rich harmonies.

These analytical observations on the five-voice *Salve regina* setting by Vinders can be summarized in three general points that are relevant to assessing the purpose and import of the repertoire in MunBS 34. First, the *Salve regina* settings written in the Low Countries share a clearly defined set of musical conventions that imply that their composers were working within a well-defined tradition. Recurring musical decisions, such as the setting of the phrases 'Et Jesum' and 'O pia' in long-note texture, suggest that composers who set the *Salve regina* understood themselves to be working within a previously defined set of generic conventions. Second, the musical conventions of the *Salve regina* interestingly parallel those of the mass and of other genres: just as composers of mass settings often set phrases such as the 'Jesu Christe' of the Gloria and 'Et incarnatus' of the Credo in slow-moving homophony, composers of northern Europe used a similar texture for the 'Et Jesum' and 'O pia' of the *Salve regina*. Third, the relatively loose paraphrase of the plainchant melody, and its low prominence compared to the other musical material, suggest that the *Salve regina* genre was capable of transcending its original function as a paraphrase of plainchant. Instead of being the focus of attention, the plainchant melody of the *Salve regina* was relegated to the musical background, allowing secular song melodies or other striking musical ideas to come to prominence. This flexibility of meaning implies that a wide variety of musical possibilities and theological emphases were possible within the single genre of the polyphonic *Salve regina*.

If the repertoire in MunBS 34 is representative of repertory performed at *Salve* or *lof* services in the Low Countries—presumably including repertoire from the Habsburg-Burgundian court itself along with other performing institutions in the region—then it can be assumed that the most commonly performed settings there were the *alternatim* settings (which dominate the manuscript) written in four voices rather than five or six. If motet-like settings with five or six voices were less frequently performed, though, it does not follow that the music for the services was simple or unimpressive. Because only four of the nine verses of the *Salve regina* are set polyphonically, the remaining five verses could either be sung to the chant melody or played by the organ, and thus a variety of textural combinations was possible: chant only, chant and organ, chant and vocal polyphony, or vocal polyphony and organ. Such performing possibilities provided ample opportunities for varied musical expression in a text that was performed in *lof* services every evening. The use of these contrasting musical forces also spoke to the elevated status of the *Salve regina* in its Habsburg-Burgundian context, since *alternatim* settings including polyphony, chant, and/or organ were most typically written for the central elements of the liturgy, particularly the hymns and canticles of the office.[73]

Polytextual Symbolism in the Secular-Song Settings

Vinders's five-voice setting of the *Salve regina*, described above, is one of several settings in MunBS 34 to employ an added secular melody, usually a love song in either French or Flemish (see Table 1). This category accounts for nine of the manuscript's *Salve regina* settings, just under a third of the total; with the single exception of the setting by Divitis, all of these are *alternatim* settings. One purpose of these secular songs may be purely musical: they often serve to create a sense of cyclic unity within the four *alternatim* verses of the *Salve regina*, creating a greater sense of continuity and musical interest.[74] The addition of a secular melody created opportunities for polytextual commentary and demonstrations of contrapuntal skill, as the composer faced the technical and literary challenges of integrating two distinct musical melodies.

The possible meanings implied by the use of secular chansons have been much discussed in the literature on the polyphonic mass; even when its melody is sung to different words, a secular chanson melody carries the association of its original text, creating an effect that Jennifer Bloxam has called 'inaudible polytextuality'.[75] In adopting this established language of symbolism, composers of *Salve regina* settings allied themselves with a venerable compositional tradition, exploiting the 'highly propitious' congruence between the language of Marian devotion and of the love lyric.[76] In contrast to the general practice of the cantus-firmus mass, however, in which the chanson melody is quoted in the tenor voice, the song melody is usually placed in the discantus voice, as in the five-voice setting by Vinders. (Only two settings use the more old-fashioned technique of quoting the chanson melody in the tenor: the setting by Divitis, with its careful adherence to Josquin's chanson tenor, and the anonymous setting No. 25, based on *Myns liefkens bruyn ooghen*). This treatment ensures that the secular song melody is

---

[73] This tradition of *alternatim* polyphony is most familiar through the large repertory of Magnificat settings and the many collections of office hymnody, but it also included settings of the Te Deum, Benedictus, and Nunc dimittis.

[74] In *alternatim* settings that lack a secular song melody, composers sometimes create this sense of unity through other means; for example, the anonymous setting No. 24 is based around a repeated melodic motive in the bassus that appears in all four sections.

[75] M. Jennifer Bloxam, 'A Cultural Context for the Chanson Mass', in *Early Musical Borrowing*, ed. Honey Meconi (Oxford, 2003), 23; the term is taken up in David J. Rothenberg, *The Flower of Paradise* (Oxford, 2011), 185.

[76] Andrew Kirkman, *The Cultural Life of the Early Polyphonic Mass* (Cambridge, 2010), 50.

prominently audible, inviting the listener to draw connections between the song melody and the *Salve regina* text.

As Jacobijn Kiel has shown, these secular borrowings occasionally relate to specific elements in the existing sacred text; when Pierre de la Rue quotes Du Fay's song *Par le regard des vos beaux yeux* ('For the look in your sweet eyes') in his *Salve regina* IV (No. 17),[77] the listener familiar with both texts will connect the 'sweet eyes' of the lover to the 'merciful eyes' ('illos tuos misericordes oculos') of the Virgin Mary.[78] David Rothenberg has noted a similar phenomenon in a *Salve regina* setting by Alexander Agricola (not in MunBS 34), which quotes Walter Frye's *Ave regina caelorum*. In Agricola's setting, the final plea to Mary in the *Salve* text ('O clemens, O pia, O dulcis virgo Maria!') coincides with the parallel invocation of Mary at the close of Frye's text ('O Maria flos virginum, velut rosa vel lilium').[79] Such polytextual links could be created by a skilful composer willing to draw thematic connections between sacred and secular repertories, and would be appreciated by an audience or performer familiar with both texts.

In many cases, however, specific thematic connections between the sacred and secular texts are not immediately obvious. The chanson *Je ne vis onques la pareille*, for example, attributed variously to Du Fay and Gilles Binchois, appears in two *Salve regina* settings in MunBS 34: the previously mentioned *Salve regina* IV by La Rue and the setting by Ghiselin (No. 27).[80] Yet the text of the song does not contain any images with obvious connections to the *Salve regina* text:

Je ne vis onques la pareille	I have never seen any equal
de vous, ma gracieuse dame,	to you, my gracious lady;
car vo beaulté est, par mon ame,	For your beauty is, by my soul,
sur toutes aultres nonpareille.	above all others unequalled.[81]

The ascription of unparalleled beauty to Mary had ample precedent in medieval devotion, but it is not a prominent theme in the *Salve regina* text, which focuses on Mary as a merciful intercessor rather than a figure of heavenly beauty.[82] Songs like *Je ne vis onques*, therefore, were applied to the *Salve regina* text not because they aligned precisely with the existing textual content of the antiphon but because they added new layers of meaning to the text that resonated with the existing discourses of Marian theology and devotion. Ingram has argued that such secular borrowings 'serve as commentary to the text of the motet itself', enriching its scope of reference beyond the appointed liturgical text to include a wide variety of possible composite meanings.[83] Although not every listener would pick up on such subtle shades of meaning, the settings in MunBS 34 could be appreciated on multiple levels, including the simple pleasure of recognizing a familiar song melody.[84]

[77] Modern edition in Pierre de la Rue, *Opera Omnia*, vol. 9, 149-56.
[78] Kiel, 'Songs and Salves', 45-46.
[79] Rothenberg, *The Flower of Paradise*, 140.
[80] Modern edition in Ghiselin, *Opera Omnia*, vol. 1, 17-20.
[81] French text quoted in Ingram, 'The Polyphonic *Salve Regina*', 112; translation mine.
[82] A more obvious parallel, perhaps, would be with the text of the antiphon *Ave regina caelorum*, which hails Mary as 'super omnes speciosa' ('beautiful above all others').
[83] Ingram, 'The Polyphonic *Salve Regina*', 107.
[84] Some of the songs in MunBS 34 would have had a greater popular appeal than others, however. Such Flemish songs as *Mijn hert altijt heeft verlanghen* were at the height of their popularity in the Low Countries when the manuscript

The majority of the songs in MunBS 34, like *Par le regart* and *Je ne vis oncques*, are in a courtly-love register praising the beloved for her beauty and grace. A second group of songs, however, take estrangement from the beloved as their subject matter, emphasizing the distance between Mary and her petitioner. Such songs bring out the supplicatory tone already present in the *Salve regina* text, begging Mary to look upon her petitioner with favour. In juxtaposing the antiphon text with a song such as *Myns liefkens bruyn ooghen* or *Adieu, mes amours*, a listener would be reminded that the *Salve regina* describes humanity as 'weeping and mourning in this vale of tears'.[85] Finally, the song *Je nay deuil*, used in the *Salve regina* setting by Noel Bauldeweyn, expresses an even deeper mood of desolation and sorrow, in which the beloved is not merely distant but entirely absent.[86] Such settings remind us that Mary was also venerated in the Low Countries as Our Lady of Sorrows, a title that embodies the inextricable connection between Marian devotion and the corporate expression of grief.[87]

These different uses of added secular material, along with the already noted variety in approaches to text setting, imply a wide variety of potential musical possibilities and theological meanings within the genre of the polyphonic *Salve regina*. A more motet-like setting such as the five-voice *Salve regina* of Josquin, with its ostinato repetition of the opening motive of the chant, would draw the attention of listeners to the familiar mode 1 chant melody, while a setting employing a secular chanson had the ability to suggest complex shades of polytextual meaning.[88] Some of these differences can be quite subtle. As previously mentioned, both Ghiselin and La Rue wrote *Salve regina* settings based on the song *Je ne vis oncques*, but the settings are very different in effect; Ghiselin's setting is dominated by the chanson melody and contains no clear reference to the *Salve regina* chant, while La Rue's setting juxtaposes the song melody with a clear paraphrase of the chant melody in the lower voices. A listener familiar with the song would hear the two settings very differently; Ghiselin's setting could almost be heard as a straightforward setting of the chanson melody, while La Rue's setting creates a sense of interplay between the chanson melody in the discantus and the chant melody paraphrased beneath.

was copied, as attested by numerous other sources, and would have been familiar to a wide audience; on this song, see Eugeen Schreurs and Bruno Bouckaert, 'The Dutch Song *Mijn hert altijt heeft verlanghen* as a Model' in *BHCC*, 259-84. The French songs written in the generation of Du Fay and Binchois, on the other hand, were seventy years old in the 1520s; a song like *Par le regart* would presumably be familiar only to an audience of connoisseurs. Sources for *Par le regart* are listed in David Fallows, *A Catalogue of Polyphonic Songs, 1415-1480* (New York, 1999), 306-7.

[85] In some cases, this supplicatory tone can be seen as a reference to the immediate circumstances of the work's composition. Lewis Lockwood argues such a connection for Johannes Martini's *Salve regina*, whose nine sections juxtapose the antiphon text with non-Marian cantus firmi, including the antiphon *Da pacem, Domine*. In this context, the antiphon's cry to Mary for aid can be understood in the specific context of the devastating war between Ferrara and Venice in 1482-84. See Lewis Lockwood, *Music in Renaissance Ferrara* (Oxford, ²2009), 287. Martini's setting of the antiphon in nine sections aligns with his early training in Germany; he is referred to in Ferrarese court chapel records as 'Giovanni d'Alemagna'.

[86] This category would also include the song *Fors seulement*, which is not used in MunBS 34; there is an incomplete *Salve regina* setting based on *Fors seulement* in the manuscript LeidSM 1440, however.

[87] The possibility of a connection to the Our Lady of Sorrows cult is a particularly intriguing possibility because of the Burgundian origin of the cult, and the existence of BrusBR 215-216, an Alamire manuscript dedicated to music for this feast. On Our Lady of Sorrows, see Emily Catherine Snow, 'The Lady of Sorrows: Music, Devotion, and Politics in the Burgundian-Habsburg Netherlands' (Ph.D. diss., Princeton University, 2010).

[88] The actual audibility of the chant ostinato in Josquin's setting would depend on how it was performed; in many modern performances, it cannot be clearly distinguished from the surrounding counterpoint. David Fallows argues for its inaudibility in his *Josquin* (Turnhout, 2009), 216.

The *Salve regina*: from the Low Countries to Bavaria

The richly varied *Salve regina* settings in MunBS 34 constitute a mature and well-developed musical repertory, one with a well-established tradition of *alternatim* musical treatment that could be further enhanced by the addition of secular song melodies. This elevated significance of the *Salve regina* makes it less surprising that the repertory of MunBS 34 would be considered suitable for a presentation manuscript. As I have argued above, the physical condition, notational conventions, and musical contents of the manuscript make it unlikely that MunBS 34 was intended primarily as a performing score, and suggest instead that its significance relates to the political relationship between the Habsburg-Burgundian and Bavarian courts. The exalted status of the Burgundian court, with its close ties to the Habsburg monarchy, gave the activities of the Alamire workshop a heightened political significance in which context musical manuscripts like MunBS 34 served as valuable diplomatic gifts.[89] At the same time, the manuscript exploits the popularity of the recently deceased Josquin, giving precedence to Josquin's ingenious ostinato-based *Salve regina* setting and to compositions by Divitis and La Rue that demonstrate equally impressive contrapuntal virtuosity. Finally, the manuscript offered an opportunity for the Habsburg-Burgundian court to advertise the works of their leading court composer, Pierre de la Rue, who is represented by five settings.

None of these observations, however, explain specifically why a book of *Salve regina* settings would be sent to Wilhelm IV. A third book of masses like MunBS 6 or 7 could also have served as a diplomatic gift, anthologize works by Josquin or promote works by La Rue, and the ubiquity of the mass ordinary texts would ensure a practical use for the works it contained. No such guarantee can be made for the *Salve regina*, a text that seems to have varied considerably in performance practice in different geographical areas. As previously mentioned, the three main patterns of text setting in MunBS 34 (nine-sectioned, motet-type, and *alternatim*) can be roughly divided by geographical area, associated respectively with Germany, with the French and papal courts, and with the Low Countries. If the surviving sources are an accurate indication, there seems to have been relatively little interchange between these performance traditions: *alternatim Salve regina* settings do not generally appear in German sources, nor do nine-sectioned settings appear in northern sources.[90] In this respect, it is instructive to compare the repertory of MunBS 34 to that of RegB C98, a choirbook of early sixteenth-century south German provenance which is second only to MunBS 34 as a source of polyphonic *Salve regina* settings of this period.[91] RegB C98 contains eighteen *Salve regina* settings, of which only three are of the *alternatim* type; the most common settings in the manuscript are divided into nine parts, and several settings leave

[89] On musical manuscripts as gifts, see Rob C. Wegman, 'Musical Offerings in the Renaissance', in *Early Music* 33 (2005), 425-37; and Tim Shephard, 'Constructing Identities in a Music Manuscript: The Medici Codex as a Gift', in *Renaissance Quarterly* 63 (Spring 2010), 84-127.

[90] To my knowledge, the only *alternatim Salve regina* settings in any source of German provenance prior to the mid-sixteenth century are those in MunBS 3154 and RegB C 98 (date unknown). Jacobijn Kiel suggests that some of the *Salve regina* settings in RegB C98 may have been copied from a source of non-German origin; see her 'A Sixteenth-Century Manuscript in Regensburg', *Early Music* 37 (2009), 49-59.

[91] For the contents of RegB C98, see Ingram, 'The Polyphonic *Salve Regina*', 155-61; and Kiel, 'A 16th-Century Manuscript in Regensburg.' The manuscript has not been precisely dated, nor do its few concordances with other sources suggest a strong connection to any other known manuscript tradition.

the word 'Salve' unset, expecting it to be intoned by a cantor. MunBS 34, by contrast, contains only one nine-sectioned setting and does not contain any settings with the word 'Salve' unset. The dramatic differences in repertory contained in these two roughly contemporaneous manuscripts suggest that they represent very different traditions of performance practice. Performances of the antiphon would have varied between regions depending on local traditions involving the inclusion of the organ, the traditional divisions of the text, the use of tropes on the *Salve regina* chant, and the number and disposition of singers available. If the records of the Church of Our Lady in Antwerp are representative, local performing institutions would have had their own specially commissioned 'Virgo books' containing their own performing repertoire, which would not have circulated far beyond their immediate surroundings.[92] Given this wide diversity in treatment of the *Salve regina* across Europe, it is probable that much of the repertory of MunBS 34 would simply have been incompatible with Bavarian performance traditions.[93]

These factors suggest that, in the context of the Burgundian court, the *Salve regina* genre had developed a significance transcending its immediate practical context. It was in the Low Countries, after all, that Marian confraternities were most active; cities such as Antwerp and Bruges boasted centuries-old traditions of daily *Salve* services, which by the sixteenth century offered the opportunity for generations of composers to set the text polyphonically. With such widespread opportunities for performances of this genre, the repertory performed at *Salve* services presumably included many more pieces than those available in extant sources. Such a compositional tradition no doubt ran the risk of becoming formulaic, since settings of the *Salve regina* were expected to incorporate not only a set text but also a set plainchant melody. Instead, however, confraternities in the Low Countries developed a remarkably diverse repertoire of music that could employ different approaches to text setting, different *alternatim* arrangements of choir, chant and instruments, and a variety of polytextual reference made possible by the incorporation of secular song melodies. Pierre de la Rue, who set the *Salve regina* text six times, is a fine example of this: his settings of the text include versicular and through-composed text treatment, settings with and without added secular melodies, and the use of strict canon.[94] The choice to fill a manuscript with this repertoire, which might or might not be useful to foreign musicians with different liturgical traditions, suggests that by the 1520s the Habsburg-Burgundian court was justifiably proud of the accomplishments of their composers within this genre and viewed the *Salve regina* as a genre with sufficient potential to be of interest to foreign musicians. The twenty-nine *Salve reginas* in MunBS 34 should thus be viewed not as twenty-nine motets on the same text, but as part of a distinct genre with its own musical conventions and possibilities.

When considered as a genre in its own right, the *Salve regina* can helpfully be compared with genres that use the same polyphonic models, notably the mass ordinary

---

[92] See Forney, 'Music, Ritual and Patronage', 33-34.

[93] The only large surviving collection from southern Germany or Austria at the turn of the sixteenth century is MunBS 3154 (Innsbruck, c. 1466-1511); although it contains one brief *alternatim* setting of the *Salve regina*, all of the other settings it contains are in the typical German nine-sectioned form. On this manuscript, see Thomas Noblitt, 'Die Datierung der Handschrift Mus. ms. 3154 der Staatsbibliothek München', in *Die Musikforschung* 27 (1974), 36-56, as well as Thomas Noblitt (ed.), *Der Kodex des Magister Nicholaus Leopold: Staatsbibliothek München Mus. MS 3154*, Das Erbe deutsche Musik 80-83 (Kassel, 1987-96).

[94] For a more detailed study of La Rue's settings, see Just, 'Das Salve-Regina Repertoire'.

setting. As Table 3 shows, the same secular songs used in early sixteenth-century *Salve regina* settings also appear in mass settings from the same period and, in many cases, from manuscript sources of the same provenance. As Eric Jas has pointed out, one of these mass settings even quotes directly from a corresponding setting of the *Salve regina*; the Vinders mass on *Myns liefkens bruyn ooghen* includes substantial sections of polyphony lifted directly from Appenzeller's *Salve regina* on the same tune.[95] By using the same repertory of secular song melodies cultivated in the mass setting, and by filling their *Salve regina* settings with complex canons, ostinati, and other demonstrations of contrapuntal virtuosity, Franco-Flemish composers adorned their *Salve regina* settings with some of the reflected glory of the many mass settings that used the same techniques. This early sixteenth-century apotheosis of the *Salve regina* reflects the devotional culture of the time, in which paraliturgical services such as *lof* were at the height of their popularity as a center of the community's spiritual life.[96]

Table 3. Secular songs used in early sixteenth-century *Salve regina* settings
with masses composed on the same melodies

Song	*Salve regina* setting	Mass
Adieu, mes amours	Divitis (MunBS 34)	Obrecht (JenaU 32)
		Rener (RISM 1541¹)
Fors seulement	Anon. (LeidGA 1442)	Obrecht (MunU 239)
		Ockeghem (VatC 234)
		Pipelare (JenaU 2, MechAS s.s.)
		Vinders ('s-HerAB 74)
Ghy syt de lefte	Vinders (MunBS 34)	Ghiselin (VienNB 11883)
Je nay deuil	Bauldeweyn (MunBS 34)	Brumel (*Misse Brumel*, 1503)
		Ghiselin (VienNB 1783)
Je ne vis oncques	Ghiselin (MunBS 34)	Agricola (two Credo settings)
	La Rue IV (MunBS 34)	
Myn hert	Anon., No. 21 (MunBS 34)	Gascogne (MunBS 7, MunBS F)
Myns liefkens bruyn ooghen	Anon., No. 25 (MunBS 34)	Bauldeweyn (JenaU 8, MunBS 7)
	Appenzeller (LeidGA 1442)	Vinders? ('s-HerAB 75)
O werde mont	Molinet (MunBS 34)	Anonymous (MunBS F)
	Anon., No. 23 (MunBS 34)	

[95] Eric Jas, 'A Rediscovered Mass of Jheronimus Vinders?', in *From Ciconia to Sweelinck: Donum Natalicium Willem Elders*, ed. Albert Clement and Eric Jas (Amsterdam, 1994), 223-27.

[96] The prominence of the *Salve regina* in the Low Countries is supported by several other sources from later in the sixteenth century. The manuscript LeidGA 1442, for example, contains a series of twelve consecutive *Salve regina* settings, one of the largest groupings in the six Leiden choirbooks. Jacobus Vaet, a chapel musician at the Habsburg court in the generation after Pierre de la Rue, composed eight *Salve regina* settings, all of which were published in a Gardane print (RISM 1568⁵). Finally, two additional collections consisting entirely of *Salve regina* settings, both now lost, are recorded in the inventories of Mary of Hungary (1559) and the Fugger family (1566); descriptions of the manuscripts in the surviving inventories suggests that their repertory may have overlapped with that of MunBS 34. On Mary of Hungary, see Edmond vander Straeten, *La Musique aux Pays-Bas avant le XIXᵉ siècle*, 8 vols. (Brussels 1867-88; reprint ed., New York, 1969), vol. 7, 492; and Eric Jas and Herbert Kellman, 'JenaU 20', in *Treasury*, 102. According to Mary of Hungary's inventory, the manuscript she possessed was a parchment choirbook decorated with the arms of the Duke of Saxony, leading Jas and Kellman to suggest that this manuscript may have been intended as a gift for the Saxon court in Jena. On the Fugger inventory, see Richard Schaal, 'Die Musikbibliothek von Raimund Fugger d. J.: Ein Beitrag zur Musiküberlieferung des 16. Jahrhunderts', in *Acta musicologica* 29 (1957), 126-37.

Such an understanding of the *Salve regina* seems to have been unique to the Low Countries, particularly the circle surrounding the Habsburg-Burgundian court. In foreign manuscripts where the polyphonic *Salve regina* appears, it does not receive the same rich treatment given to it in MunBS 34. RegB C98, for example, seems to have been compiled for practical use: although it collects a large number of *Salve regina* settings, it does not identify any composers, even though it contains famous settings by Josquin, Obrecht, and La Rue. Most other manuscripts from southern Europe that contain settings of the *Salve regina* place it within a much larger selection of Marian and other devotional texts. The Sistine chapel choirbooks VatS 15 and 42, for example, compiled around the turn of the sixteenth century, are typical in their treatment of the *Salve regina*—in these sources, *Salve regina* settings are surrounded by settings of other Marian antiphons and motet texts, making it clear that in this context the *Salve regina* is regarded as one of many motet texts suitable for performance at Vespers. The prestige attached to the *Salve regina* by the Burgundian-Habsburgs seems to have been confined to a relatively small geographical area and to a particular historical moment in the late fifteenth and early sixteenth centuries.

Did the Bavarians realize the devotional and symbolic significance of the manuscript that was sent to them? The apparent disuse of the manuscript might initially suggest not, but MunBS 34 arrived at a propitious time for the Bavarian court: in the 1520s, Wilhelm IV was in the midst of cementing his own power, building up a musical establishment able to compete with the most prominent court chapels in Europe. Given his aspirations to establish his court as a rival power to the Habsburg imperial court, the duke's political purposes were well served by the possession and imitation of a prestigious musical repertory from the emperor's home country.[97] Hints of this political project can be seen in the repertory of a second manuscript in the Bayerische Staatsbibliothek, MunBS 19.[98] This choirbook contains two consecutive settings of the *Salve regina*, both probably by Ludwig Senfl, although only the first is attributed to him.[99] Senfl arrived at the court of Wilhelm IV in 1523, around the same time that MunBS 34 must have arrived in Bavaria, and the two *Salve regina* settings that he wrote for the chapel choir seem to reflect the influence of Franco-Flemish traditions. Senfl's first setting in MunBS 19 is in the typical German nine-sectioned form, but like many of the settings in MunBS 34 it employs an added melody—not a secular song, which would be uncharacteristic of Senfl's sacred music, but the Magnificat antiphon *Stella maris a trimatu*, sung on the feast of Mary's Presentation.[100] Because the added melody alternates between the tenor and discantus voices, the textural clarity of this setting is remarkably similar to the secular-song settings in MunBS 34. Senfl's second setting does not employ an added melody but is written in the *alternatim* style, a

---

[97] Armin Brinzing argues that this process began as early as 1515; see his 'Bemerkungen zur Hofkapelle Herzog Wilhelms IV: Mit einer provisorischen Liste der Hofmusiker', in *Die Müncher Hofkapelle des 16. Jahrhunderts im europäischen Kontext*, ed. Theodor Göllner and Bernhold Schmid (Munich, 2006), 20-46, and Birgit Lodes, 'Ludwig Senfl and the Munich Choirbooks: The Emperor's or the Duke's?' in ibid., 224-33.

[98] According to Martin Bente, this choirbook was copied in two layers, with the first layer complete by 1531 and the subsequent layers added between 1531 and 1540; see his *Neue Wege der Quellenkritik und die Biographie Ludwig Senfls* (Wiesbaden, 1968), 169-71. Bente's datings, based on a study of the watermarks in the manuscripts, have been challenged in Birgit Lodes, 'Ludwig Senfl and the Munich Choirbooks.'

[99] Alexander Heinzel attributes the second setting to Senfl on the basis of style; see his, 'Orlando di Lasso und die Münchner Salve Regina-Tradition', in *Musik in Bayern* 55 (1998), 145-46. The attribution is plausible, since MunBS 19 was copied under Senfl's direction and contains primarily works by him.

[100] Heinzel, 'Orlando di Lasso', 145.

rare example of an *alternatim Salve regina* setting by a German composer.[101] These features suggest that, even if MunBS 34 was not directly used for performance, there was at least one musician in Munich who carefully studied its contents and incorporated aspects of the northern style into his own compositions.

While it cannot be proved whether or not Senfl knew the repertory in MunBS 34, his decision to compose two *Salve regina* settings in a style characteristic of the Low Countries suggests inspiration from an outside source, with Alamire's manuscript as a likely channel of influence. The influence of MunBS 34 may also explain the presence in the ducal chapel choirbooks of a mass on the tune *Myns liefkens bruyn ooghen* by one of Senfl's successors as Kappellmeister to the Bavarian court, Ludwig Daser, who would likely not have encountered this Flemish song elsewhere in Munich.[102] Speculation about the subsequent influence of the repertory of MunBS 34 on Bavarian composers would require a more extensive survey of repertoire, but it is at least suggestive that *alternatim* settings of the *Salve regina* begin to appear in manuscripts of Bavarian provenance from the 1530s onwards.[103] Such a trend cannot be attributed solely to the single manuscript MunBS 34, but it at least raises the possibility that the Habsburg-Burgundian *Salve regina* repertory, with its distinctive *alternatim* style, attracted interest beyond the immediate context of the Bavarian court, perhaps circulating in manuscript copies that were used for study and performance.

Conclusion

The precise circumstances of the production of MunBS 34, an unusual gift from the Habsburg-Burgundian court to the Duke of Bavaria, cannot be reconstructed with certainty. Nonetheless, an examination of the manuscript and its contents suggests that it has greater importance than has been hitherto supposed, anthologizing a prestigious repertory with its own clearly defined musical and generic conventions. Within the boundaries of these conventions, the repertoire in MunBS 34 is remarkably varied in musical style and theological import, moving beyond the well-known text and melody of the *Salve regina* antiphon to evoke the prestigious musical traditions associated with the polyphonic mass. In its historical context, the *Salve regina* repertory can thus be seen as a musical link serving distinct musical and political functions at two prestigious European courts. For the Habsburg-Burgundian court, the *Salve regina* represented a prestigious export product, showcasing a highly-developed native tradition of Marian devotion and symbolism; at the Bavarian court, acquiring and emulating this foreign repertory enhanced the duke's project of creating a prestigious musical center that could stand comparison to the most important courts of Europe. While many composers from this period wrote settings of the *Salve regina*, both for voices and for organ, only the Habsburg-Burgundians had the influence and resources to create a deluxe manuscript showcasing their unparalleled tradition of Marian devotion, offering this repertoire to foreign musicians in a form designed to impress and to encourage careful study and imitation.

---

[101] See note 90 above.

[102] This mass is found in MunBS 18, fols. 58v-86r.

[103] Specifically, the anonymous *alternatim* settings in Ulm, Münster Bibliothek, Von Schermar'sche Familienstiftung, Ms. 237 (c. 1530-40), and one in Stuttgart, Württemberische Landesbibliothek, Ms. Musica folio I.39 (c. 1540-50). That this repertory is representative of a broader trend can be seen by the presence of anonymous *alternatim* settings in Dresden, Sächsische Landesbibliothek, Ms. Mus. 1/D/505 and 1/D/506 (both c. 1530), presumably copied in Wittenberg and far from the influence of the Bavarian court.

Appendix. Jheronimus Vinders, *Salve regina/Ghy syt de liefte*

[8.] Jheronimus Vinders

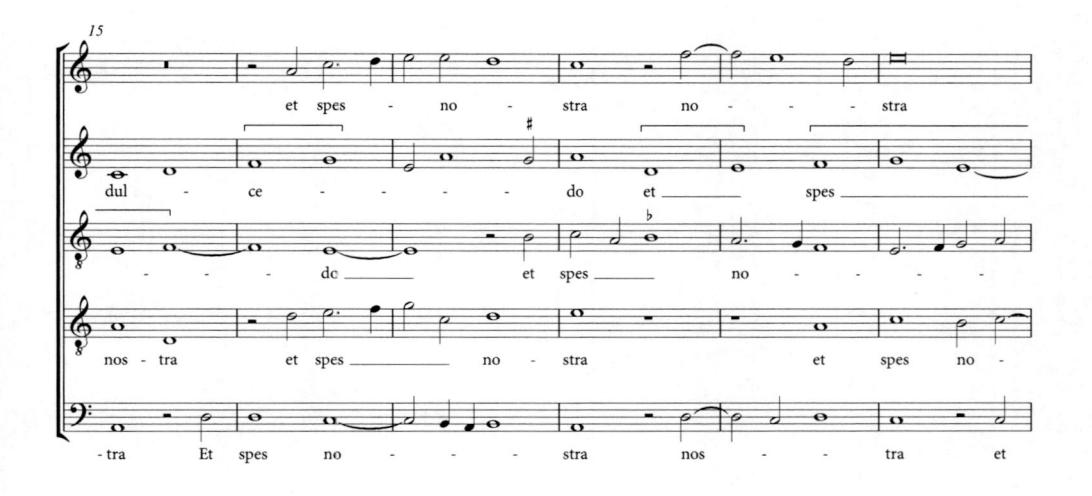

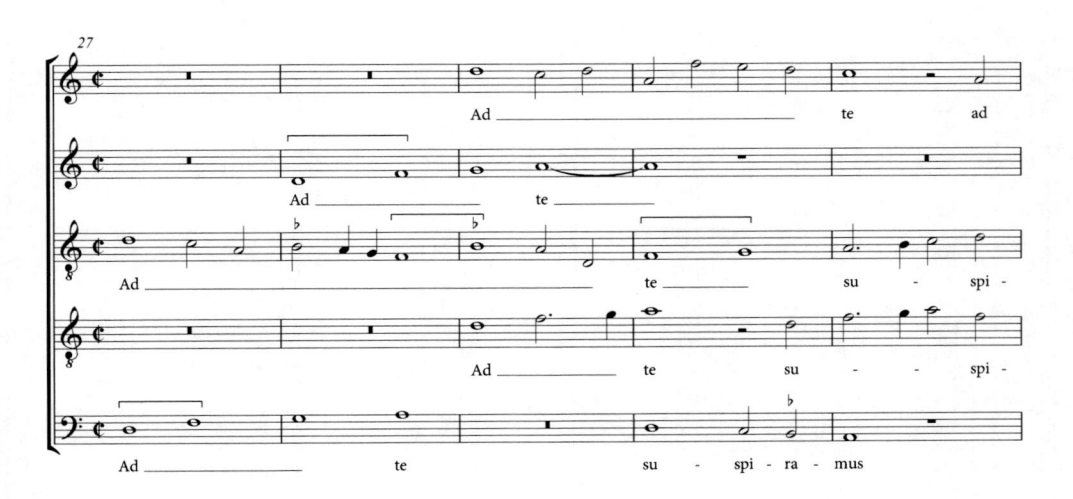

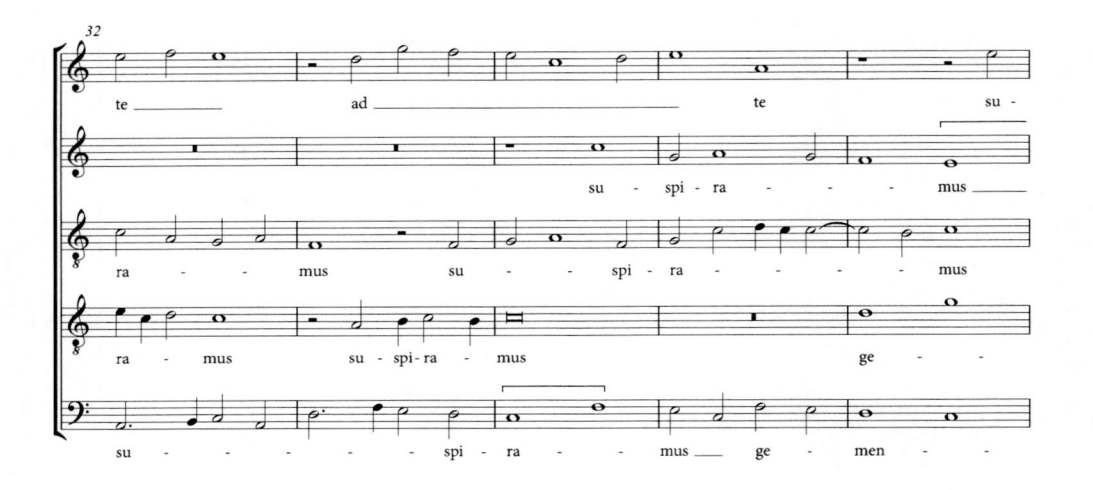

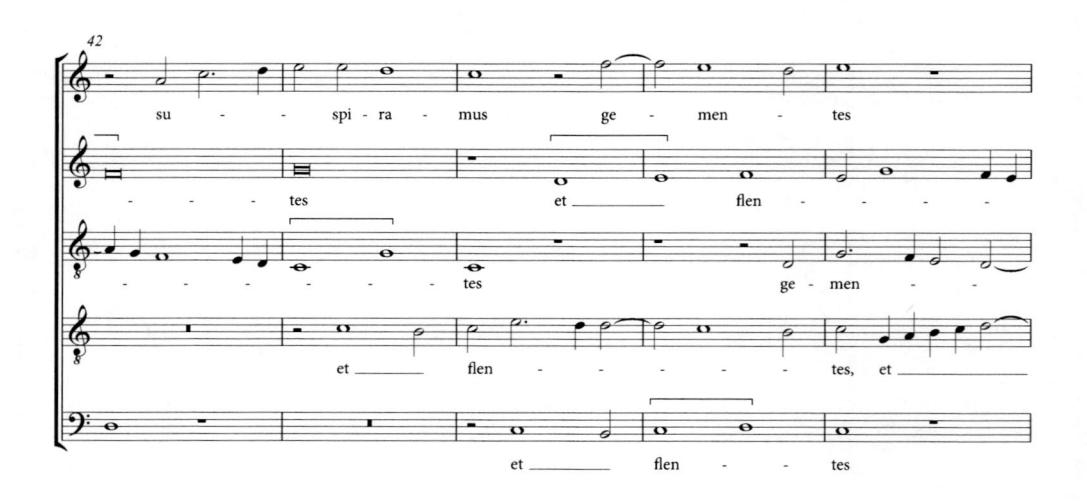

62 ■ AARON JAMES

THE APOTHEOSIS OF THE *SALVE REGINA* ■ 63

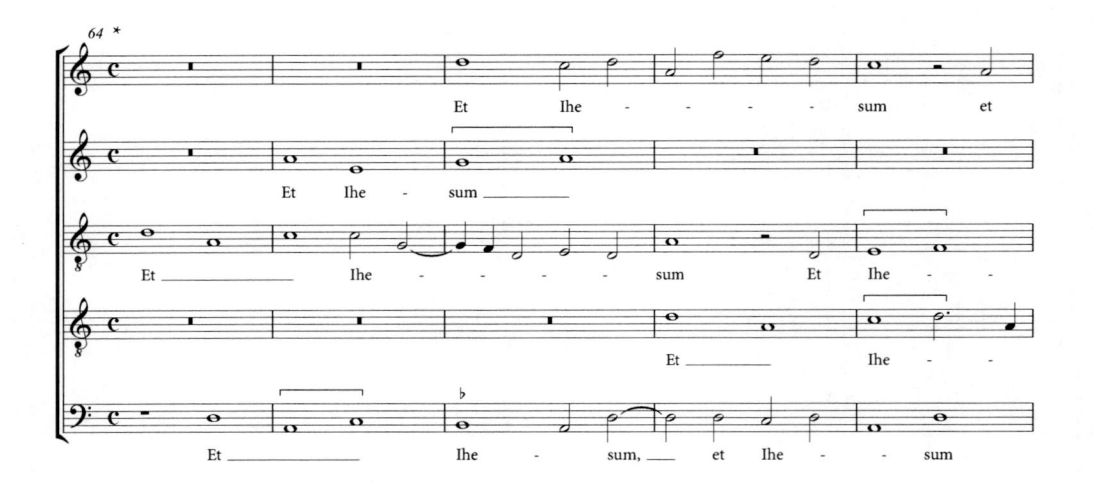

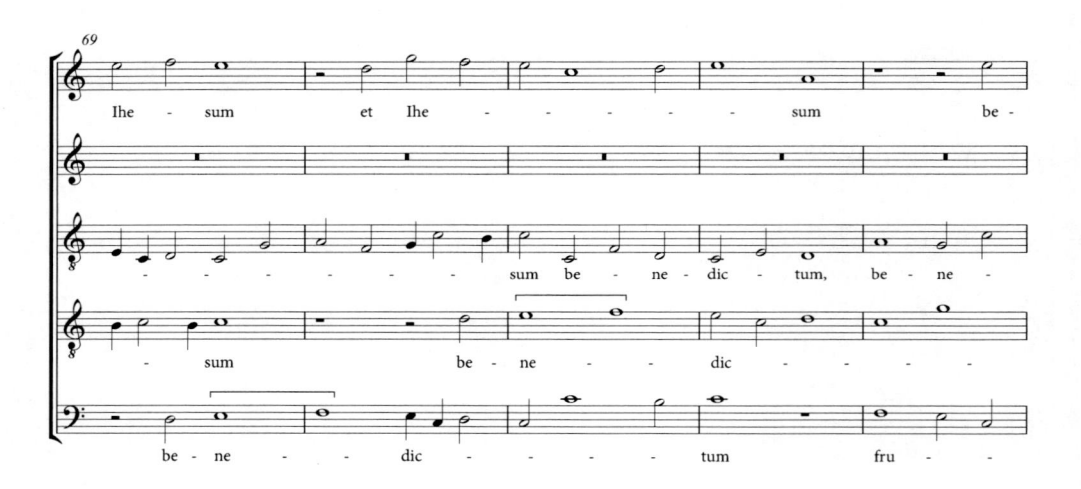

* D and T1 parts throughout this section have incomplete text (texted only through 'ventris tui'; B part concludes with incorrect text, 'nobis post hoc tui.'). The text underlay for these three voices has been reconstructed based on that of the two completely texted voices as well as the *Salve* chant melody.

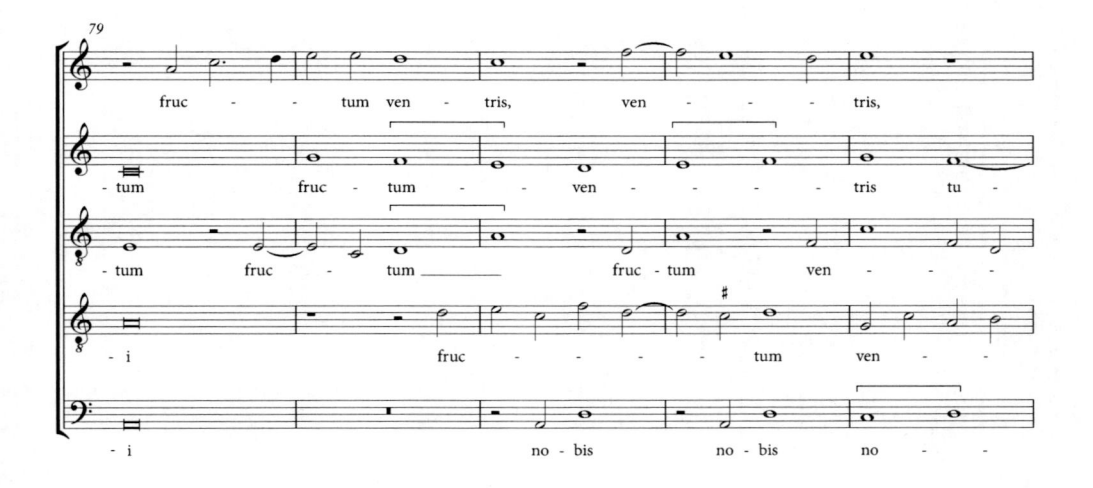

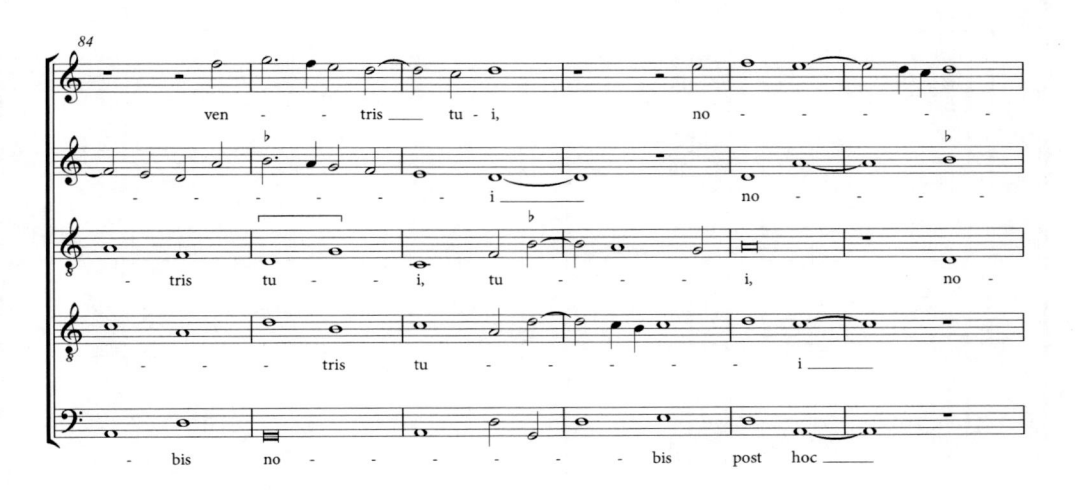

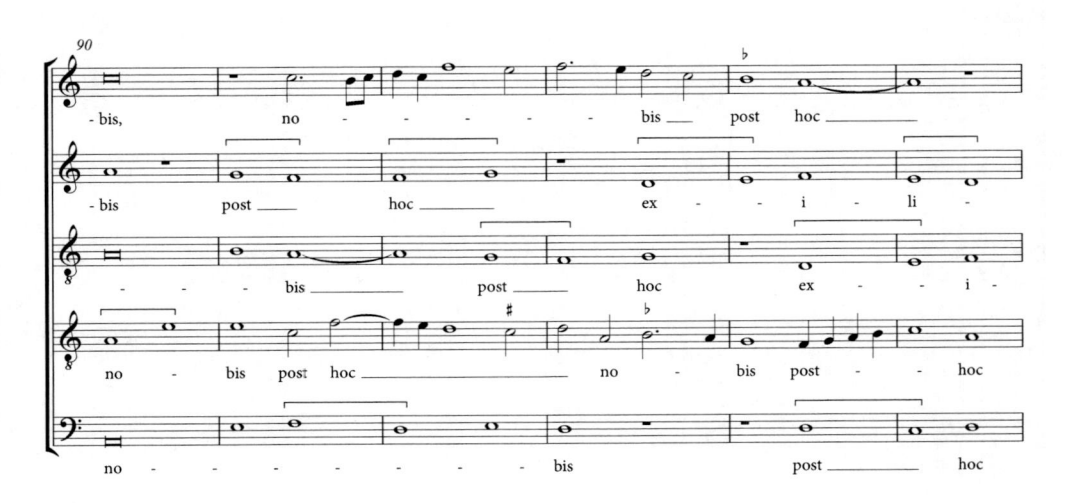

* B: MS has text 'Salve' here (rather than 'pya' as in all other voices).

Abstract

The richly decorated musical manuscripts produced in the famous workshop of Petrus Alamire represent the highest standard of craftsmanship in early sixteenth-century manuscript production, serving not only as practical performing scores but also as political gifts symbolizing Habsburg prestige. Among Alamire's manuscripts, however, is a collection whose contents set it apart from its neighbours: Munich, Bayerische Staatsbibliothek, Mus. Ms. 34 [MunBS 34], a choirbook containing twenty-nine settings of the Marian antiphon *Salve regina*. Because of the repertory it contains, the manuscript has typically been linked to the practical needs of Marian devotional culture, particularly the *Salve* service. However, close examination of the layout of the manuscript and conspicuous clues left by the scribe suggest that the manuscript was not intended primarily as a performing score, nor does it show signs of having been used in the chapel of Wilhelm IV of Bavaria, the manuscript's recipient. Instead, the collection's significance lies in its demonstration of a wide range of approaches to setting the venerable *Salve regina* text, deploying the chant melody independently or in combination with secular chanson tunes to imply numerous possible intertextual meanings. This lavish and varied elaboration of a single text suggests that, for the aristocratic owners of MunBS 34, the *Salve regina* was understood as a distinct and prestigious genre capable of sustaining a rich and varied theological discourse.

A Virgin, a Lineage, and an Elector: Ancestry and Imagery in Thüringer Universitäts- und Landesbibliothek Ms. 22 [*]

Hannah Mowrey Clarke

The splendid Habsburg-Burgundian manuscripts sent forth from the scriptoria[1] of Petrus Alamire found their way into the collections of many prominent sixteenth-century leaders, include Henry VIII, Emperor Maximilian I, Margaret of Austria, Pope Leo X, Charles V, and Frederick the Wise, Elector of Saxony.[2] While providing a glimpse into the magnificent artwork of the Ghent-Bruges school, the manuscripts serve as rich anthologies of music by such Renaissance luminaries as Pierre de la Rue, Josquin des Prez, Jacob Obrecht, and many others. By his death in 1525, Frederick the Wise owned eleven of these Alamire manuscripts.[3] Several of these were made explicitly for Frederick, while others were somehow acquired.[4] As a whole, the collection supplies the elector with some of the best-known and most innovative music of the time. Most of the elector's manuscripts were created between 1515 and 1525—a period marked by increasing religious tension, since Martin Luther sounded a call for reform within the Catholic church. Frederick's court became the epicentre of this religious movement. Filled with symbols of decisively Catholic theology—particularly Mary's Immaculate Conception, a prominent and controversial doctrine of the time period—these eleven Alamire manuscripts came to the elector just as Protestantism began to split the church apart.

---

[*] Earlier versions of this paper were presented at the 2010 American Musicological Society meeting in Indianapolis, and the 2010 Forum on Music and Christian Scholarship in Boston. I am grateful for the helpful comments of Honey Meconi and M. Jennifer Bloxam, as well as of the anonymous readers of this Journal. All sigla throughout this article come from *Census-Catalogue of Manuscript Sources of Polyphonic Music 1400-1550*, 5 vols., ed. Herbert Kellman and Charles Hamm, Renaissance Manuscript Studies 1 (Neuhausen-Stuttgart, 1979-88). This manuscript has been digitized and is available online at <http://archive.thulb.uni-jena.de/hisbest/receive/HisBest_cbu_00014267>.

[1] Though 'Alamire Scriptorium' (implying one location) is commonly used, the term is misleading, as Petrus Alamire certainly had multiple venues for manuscript production. Unfortunately, the precise location of these scriptoria remains a mystery.

[2] For a summary and overview of the surviving Habsburg-Burgundian manuscripts, see Herbert Kellman (ed.), *The Treasury of Petrus Alamire: Music and Art in Flemish Court Manuscripts 1500-1535* (Ghent-Amsterdam, 1999); hereafter *Treasury*.

[3] Frederick owned eleven of the Habsburg-Burgundian manuscripts, as well as an additional set of eight choirbooks, often called the 'paper' choirbooks. The two sets of manuscripts have a variety of distinctions, including physical (the Alamire manuscripts are primarily parchment; the non-Alamire manuscripts are paper), aesthetic (the Alamire manuscripts display rich illumination; the paper manuscripts are very plain in appearance), and musical (the Alamire manuscripts are filled primarily with music for the mass ordinary; the paper manuscripts have mostly music for the mass proper). For extensive discussion of the paper choirbooks, see Kathryn Duffy, 'The Jena Choirbooks: Music and Liturgy at the Castle Church in Wittenberg Under Frederick the Wise, Elector of Saxony' (Ph.D. diss., University of Chicago, 1995); and Jürgen Heidrich, *Die Chorbücher aus der Hofkapelle Friedrichs des Weisen: Ein Beitrag zur mitteldeutschen geistlichen Musikpraxis um 1500*, Sammlung Musikwissenschaftlicher Abhandlungen 84 (Baden-Baden, 1993). Throughout this article any reference to Frederick's choirbooks/manuscripts refers to those from the Alamire workshop.

[4] JenaU 2, JenaU 3, JenaU 5, JenaU 8, JenaU 12, and JenaU 20 were created for Frederick the Wise. JenaU 4, JenaU 7, JenaU 9, JenaU 21, and JenaU 22 were acquired by the elector.

One of the more modest manuscripts—JenaU 22—found its way into Frederick's collection. As a whole, the Alamire manuscripts display an impressive amount of artwork, leading scholars to pore over the collection's visual gems and compilation of early sixteenth-century sacred and secular repertoire. Therefore, is almost understandable that the sole miniature in JenaU 22,[5] accompanying Obrecht's *Missa Sicut spina rosam*, has received less attention, in favour of 'miniature rich' choirbooks such as JenaU 3 or JenaU 4.[6] But as a result, important themes in JenaU 22 have been overlooked. Close examination of the interwoven visual and aural symbols in JenaU 22 will reveal that the message in this relatively unassuming manuscript foreshadows many themes found not only in Frederick's later manuscripts, but in the entire Habsburg-Burgundian collection as well.

Physical Appearance and Dating

JenaU 22 has the smallest folio dimensions of any choirbook in Frederick's collection (measuring 397 x 290 mm). It also has the most folios (163 parchment folios). The expression 'Alamire Manuscripts' traditionally includes several manuscripts that were most likely created in the workshop of Alamire's predecessor, so-called 'Scribe B', for Alamire did not begin overseeing scribes until c. 1508.[7] Scribe B's output includes two manuscripts that share numerous similarities: JenaU 22 and VienNB 1783. VienNB 1783 seems to have been created between 1500 and 1505, with compelling evidence pointing to the latter two years.[8] This dating has helped determine JenaU 22's date, as the two manuscripts have numerous affinities, leading Herbert Kellman to conclude they were created together. The two choirbooks share scribes, dimensions, and layout, and ten of the compositions in JenaU 22 are also found in VienNB 1783.[9] Furthermore, the calligraphic initials are exceptionally elaborate in both manuscripts; painted calligraphic initials open every mass, and, in the case of JenaU 22's opening mass, La Rue's *Missa de Sancto Antonio*, painted initials also appear at the opening of the Gloria. There is only

[5] JenaU 22's miniature is reproduced in *Treasury*, 106.

[6] See, for example Bonnie J. Blackburn, 'For Whom do the Singers Sing?', in *Early Music* 25 (1997), 593-609; 'The Virgin and the Sun: Music and Image for a Prayer Attributed to Sixtus IV', in *Journal of the Royal Musical Association* 124 (1999), 157-95; 'Messages in Miniature: Pictorial Programme and Theological Implications in the Alamire Choirbooks', in *The Burgundian-Habsburg Court Complex of Music Manuscripts (1500-1535) and the Workshop of Petrus Alamire*, ed. Bruno Bouckaert and Eugeen Schreurs, Yearbook of the Alamire Foundation 5 (Leuven and Neerpelt, 2003), 161-84, hereafter *BHCC*; and Dagmar Thoss, 'Flemish Miniature Painting in the Alamire Manuscripts', in *Treasury*, 53-62.

[7] Herbert Kellman, 'Production, Distribution, and Symbolism of the Manuscripts - A Synopsis', in *Treasury*, 11; and 'Jena, Thüringer Universitäts- und Landesbibliothek Ms. 22', in *Treasury*, 107. For more on Alamire himself, see Eugeen Schreurs, 'Petrus Alamire: Music Calligrapher, Musician, Composer, Spy', in *Treasury*, 15-27 and David Fallows, 'Alamire as Composer', in *BHCC*, 247-58.

[8] VienNB 1783 was first thought to be a wedding gift for the 1526 nuptials between Isabella of Portugal and Charles V, based upon the appearance of coats of arms for Spain and Portugal; see Helen Dixon, 'The Manuscript Vienna, National Library, 1783', in *Musica Disciplina* 23 (1969), 105-16. Kellman originally concurred with Dixon, but he later concluded that VienNB 1783 was sent from Philip the Fair to Emanuel and Maria of Spain for their 1500 wedding, and that the arms of Portugal pay homage to Emanuel. Philip the Fair's motto also appears in the manuscript. Based upon the manuscript's repertoire—three masses by Marbrianus de Orto, who is first documented in Philip the Fair's chapel in mid-1505 and who may have arrived in late 1504—and lack of evidence that the manuscript actually served as a wedding gift, however, Kellman once again revised the dates. He even muses that the concordant masses between VienNB 1783 and BrusBR 9126 and the common owner and/or commissioner—Philip the Fair—point to the later date (1505). See Herbert Kellman, 'Vienna, Österreichische Nationalbibliothek, Handschriftensammlung Ms. 1783', in *Treasury*, 141; 'JenaU 22', in *Treasury*, 107; and 'Brussels, Bibliothèque royale de Belgique Ms. 9126', in *Treasury*, 73.

[9] Kellman, 'JenaU 22', in *Treasury*, 107. Duffy has also noted the similarities between these two manuscripts in Kathryn Duffy, 'Netherlands Manuscripts at a Saxon Court', in *BHCC*, 217-18.

one grotesque in JenaU 22 (fol. 30v), but several of the large painted initials subtly feature the face of a man: in the letter 'B' of the bassus on fol. 4r (the opening of the 'Christe'), in the 'C' of the contratenor on fol. 19r, and in the 'B' of the bassus on fol. 43r.[10] While many of the physical features of VienNB 1783 are duplicated in JenaU 22, this was apparently a common practice for Scribe B. Kellman has noted that six manuscripts from Scribe B's workshop have pair relationships based on physical similarities: VatC 234 and BrusBR 9126; FlorC 2439 and VerBC 756; JenaU 22 and VienNB 1783.[11]

JenaU 22 contains thirteen masses:[12] eight by La Rue, two by Obrecht, two by Agricola/[Ghiselin],[13] and one by Pipelare. The La Rue masses in JenaU 22 are noteworthy, because by 1505 the composer had only been represented by a total of nine masses in the Habsburg-Burgundian sources.[14] With such prominent status given to La Rue, JenaU 22 became the first in a long line of court manuscripts dedicated to the composer's work. Table 1 lists the contents of JenaU 22. All thirteen masses are for four voices.[15]

Table 1. Contents of JenaU 22

Composer[a]	Mass/Mass movement	Topic	Folio
La Rue	*Missa de Sancto Antonio*	Saint Anthony	2v-18r
La Rue	*Missa de Beata Virgine*	Virgin Mary	18v-29r
La Rue	*Missa L'homme armé I*	Armed man	30v-42r
La Rue	*Missa Puer natus est*	Christ/Nativity	42v-54r
La Rue	*Missa Nunca fué pena mayor*	Secular	54v-67r
La Rue	*Missa Assumpta est Maria*	Mary's Assumption	68v-78r
Agricola / [Ghiselin]	*Missa in die pasce* [K-G]	Easter	78v-84r
[Isaac]	Credo from *Missa Tmeiskin was jonck*	Secular (Dutch song)	84v-86r
Agricola / [Ghiselin]	Missa in die pasce [S-A]	Easter	86v-90r
Obrecht	*Missa O quam suavis est*	Corpus Christi?[b]	90v-102r
Obrecht	*Missa Sicut spina rosam*	Mary's Nativity / Conception	102v-113r
Barbireau	Kyrie from *Missa Pascale*	Easter	113v-116r
Pipelare	*Missa L'homme armé*	Armed man	116v-128r
Agricola	*Missa Le serviteur*	Secular (Dufay's chanson)	128v-141r
La Rue	*Missa Cum iocunditate*	Mary's Nativity / Conception	141v-152r
La Rue	*Missa Almana*	Unknown model[c]	152v-163r

[a] The following chart comes from *Treasury*, 107.
[b] The liturgical function of the cantus firmus in this mass is difficult to identify. JenaU 22 and LeipU 51 use *O quam suavis* in the tenor and title; this was a Corpus Christi antiphon. However, VatSM 26 uses the title *O lumen ecclesie*—a chant used almost exclusively in the Dominican rite to honour St. Dominic. While the two chants are related, it is impossible to determine which one Obrecht used. See Rob Wegman, *Born for the Muses: The Life and Masses of Jacob Obrecht* (Oxford, 1994), 109, especially note 18. Also see Jacob Obrecht, *Missa O lumen ecclesie* and *Missa Petrus apostolus*, ed. Barton Hudson, New Obrecht Edition 8 (Utrecht, 1988), xvii.
[c] This model has not been identified. One source incorrectly refers to this mass as *Missa Pourquoy non*, though the mass is not based on the *Pourquoy non* chanson. See Honey Meconi, *Pierre de la Rue and Musical Life at the Habsburg-Burgundian Court* (Oxford, 2003), 314.

[10] Kellman, 'JenaU 22', in *Treasury*, 108-9. Fol. 19r, which features the 'C' in the contratenor, is reproduced in *Treasury*, 109.
[11] The Scribe B manuscript OxfBA 831 survives only as a fragment, and does not have a match. See Kellman, 'JenaU 22', 107.
[12] JenaU 22 also contains the Kyrie from Barbireau's *Missa Pascale*.
[13] Isaac's Credo from *Missa Tmeiskin was jonck* was inserted between the Gloria and Sanctus in Agricola's *Missa in die Pasce*.
[14] Kellman, 'JenaU 22', 107.
[15] La Rue's *Missa Cum iocunditate* expands to five voices in the Credo.

The manuscript has one partial border that appears with the miniature, on fol. 102v (see Plate 1). This sole miniature features the Virgin Mary holding her infant son, standing on a crescent moon and emanating rays. Red and white roses surround both mother and child. The important symbolism in this miniature will be addressed shortly.

We do not know how the elector acquired JenaU 22. In an effort to determine the provenance of JenaU 22, Kellman has called attention to an unusual decoration on fols. 18v-19: a rose (a Tudor emblem) along with a daisy or marguerite (perhaps referring to Margaret of Austria), a very strange headpiece, and a blank shield.[16] Presumably a coat of arms was to have been placed in the shield. Kellman speculates that perhaps this was meant to reflect some relationship between the Tudors (England) and Habsburgs; a similar mixture of emblems is found in JenaU 4.[17]

While Kellman's suggestion of the Tudor connection is intriguing, it leaves us wondering why the shield was not placed at the beginning of the manuscript, where coats of arms tended to appear. With the exception of the blank arms in JenaU 22, all surviving manuscripts from the workshop of Scribe B that have coats of arms couple the first coat of arms with the first composition in the manuscript. The following Scribe B manuscripts identify their respective owners with a coat of arms: VatC 234, BrusBR 9126, VienNB 1783, and FlorC 2439.[18] VerBC 756 features an unidentified coat of arms; the recipient of this manuscript is also unknown, though Kellman speculates that the original owner was probably Italian.[19] No coat of arms appear in the OxfBA 831 fragment, though it is quite possible that in its original state, the manuscript did feature an identifying emblem. JenaU 22 lacks a coat of arms or other royal emblems, thus the original owner of this manuscript is difficult to identify. The lack of arms coupled with the unusual placement of the blank shield makes it difficult to convincingly posit that a Tudor coat of arms was meant to adorn the manuscript. Discounting the Habsburg-Burgundian/Tudor connection, however, does not suggest that Frederick was the original owner.

In trying to determine for whom JenaU 22 was originally intended, we should also consider Frederick's travels, and how they might have influenced the elector's manuscript collection. Frederick journeyed to the Low Countries in 1494, spending time first at the court of Philip and Fair, and then at Maximilian's court from 1494-98. In this four-year time span, the elector would have been exposed to extremely sophisticated music, composed by the period's most prominent composers.[20] While visiting the splendid chapel of Philip the Fair, Frederick would have heard a young and talented composer named Pierre de la Rue. He also would have heard Heinrich Isaac who served Maximilian's court from November 1496 until the composer's death in 1517.[21]

Inspired by what he saw and heard during his travels, Frederick increased the size of his court chapel when he returned home. He also rebuilt and beautified Wittenberg

---

[16] The images are reproduced in *Treasury*, 108-9.
[17] See Kellman, 'JenaU 22', in *Treasury*, 108.
[18] FlorC 2439 has the Agostini Ciardi family coat of arms and went to some member of that family, though the particular recipient is unknown. See Honey Meconi, 'Florence, Biblioteca del Conservatorio di Musica Luigi Cherubini, Ms. Basevi 2439 ("Basevi Codex")', in *Treasury*, 78-79; and 'Sacred Tricinia and Basevi 2439', in *I Tatti Studies: Essays in the Renaissance* 4 (Florence, 1991), 153.
[19] See Herbert Kellman, 'Verona, Biblioteca Capitolare Ms. 756', in *Treasury*, 137.
[20] Kellman, 'JenaU 22', in *Treasury*, 108.
[21] Kellman, 'JenaU 22', in Treasury 107-8.

Castle (construction had started in 1496). The University of Wittenberg was established in October 1502, and shortly thereafter in January 1503, the Castle Church was dedicated. As his chapel, university, and political presence in early sixteenth-century Europe continued to blossom, no doubt Frederick would have been interested in acquiring music manuscripts—particularly such manuscripts that featured some of the most well-known and accomplished composers of the time. Perhaps Frederick ordered the manuscript himself, or perhaps it came as a gift. Regardless of acquisition, it seems plausible to suggest that this choirbook was one of the earliest to appear in Frederick's burgeoning collection.

Jacob Obrecht's *Missa Sicut spina rosam*

Missa Sicut spina rosam appears in only two sources: JenaU 22 and VatS 160. Both choirbooks originated in Alamire's workshops, though the Jena manuscript predates the Vatican manuscript by at least ten years. Unfortunately, VatS 160 fell victim to vandals, as five of its seven masses are missing folios—presumably folios that featured expensive and coveted miniatures. However, we can imagine what the missing artwork might have looked like, since masses appearing in multiple choirbooks would routinely feature a miniature on the same subject. For example, La Rue's *Missa Ave sanctissima Maria* is found in JenaU 4 and JenaU 5. Both manuscripts have miniatures of the Virgin, *in sole* and standing on a crescent moon, crowned by angels. Furthermore, the composer's Marian motet that served as the basis for his mass—*Ave sanctissima Maria*—appears in BrusBR 228 with an image of the same subject.[22] A similar scenario occurs with Josquin's *Missa Ave maris stella*. This mass is found in BrusBR 9126 and JenaU 3, both manuscripts featuring a splendid image of the enthroned Virgin and Child. Therefore, it is reasonable to assume that the miniature missing from VatS 160's *Missa Sicut spina rosam* was similar to the one that survives in JenaU 22. The incomplete *Missa Sicut spina rosam* in VatS 160 led Barton Hudson to conclude that JenaU 22 remains the most reliable and complete source for Obrecht's mass.[23]

Missa Sicut spina rosam is based on the repetendum section of the responsory *Ad nutum Domini*, a chant often associated with both the Feast of Mary's Nativity (September 8) and the Feast of Mary's Conception (December 8). Obrecht used the chant in a variety of innovative ways throughout the mass: it is paraphrased, treated as canon, and often quoted directly in all of the movements.[24] In addition to its creative use of chant, the mass also quotes directly from Ockeghem's *Missa Mi mi* throughout portions of the Kyrie and Agnus Dei, leading scholars to speculate that Obrecht may have been paying tribute to the older composer, as the mass takes on an especially commemorative role.[25]

---

[22] The image in JenaU 5 is reproduced in *Treasury*, 94, and the image in BrusBR 228 can be found in *Treasury*, 70.

[23] Barton Hudson, 'Obrecht's Tribute to Ockeghem', in *Tijdschrift van de Vereniging voor Nederlandse Muziekgeschiedenis* 37 (1987), 3.

[24] For a thorough analysis of this mass, see Wegman, *Born for the Muses*, 118-30. Also see Hudson, 'Obrecht's Tribute to Ockeghem', 3-13; and Edgar H. Sparks, *Cantus Firmus in Mass and Motet 1420-1520* (Berkeley and Los Angeles, 1963), 274-76.

[25] Hudson, 'Obrecht's Tribute to Ockeghem', 8; Wegman, *Born for the Muses*, 129-30; and M. Jennifer Bloxam, 'Plainsong and Polyphony For the Blessed Virgin Mary: Notes on Two Masses by Jacob Obrecht', in *Journal of Musicology* 12 (1994), 61 and 63.

The date of *Missa Sicut spina rosam* has been disputed, though the most compelling evidence points to Obrecht's time at Antwerp (either from 1492-97 or from 1501-1503). Based upon stylistic comparisons with other works, Barton Hudson first suggested that *Missa Sicut spina rosam* was created sometime in the early 1490s.[26] Rob Wegman has speculated that the mass was composed for the celebration of Mary's Nativity at Cambrai cathedral on 8 September 1484, since Obrecht had just been hired by the cathedral on 6 September 1484.[27] M. Jennifer Bloxam disagrees with Wegman's scenario, arguing instead that the mass was composed during one of Obrecht's stays in Antwerp—either from 1492-mid-1497, or 1501-03, commenting that 'A polyphonic Mass based on this snippet of plainsong [*Ad nutum Domini*] would have likely held a special association for the churchmen and the populace of Antwerp, especially if the proper text of the plainsong segment was retained in performance, as it is in Obrecht's *Missa Sicut spina rosam*.'[28] Bloxam's careful consideration of the liturgical context, as well as stylistic features of the mass and cantus firmus, results in the most compelling argument—an argument that has implications for the dating not only of *Missa Sicut spina rosam*, but also for JenaU 22. If Obrecht composed the mass during his 1501-3 stay in Antwerp, then the manuscript could not have been completed before at least 1501. Regardless of the precise date, the mass is commemorative, not only of Ockeghem (via direct quotation), but also of the Virgin Mary's Conception and Nativity (via the model itself).

JenaU 22 contains several puzzling physical features. First, it is unusual for a heavily Marian manuscript to open with a mass by St. Anthony (La Rue's *Missa de Sancto Antonio*). It is tempting to posit that the St. Anthony mass was originally later in the manuscript, but the gathering structure of the choirbook leaves little doubt that the current sequence of compositions likely mirrors the manuscript's original ordering.[29] Second, based on the pattern set forth by other Alamire manuscripts—and in fact most illuminated manuscripts of the late fifteenth and early sixteenth centuries—one would expect the sole miniature to accompany the manuscript's opening composition. It is therefore unusual that a later mass in the choirbook would receive such beautiful artwork, since the first composition was deprived of a miniature (though, as noted earlier, *Missa de Sancto Antonio* did have several elaborate calligraphic initials). The sudden appearance of an image on the verso of fol. 102 is visually striking, particularly after turning 101 non-illuminated folios. If the scriptoria were to provide only one miniature for the manuscript, why not simply place a St. Anthony miniature with the opening mass? Why deviate from a common practice? Yet the scribes appear to deliberately skip the St. Anthony mass, instead singling out the Obrecht mass. Considering this unusual diversion from standard miniature placement, we should turn to the mass itself, and examine what was so special about it, and whether the theological implications of *Missa Sicut spina rosam*, particularly the chant upon which it was based, offer a clue.

[26] Hudson, 'Obrecht's Tribute to Ockeghem', 8.
[27] Wegman, *Born for the Muses*, 129-30.
[28] Bloxam, 'Plainsong and Polyphony For the Blessed Virgin Mary', 61; also see 63.
[29] See Kellman, 'JenaU 22', in *Treasury*, 107, for the gathering structure of JenaU 22.

Controversy over the Immaculate Conception

Before examining the connection between chant and image, which will shed light upon the miniature's unusual placement within the manuscript, it will be helpful to visit a theological debate that is woven throughout many of the Habsburg-Burgundian choirbooks (Frederick's collection especially): the Virgin Mary's Immaculate Conception.

While the early church fathers (St. Ambrose, St. Jerome, and others) spoke of Mary's exemplary life,[30] it was St. Augustine's emphasis on the original sin of all humanity that thrust the debate over Mary's nature to the forefront. How could one reconcile Mary's sinless state with humanity's original sin? Augustine himself attempted to justify Mary's sanctity, ultimately arguing for her special status and even exemption from sin.[31] Though Augustine had argued (against Pelagius) that every human was plagued by Adam's original sin, Mary, he asserted, did not possess such a stain: 'The holy Virgin Mary, about whom, for the honor of the Lord, I want there to be no question where sin is mentioned, for concerning her we know that more grace for conquering sin in every way was given to her who merited to conceive and give birth to him, who certainly had no sin whatsoever—this virgin excepted.'[32] By the thirteenth century, two distinct camps had formed: the Dominicans, who, following in the footsteps of Thomas Aquinas, believed that Mary was conceived in original sin and then immediately sanctified in her mother's womb, and the Franciscans, who championed John Duns Scotus's insistence that Mary was conceived sinless.[33] While the debate remained primarily among theologians in the twelfth, thirteenth, and fourteenth centuries, the fifteenth century hosted a wider audience, including kings and other rulers. A letter exchange between the king of Aragon and Emperor Sigismund in 1417 indicates that leaders were discussing the issue. The king of Castile went so far as to send a representative to the Council of Basel in 1436, urging the council to side with immaculists.[34] The Council of Basel (1431-1449) did intervene, but the controversy only deepened, with Franciscans and Dominicans attempting to have some from the opposing side excommunicated over the issue.[35] Even after Pope Sixtus IV, himself an ardent immaculist, issued the bull *Grave nimis* in 1485 forbidding both Franciscans and Dominicans from attempting to have excommunicated or declaring the other heretical, the controversy continued.[36] With the

---

[30] For more on Mary and the early church fathers, see Hilda Graef, *Mary: A History of Doctrine and Devotion* (London, 1963; repr. 1985), 32-94.

[31] Augustine, *De natura et gratia*, XXXVI, 42, as discussed in Georges Jouassard, 'The Fathers of the Church and the Immaculate Conception', in *The Dogma of the Immaculate Conception: History and Significance*, ed. Edward Dennis O'Connor (Notre Dame, 1958), 70. There was considerable debate among Augustine's successors regarding his position on Mary and original sin. See Jouassard, 'The Fathers of the Church and the Immaculate Conception', 70-73.

[32] Augustine, *De natura et gratia*, 42, as quoted in Graef, *Mary: A History of Doctrine and Devotion*, 98-99.

[33] For an extremely thorough yet accessible account of the Immaculate Conception issues, see Graef, *Mary: A History of Doctrine and Devotion*, 98-99. See also Carlo Balic, 'The Mediaeval Controversy over the Immaculate Conception up to the Death of Scotus', in *The Dogma of the Immaculate Conception: History and Significance*, ed. Edward Dennis O'Connor (Notre Dame, 1958), 161-211; and Wenceslaus Sebastian, 'The Controversy over the Immaculate Conception after Scotus to the End of the Eighteenth Century', in *The Dogma of the Immaculate Conception: History and Significance*, ed. idem (Notre Dame, 1958), 213-69.

[34] Nancy Mayberry, 'The Controversy over the Immaculate Conception in Medieval and Renaissance Art, Literature, and Society', in *Journal of Medieval and Renaissance Studies* 21 (1991), 208.

[35] Mayberry, 'The Controversy over the Immaculate Conception', 208-9.

[36] For more on Sixtus IV, see Blackburn, 'For Whom do the Singers Sing?', 593-609; and 'The Virgin and the Sun', 157-95.

papacy refusing to take an official stand, both immaculists and maculists claimed victory.[37]

The Immaculate Conception debate infiltrated art and music. In an important study on Marian iconography, Mirella D'Ancona has traced the theological controversy as it pervaded art, noting the formidable challenge that portraying Mary's spiritual state *in utero* posed to artists.[38] She argues that art reflected the changing, and at times ambiguous, attitude toward the doctrine. D'Ancona's study is important because she reminds us that the doctrine, and by extension, the iconography, was not solidified: indeed, the Immaculate Conception was not official Catholic dogma until 1854. Through a study of prayer books and other manuscripts dating from the fifteenth and early sixteenth centuries, D'Ancona has demonstrated how various symbols used to represent the Immaculate Conception often overlap, as artists looked for ways to visually depict the subtle doctrinal features of a heated and long-standing debate:

> The symbolism and imagery of the feasts of the Nativity and Assumption of the Virgin gave important contributions to the development of the Immaculist iconography. Images, such as the Tree of Jesse, the Assumption and Coronation of the Virgin, the Nativity of Mary, the Virgin of Mercy, and Annunciation, the Apocalyptic Woman, and others, were at one time or another applied to the Immaculate Conception by Immaculist artists.[39]

In addition to the images D'Ancona describes, the Virgin standing on a crescent moon with emanating rays had also come to represent Immaculate Conception doctrine. Both sun and moon metaphors equated Mary with the apocalyptic woman of Revelation 12, which describes 'A woman, clothed with the sun and the moon at her feet, and on her head a crown of twelve stars.' An artist, therefore, had a list of options when deciding how to represent the Immaculate Conception.

It is often difficult to determine whether a music manuscript's theological component was tailored for its recipient. Yet regardless of whether or not the original intended recipient is known, we must give serious consideration to theological implications in the choirbooks, and, if possible, connections between the recipient and the theology. It is also plausible to assume that the scriptoria may have played a role in determining the content and presentation of individual manuscripts. Regardless of who was overseeing content and who was to receive the manuscripts, theological implications in many of the choirbooks are profound.

Take for instance JenaU 4, another Alamire manuscript that, like JenaU 22, appeared in Frederick's collection, though the identity of its original recipient is unknown. Scholars have devoted significant energy to the extensive artwork in JenaU 4, and Blackburn's discussion of Pierre de la Rue's *Missa Conceptio tua* in JenaU 4 is of special significance to any discussion of JenaU 22.[40] In addition to an imposing miniature of Mary, Eve, and the Tree of Life, the opening folios of this mass in JenaU 4 feature the

[37] René Laurentin, 'The Role of the Papal Magisterium in the Development of the Dogma of the Immaculate Conception', trans. Charles H. Sheedy and Edward S. Shea, in *The Dogma of the Immaculate Conception: History and Significance*, ed. Edward Dennis O'Connor (Notre Dame, 1958), 298-99.

[38] Mirella Levi D'Ancona, *The Iconography of the Immaculate Conception in the Middle Ages and Early Renaissance* (New York, 1957), 15-16.

[39] D'Ancona, *The Iconography of the Immaculate Conception in the Middle Ages and Early Renaissance*, 15.

[40] Blackburn, 'Messages in Miniature', 170-84.

portraits of four popes, three of whom were important proponents of the Immaculate Conception doctrine. The three pro-immaculate conception popes in JenaU 4 include Pope Girolamo Masci (Nicholas IV), Pope Alexander V, and Pope Sixtus IV. Yet woven into the fabric of these very pro-Franciscan folios is a Dominican pope—Innocent V.[41] An almost identical situation occurs in another Habsburg-Burgundian manuscript— Mechelen, Archief en Stadsbibliotheek Ms. s.s.—where miniatures of popes, including Innocent V, once again accompany La Rue's Conception mass. The inclusion of the Dominican pope, argues Blackburn, is most likely 'a sleight of hand, familiar from recent politics, to give a false impression of consensus.'[42] Blackburn further concludes that both JenaU 4 and MechAS s.s. reflect staunch Immaculate Conception doctrine, even embodying an element of propaganda.[43] And perhaps these manuscripts, though certainly in favour of the Franciscan viewpoint, offer a politically expedient nod to the 1485 *Grave nimis* bull and the official position of a papacy that had not, by the early sixteenth century, declared allegiance to either the Franciscan or Dominican position. JenaU 22 provides similar, acute theological commentary. Returning to the cantus firmus and miniature of *Missa Sicut spina rosam*, one encounters a similar case of theological insight and overlapping symbols.

Aural and Visual Symbols in JenaU 22

The section of chant that Obrecht used throughout the *Missa Sicut spina rosam* speaks figuratively of Mary as a 'rose' and literally of Mary's lineage: 'Sicut spina rosam, genuit Iudea Mariam' ('Just as a thorn brings forth a rose, so did Judea bring forth Mary'). Two important themes emerge from this chant snippet. First, as Bloxam has observed, the image of Mary as a rose (or flower) surrounded by thorns was a popular one, prompted not only by the rise of the Virgin's cult, but also by the 'ever increasing popularity of the Song of Songs, whose erotic images and metaphors often reappear in Latin religious poetry, popular publications such as the blockbooks entitled *Canticum Canticorum*, and devotional art.'[44] But the words also evoke another image—that of Mary descending from the line of David and Solomon. Both kings of Israel came through the tribe of Judah. Christ's lineage was also through David and the tribe of Judah, so establishing Mary's lineage as equal to Christ's added another piece to the Immaculate Conception puzzle: just as Christ was conceived sinless through this lineage, so too was Mary conceived sinless. Both David and Solomon often appear in Immaculate Conception paintings,[45] and the Virgin's lineage was a common theme within formularies for Marian feasts in general.[46] The prophet Isaiah also foretold Christ's descent from the tree of Jesse: 'There shall come forth a shoot from the stump ['tree'] of Jesse, and a branch from his roots shall bear fruit.'[47] The first chapter of Matthew's gospel offers a detailed (and less

---

[41] Blackburn, 'Messages in Miniature', 177.
[42] Blackburn, 'Messages in Miniature', 179.
[43] Blackburn, 'Messages in Miniature', 182.
[44] Bloxam, 'Plainsong and Polyphony', 60.
[45] Blackburn, 'Messages in Miniature', 173; see also 173 n. 48 and 49.
[46] I am grateful to Jennifer Bloxam for this observation.
[47] Isaiah 11:1, English Standard Version (ESV).

allegorical) lineage of Christ, tracing his ancestry back to Abraham,[48] Isaac, Jacob, and Jacob's son Judah (hence the 'tribe of Judea').[49] By describing Mary's descent from the line of Judea, the chant equates her lineage with that of Christ.

As theologians debated the Virgin's Immaculate Conception, Mary's lineage became an important issue. As early as the thirteenth century, the Tree of Jesse had become a standard iconographical portrayal of the Immaculate Conception.[50] Artists quickly picked up on this theme of ancestry as an allusion to the Virgin's Immaculate Conception, using images of David, Solomon, or the Tree of Jesse in their work to represent the doctrine. D'Ancona explains the significance of Mary's lineage:

> At the end of the eighth century Paul Winfrid, Deacon of Aquileia, calls Mary 'the Tree of Jesse which is totally exempt from the knots of sin,' and this metaphor was illustrated in connection with the Virgin Immaculate as early as the twelfth century. To identify Mary with the Tree of Jesse, which is the genealogical tree of Christ, and to say that she was completely exempt from sin, means that Mary was immaculate at her origin: in substance this is a rough definition of the Immaculate Conception...Artists who wanted to depict the Immaculist belief chose the Tree of Jesse because in it Mary was sanctified: Mary was sanctified in her genealogical tree, therefore, before her conception.[51]

The chant excerpt used in the *Missa Sicut spina rosam* also invokes Mary's lineage, though instead of referring to the Tree of Jesse, it refers to another name in her lineage, that of the line of Judah. Mary's ancestry would have been a natural topic for the Feast honoring her Nativity—a Feast that the Conception liturgy closely resembled.[52] The celebration of Mary's Nativity obviously raised questions about her status prior to birth (i.e., was she ever stained with original sin?), so it was logical for the two feasts to share liturgical similarities. It was not uncommon for a section of chant used for either the Nativity or Conception to speak of Mary's lineage (in this case, as one coming forth from Judea) and an educated fifteenth- or sixteenth-century listener would have recognized not only the reference to Mary's lineage in *Sicut spina rosam*, but the important implications of such a reference.

The miniature accompanying the *Missa Sicut spina rosam* reinforces the concepts highlighted in the chant, and plays directly into the Immaculate Conception debate. First, the Virgin's placement—*in sole*, on an upturned crescent moon—immediately alluded to her Immaculate Conception.[53] Second, large red and white roses surround the miniature, undoubtedly representing the 'rose among thorns' spoken of in the chant,

---

[48] The ancestry in Matthew's gospel traces the line of Joseph, 'the husband of Mary' (Matt. 1:16). Though Joseph was not Christ's physical father, the genealogy is still understood as the lineage of Christ.

[49] Matthew 1:1-17.

[50] D'Ancona, *The Iconography of the Immaculate Conception in the Middle Ages and Early Renaissance*, 48.

[51] D'Ancona, *The Iconography of the Immaculate Conception in the Middle Ages and Early Renaissance*, 7 and 47. For more on the development of Marian iconography, see Maurice Vloberg, 'The Iconography of the Immaculate Conception', in *The Dogma of the Immaculate Conception: History and Significance*, ed. Edward Dennis O'Connor (Notre Dame, 1958), 463-504.

[52] David Rothenberg, 'Marian Feasts, Seasons, and Songs in Medieval Polyphony: Studies in Marian Symbolism' (Ph.D. diss., Yale University, 2004), 56. A third feast—the Feast of the Assumption—also had much in common with the Feast of the Nativity and the Feast of the Conception.

[53] See Blackburn, 'The Virgin and the Sun', 185-89.

but also the image of a rosary.[54] The rosary had long been associated with the Dominicans, one of the most vocal anti-Immaculate Conception groups.[55] The Dominicans created the Confraternity of the Rosary, which encouraged devotion to the rosary.[56]

Thus we find in JenaU 22 a mixed message, for while both image and chant point to Mary's lineage, favouring the Franciscan point of view, the appearance of the rosary hints at unresolved tension that still existed between the two orders, and the deeper theological tensions behind Mary's Immaculate Conception. JenaU 4, though probably created at least a decade after JenaU 22, features a similar, theologically astute detail to doctrinal concerns surrounding the Immaculate Conception, as Blackburn has noted.[57] But this brings us back to the question raised earlier: why was Obrecht's mass the only composition in the manuscript to receive such an image? The peculiar placement of the miniature, 102 folios into the choirbook, is extraordinary. As we shall see, the subject of the miniature, in conjunction with the mass theme, suggests the solution.

JenaU 22 and the Immaculate Conception

To undertsand why Obrecht's mass is the one adorned with a miniature in JenaU 22, we must briefly consider the Marian themes—particularly that of the Immaculate Conception—first in the entire corpus of surviving Habsburg-Burgundian manuscripts, and then in Frederick's individual Alamire collection. Themes of Mary's life and particularly her Conception run prominently throughout many of the Habsburg-Burgundian manuscripts, with just over half of the surviving miniatures featuring various moments in the Virgins' life—most prominently her Conception.[58] The surviving miniatures alone present compelling visual evidence of Mary's prominent role. Table 2 shows the breakdown of Marian Conception masses (along with one Marian motet), accompanied by their correlating miniatures, found in the Habsburg-Burgundian manuscripts (including masses with presumably stolen images).[59]

Since Marian themes dominate the entire Habsburg-Burgundian collection, it comes as no surprise that within Frederick the Wise's collection, Mary also stands front and centre. Of his eleven choirbooks, nine feature at least one (and usually more) Marian-themed mass, and five of these nine choirbooks hold Conception masses.[60] Themes of Mary's life, particularly her Conception, received priority from the workshops.[61]

54 When listing various Alamire masses in a chart, Blackburn lists *Missa Sicut spina rosam* miniature as the 'Virgin of the Rosary' miniature. Blackburn, 'Messages in Miniature', 168.

55 Blackburn, 'The Virgin in the Sun', 180.

56 Irénée Henri Dalmais, Pierre Jounel, and Aimé Georges Martimort, *The Church at Prayer: An Introduction to the Liturgy*, vol. 4 , *The Liturgy and Time*, trans. Matthew J. O'Connell (Collegeville, 1983). Frederick was a devoutly religious man. It is unclear whether he was particularly sympathetic to either Franciscans or Dominicans, though such an inquiry is worth investigation.

57 Blackburn, 'Messages in Miniature', 170-84.

58 Blackburn, 'Messages in Miniature', 164-65, see particularly the chart on 165 and 168-69.

59 This table is a condensed version of the very useful charts in Blackburn, 'Messages in Miniature', 165, 167-69.

60 JenaU 4 and JenaU 5 both feature La Rue's six-voice *Missa Ave sanctissima Maria* and his five-voice *Missa Conceptio tua*. All four appearances of these masses have, or once had, miniatures accompanying the music. JenaU 2 and JenaU 8 both include Bauldeweyn's five-voice *Missa Inviolata*, and JenaU 7 contains La Rue's *Missa Inviolata*, though these masses do not have accompanying miniatures.

61 For a detailed categorization of these masses, see Mowrey, 'The Alamire Manuscripts of Frederick the Wise', 149-56.

Table 2. Immaculate Conception masses and motet in surviving Alamire manuscripts

Composer and mass or motet	Manuscript	Owner or commissioner[a]
La Rue, *Ave sanctissima Maria*	BrusBR 228	Margaret of Austria
La Rue, *Missa Ave sanctissima Maria*	BrusBR15075	Intended for Margaret of Austria?[b]
La Rue, *Missa Conceptio tua*	BrusBR 15075	Intended for Margaret of Austria?
La Rue, *Missa Conceptio tua*	MechAS s.s.	Margaret of Austria, Maximilian, or Archduke Charles[c]
La Rue, *Missa Conceptio tua*	JenaU 4	Maximilian or Henry VIII (eventually acquired by Frederick the Wise)
La Rue, *Missa Ave sanctissima Maria*	JenaU 4	Maximilian, Henry VIII (eventually acquired by Frederick the Wise)[d]
La Rue, *Missa Ave sanctissima Maria*	JenaU 5	Frederick the Wise
Missing (presumed) Immaculate Conception images		
La Rue, *Missa Ave sanctissima Maria*	BrusBR 6428	Margaret of Austria or Maximilian?
La Rue, *Missa Conceptio tua*	BrusBR 6428	Margaret of Austria or Maximilian?
La Rue, *Missa Conceptio tua*	JenaU 5	Frederick the Wise
La Rue, *Missa Conceptio tua*	VatS 34	Pope Leo X or Margaret of Austria?
La Rue, *Missa Ave sanctissima Maria*	VatS 36	Margaret of Austria or Pope Leo X

[a] Margaret of Austria as owner or commissioner appears numerous times in this table. Margaret's involvement in the manuscript collection—in particular her possible involvement in Frederick's collection—is significant, but well beyond the scope of this paper. For an extended discussion of the issue, see Hannah Mowrey, 'The Alamire Manuscripts of Frederick the Wise: Intersections of Music, Art, and Theology' (Ph.D. diss., University of Rochester, 2010), 383-402.

[b] There has been debate over the original intended recipient. See Herbert Kellman, 'Brussels, Bibliothèque royale de Belgique MS 15075', in *Treasury*, 74-75.

[c] See discussion in Flynn Warmington, 'Mechelen, Archief en Stadsbibliotheek MS s.s.', in *Treasury*, 112-13. Based on the Immaculate Conception imagery, Blackburn suspects that Margaret was behind the Mechelen manuscript: 'But the Mechelen manuscript (MechAS s.s.) seems destined as a court manuscript, not a gift. It is the only manuscript of the complex that remained in its place of origin. Can we see the hand of Margaret behind it?' Blackburn, 'Messages in Miniature', 183.

[d] Jas and Kellman assert that JenaU 4 was likely prepared for either Maximilian or Henry VIII. (Eric Jas and Herbert Kellman, 'Jena, Thüringer Universitäts- und Landesbibliothek MS 4', in *Treasury*, 90-91.) Based on the unusual flags in the manuscript, Flynn Warmington suspects that Charles may have been behind the manuscript. My thanks to Ms. Warmington for kindly sharing with me her unpublished work on JenaU 4.

Returning to JenaU 22, eight of the thirteen masses take sacred cantus firmi, and of those eight, four are Marian: *Missa de Beata Virgine* uses a variety of chant models, creating a litany of praise to the Virgin; *Missa Assumpta est Maria* draws on the first antiphon for the second Vespers on the Feast of Mary's Assumption; *Missa Sicut spina rosam* uses a responsory for the Feast of Mary's Nativity and the Feast of Mary's Conception; and *Missa Cum iocunditate* uses the fifth antiphon from the second Vespers of the Feast of the Nativity. The chant models for the latter two masses traditionally serve both Conception and Nativity feasts, though unlike *Cum iocunditate*, the *Sicut spina rosam* responsory specifically invokes Mary's lineage.

It is unknown whether Obrecht's mass was intended for use during the Conception liturgy or the Nativity liturgy, and the composer's original intentions elude us. The versatility of the chant would have allowed the mass to be used in either liturgy. The miniature, however, provides an interesting clue. The mass's miniature—supplied by the

Alamire workshops—and subsequent interaction with the chant themes emphasized the Conception feast. Mention of Judea in the *Sicut spina rosam* responsory alludes to Mary's Immaculate Conception, and the image adds another layer to the story *behind* her Nativity, linking it directly with her Immaculate Conception. Yet the miniature not only points to the Immaculate Conception, but also to the debate that encompassed the doctrine, mingling images that correspond to both sides: the Dominican stance (through the rosary) and the Franciscan stance (through the Virgin and the Sun/Revelation 12).

In the Middle Ages and Renaissance, art—both aural and visual—found intrinsic value in its ability to tell not one, but many stories. This would necessarily require meticulous and thorough planning. The Alamire choirbooks were no exception; Bonnie Blackburn, Herbert Kellman, Honey Meconi, and Flynn Warmington have shown that music and artwork were all carefully planned and thoughtfully placed within the majority of manuscripts that left the workshops. Blackburn has even shown how JenaU 4 acts as a type of Immaculate Conception propaganda, as both the aural and visual elements in this choirbook address this pertinent doctrinal issue of the early sixteenth century.[62] Frederick's remaining choirbooks are no exception, as Mary pervades the collection in both sight and sound. Whoever ordered the manuscripts for Frederick's court seemed especially interested in Marian doctrine.[63] A devout Catholic himself, Frederick would have cared deeply about such theological issues. Considered in light not only of Frederick's collection, but all of the Alamire choirbooks, we should pay careful attention to the subtle yet pertinent theological message found in JenaU 22.

JenaU 22 therefore becomes as a catalyst and early forerunner for theological themes and messages that permeate many of the Alamire manuscripts, and especially those choirbooks that found their way into Frederick's collection. Of all the masses in Frederick's choirbooks, the Marian masses, and particularly the Immaculate Conception masses, received the most elaborate artwork.[64] It appears that JenaU 22 set a Marian Conception mass/miniature precedent that was replicated in future Hapsburg-Burgundian manuscripts, including those acquired by Frederick. The care and attention given to JenaU 22 raises intriguing questions not only about the miniature's placement, but also about the workshops' potential role in determining the theological flavor of a manuscript, as they sought to match the mass and miniature theme. Correlating miniatures with certain mass themes would have been obvious in many cases: Conception masses would receive Conception miniatures; Assumption masses would receive Assumption miniatures, etc. But for a mass such as *Missa Sicut spina rosam*, the theme of which had strong associations with two similar, yet individually distinct feasts, we should consider how the workshops— or in some cases the manuscript's commissioner—shaped the manuscript's theological emphasis. JenaU 22 thus serves as a prophetic voice, as the Virgin's Immaculate Conception, tucked one hundred folios into the manuscript would become a defining and pronounced feature in the Alamire choirbooks that would follow. Whether the workshops or a commissioner gave such careful nuance to the manuscript's lone miniature, JenaU 22 becomes one of the earliest in a long and illustrious line of Habsburg-Burgundian manuscripts that gives both sight and sound to a pertinent theological debate. This should give us pause, reminding us to let the little stories, though often hidden away and easily forgotten, speak.

[62] Blackburn, 'Messages in Miniature', 161-84.
[63] Mowrey, 'The Alamire Manuscripts of Frederick the Wise', 383-402.
[64] Mowrey, 'The Alamire Manuscripts of Frederick the Wise', 149-56.

Abstract

Created between 1500 and 1505 and acquired by Elector Frederick the Wise, Jena, Thüringer Universitäts- und Landesbibliothek, Ms. 22, an early Habsburg-Burgundian manuscript, is distinguished for its large collection of masses by Pierre de la Rue. Manuscripts that left the Habsburg-Burgundian workshops often boasted impressive artwork, including splendid borders, inked calligraphic initials, and intricate miniatures. The artists who painted the miniatures frequently offered a stunning visual portrayal of the music's theme. At first glance, JenaU 22 appears slighted in this respect, since the choirbook contains only one miniature. Furthermore, this miniature, which accompanies Jacob Obrecht's *Missa Sicut spina rosam*, is placed unusually late—on fol. 102—seemingly as an afterthought. Despite much commentary on the cantus firmus, musical structure, date, and origin of the *Missa Sicut spina rosam*, the miniature accompanying this mass has been overlooked. Yet by examining the intricate correlation between the miniature and the themes in Obrecht's mass, this paper suggests that the image/mass combination reflects upon the doctrine of the Virgin Mary's Immaculate Conception, one of the most contentious theological debates of the early sixteenth century. The subtle aural and visual theological clues found in JenaU 22 point almost prophetically to important themes that run not only throughout Frederick's impressive collection, but the entire corpus of Habsburg-Burgundian manuscripts.

Free papers

Reading Hagiographic Motets:
Christi nutu sublimato, *Lamberte vir inclite*, and the Legend of St. Lambert[*]

∎

C ATHERINE S AUCIER

Two fifteenth-century motets, *Christi nutu sublimato* ascribed to Johannes Brassart (b. c. 1400-5, d. 1455) and the anonymous *Lamberte vir inclite*, have long been associated with the city of Liège on account of their common addressee—the diocesan patron, St. Lambert.[1] As tributes to a local hero, these works resemble the motets commemorating saints of importance to regions bordering the Liège diocese, such as Guillaume de Machaut's *Martyrum gemma / Diligenter inquiramus / A Christo honoratus* for St. Quintinus (the third-century missionary who evangelized the region of Amiens and lent his name to the place of his martyrdom, the northern-French town of Saint-Quentin), the anonymous motet *O sanctissime presul / O Christi pietas* for St. Donatian (patron saint of Bruges), and Jacob Obrecht's *O beate Basili / O beate pater* for St. Basil (the Church Father whose relics were venerated in Bruges).[2] From a musico-liturgical perspective, however, the two pieces for St. Lambert differ fundamentally from this other polyphony. As freely composed equal discantus motets, both *Christi nutu* and *Lamberte vir* lack a plainchant quotation.[3] Our sole point of entry into the symbolism and local function of these works, therefore, is through their texts.

[*] An earlier version of this study was presented at the Medieval and Renaissance Music Conference, Nottingham (July, 2012). My thanks to Peter Wright for his invaluable insight into the style, dating, authorship, and transmission of the two motets, as well as to Barbara Newman, Taylor Corse, Leofranc Holford-Strevens, and the anonymous reader for this Journal their generous assistance with my translations, all of which are my own unless otherwise noted. The orthography of the Latin texts follows that of the edition. All biblical passages are quoted from *The Vulgate Bible: Douay-Rheims Translation*, ed. Angela Kinney (Cambridge MA, 2010-13). Archival citations use the following abbreviations: AEL (Archives de l'État à Liège); C (Chartes); CA (Compterie des Anniversaires); CG (Compterie du Grenier); LC (Libri Chartarum); S (Secrétariat). Polyphonic manuscript sigla are as follows: D-Mbs 14274 (Munich, Bayerische Staatsbibliothek, Clm 14274); GB-Ob 213 (Oxford, Bodleian Library, Canon. misc. 213); I-AO 15 (Aosta, Seminario Maggiore, Ms. 15); I-Bc Q 15 (Bologna, Museo Internazionale e Biblioteca della Musica, Ms. Q15); I-TRmp 87-1 (Trent, Castello del Buonconsiglio, Monumenti e Collezioni Provinciali, Cod. 1374).

At first glance, the two motets appear to sketch a conventionalized portrait of St. Lambert's character and episcopal deeds (see the texts and translations in Appendices 1 and 2). Both hail Lambert as an exemplary individual whose virtuous acts are inspired by divine influence—the Holy Spirit or the heavenly Father. As a bishop, Lambert lives by and fights for the Christian faith and condemns sinful and immoral behaviour. As a martyr, identified as Christ's champion (in *Christi nutu*) and a murdered victim who has surrendered his soul to the heavens (in *Lamberte vir*), Lambert becomes an intercessor to the faithful praying for salvation.

Yet upon closer inspection, the two works share a number of enigmatic references to Lambert's youth, episcopate, and death that have eluded musicological inquiry.[4] What is the significance of the fire that Lambert carries without burning his garment (compare Appendix 1, line 9 to Appendix 2, line 10), or the adulterous acts that he spurns (Appendix 1 and 2, lines 22-24)? The seemingly cryptic language of the two motets resembles the abridged narratives of hymns and sequences sung during liturgical and votive observances that further elucidated the significance of the saint's life. These stories became familiar to the clergy and laity who attended the annual feasts and weekly devotions honouring high-ranking saints cherished by the local community, such as St. Lambert in Liège, through the varied media of lections, chants, and images (reliquaries, tapestries, paintings, and other artwork) that depicted in vivid detail the saint's heroic deeds, pious virtues, and miracles. Without immersing ourselves in this local hagiographic context, we risk misinterpreting the narrative signs and overlooking the rich symbolism embedded in these musical texts.

The key to unlocking the meaning of *Christi nutu* and *Lamberte vir* lies in the methods of reading medieval *vitae* and other hagiographic media. Scholarship on saints' lives in their literary and pictorial forms has uncovered the underlying goals and conventions of hagiographic narrative by examining the metaphors, rhetorical devices, *topoi*, and notions of time that are unique to the genre.[5] Saints' lives are not factual biographies organized in a seamless chronology nor are they fictional eulogies devoid of locational or temporal references. Rather, hagiographers seek to rouse their audiences

---

[4] These hagiographic parallels have not been adequately addressed in previous musicological scholarship, due, in part, to the fact that neither *Christi nutu* nor *Lamberte vir* has been the subject of detailed analysis. Brief discussions of these motets are found in the following: Keith Mixter, 'Johannes Brassart and his Works', 2 vols. (Ph.D. diss., University of North Carolina at Chapel Hill, 1961), vol. 1, 78, 81, 88, 96, 112, 138, 148, 152; Marian Cobin, 'The Compilation of the Aosta Manuscript: A Working Hypothesis', in *Papers Read at the Dufay Quincentenary Conference, Brooklyn College, December 6-7, 1974*, ed. Allan Atlas (Brooklyn NY, 1976), 76-101 at 85-86 and 89; Ian Rumbold, 'The Compilation and Ownership of the "St. Emmeram" Codex (Munich, Bayerische Staatsbibliothek, Clm 14274)', in *Early Music History* 2 (1982), 161-235 at 180, 190, 224; Peter Wright, *The Related Parts of Trent Museo Provinciale d'Arte, Mss 87 (1374) and 92 (1379): A Paleographical and Text-Critical Study* (New York, 1989), 38-39, 57, 60, 188-89; Cumming, *The Motet*, 229-30; Thomas Schmidt-Beste, *Textdeklamation in der Motette des 15. Jahrhunderts* (Turnhout, 2003), 224-26; Ian Rumbold, Peter Wright, and Lorenz Welker (eds.), *Der Mensuralcodex St. Emmeram: Faksimile der Handschrift Clm 14274 der Bayerischen Staatsbibliothek München* (Wiesbaden, 2006), 94 and 103; Philip Weller, Translator's notes in *The St Emmeram Codex*, Stimmwerck (CD, Aeolus, AE-10023, 2008), 34; and Ian Rumbold and Peter Wright, *Hermann Pötzlinger's Music Book: The St. Emmeram Codex and its Contents* (Woodbridge, 2009), 52.

[5] Hippolyte Delehaye's classic *Les légendes hagiographiques* (Brussels, 1906) has generated numerous studies of hagiographic narrative. My reading of the motet texts is influenced by the following: Patrick Geary, *Furta Sacra: Thefts of Relics in the Central Middle Ages* (Princeton, 1978); Alison Elliott, *Roads to Paradise: Reading the Lives of the Early Saints* (Hanover-London, 1987); Thomas Heffernan, *Sacred Biography: Saints and Their Biographers in the Middle Ages* (Oxford-New York, 1988); Cynthia Hahn, 'Picturing the Text: Narrative in the Life of the Saints', in *Art History* 13 (1990), 1-33; Hahn, *Portrayed on the Heart: Narrative Effect in Pictorial Lives of Saints from the Tenth Through the Thirteenth Century* (Berkeley-Los Angeles-London, 2001); and Laura Weigert, *Weaving Sacred Stories: French Choir Tapestries and the Performance of Clerical Identity* (Ithaca NY, 2004).

to a state of devotion and imitation through a series of tableaux or snapshots of the saint in the likeness of Christ and other holy figures, thereby inviting believers to renew their faith through the saint's example and, ultimately, to participate in the history of salvation.[6] To be effective, however, the hagiographer must adhere to generic expectations and saintly types that allow the reader to recognize the saint's extraordinary powers and to be moved to reverence. Markers of the saint's holiness are often expressed by analogy to an episode in the life of Christ or another saint, through *topoi* that represent specific characteristics of sanctity and reveal saintly powers, and through miracles that reverse normative expectations to signal the presence of the divine.[7] These modes of narrative expression and interpretation are found in the two motets for St. Lambert, providing an insightful point of entry into the complex inner workings of this hagiographic polyphony.

Christi nutu and *Lamberte vir* merit comparative textual analysis for two reasons. First, these works share previously unidentified hagiographic references to a saint whose life received ongoing, and well-documented, embellishment throughout the later Middle Ages. Revisions to the saint's *vita* over the course of some eight centuries (from c. 727-743 to the early 1500s) survive in multiple media—from prose and verse literature to liturgical chant and votive images—that testify to the prolonged vitality of the saint's cult. In our reading of the motet texts, we consider how Lambert's hybrid status as a bishop-martyr, merging the saintly types of martyr and confessor, may have been a motivating factor in these accretions, as hagiographers, musicians, and artists sought to enhance Lambert's episcopal attributes and to justify his exalted martyrial rank.

Second, noteworthy parallels in the manuscript transmission and musical style of the two motets suggest the possibility of a common origin. As shown in Table 1, *Christi nutu* and *Lamberte vir* circulated adjacently in two sources: the fourth section of I-AO 15 (in the same gathering as Johannes Brassart's motet *O rex Fridrice*),[8] and the seventh gathering of I-TRmp 87-1 (alongside Brassart's motets for St. Martin and St. John the Evangelist).[9]

In addition to this scribal pairing, the two motets share distinct motives that are characteristic of Brassart's Latin-texted works,[10] and feature a very similar two- and four-voice texture. As outlined in Table 2, both works alternate between three discantus duets, the first of which corresponds to the first tercet of the poetry, and three four-voice sections, the longest of which is the second.

---

[6] Heffernan, *Sacred Biography*, 5-6; and Hahn, 'Picturing the Text', 3-5.

[7] Hahn, *Portrayed on the Heart*, 39-45.

[8] Peter Wright notes the high concentration of Brassart's music in the fourth section of I-AO 15. In addition to the above-named motets, this section contains an anonymous Gloria-Credo pair (fols. 268v-271r) that Wright attributes convincingly to Brassart on the basis of pronounced melodic similarities to the composer's other more securely attributed mass music. See Wright, 'A New Attribution to Brassart?', in *Plainsong and Medieval Music* 3 (1994), 23-43.

[9] Peter Wright believes that an earlier (unknown) source may have prescribed the adjacency of these motets. See Wright, *The Related Parts of Trent*, 188-89. Brassart's motet *Te dignitas presularis* for St. Martin is also transmitted in the second layer of I-Bc Q 15 (fols. 266v-267r) compiled in the early 1430s. See Margaret Bent (ed.), *Bologna Q15: The Making and Remaking of a Musical Manuscript*, 2 vols. (Lucca, 2008), vol. 1, 3 and 227. Brassart's motet *Fortis cum quevis actio* for St. John the Evangelist is also found in the ninth gathering of GB-Ob 213 (fols. 131v-32r), probably copied c. 1428-c. 1434. See David Fallows (ed.), *Oxford, Bodleian Library MS. Canon. Misc. 213* (Chicago-London, 1995), 19-20.

[10] Peter Wright has identified a number of melodic figures that recur throughout Brassart's mass settings and motets in 'A New Attribution to Brassart?', 30-31. Two of these motives are common to *Christi nutu* and *Lamberte vir*: the motive of two rising fourths joined by a descending second (Wright, Figure C); and a descending second-inversion chordal figure (Wright, Figure D). *Christi nutu* also includes a four-note rising figure favoured by Brassart (Wright, Figure A), while *Lamberte vir* features a falling six-note motive, consisting of the sequential treatment of a descending second followed by a descending third, found in roughly half of Brassart's works (Wright, Figure B, discussed below in conjunction with drinking vessels).

Table 1. Manuscript sources for *Christi nutu sublimato* and *Lamberte vir inclite*

Motet	Sources
Christi nutu sublimato	I-AO 15, fols. 258v-259v (anon.) and fols. 280v-281v ('Jo Brassart')
	I-TRmp 87-1, fols. 75v-77r (anon.)
	D-Mbs 14274, fols. 116v-117v (anon.)
Lamberte vir inclite	I-AO 15, fols. 260r-261v (anon.)
	I-Trmp 87-1, fols. 73v-75r (anon.)

Table 2. Alternating two- and four-voice textures in *Christi nutu sublimato, Lamberte vir inclite,*
and *Fortis cum quevis actio*

Christi nutu sublimato	*Lamberte vir inclite*	*Fortis cum quevis actio*
Discantus duet (17 breves) = 3 lines	Discantus duet (25 breves) = 3 lines	Discantus duet (32 breves) = 3 lines
4vv. (12 breves) = 3 lines	4vv. (32 breves) = 6 lines	4vv. (26 breves) = 4 lines
Discantus duet (19 breves) = 6 lines	Discantus duet (8 breves) = 2 lines	Discantus duet (13 breves) = 2 lines
4vv. (27 breves) = 11 lines	4vv. (51 breves) = 13 lines	4vv. (68 breves) = 7 lines
Discantus duet (6 breves) = 2 lines	Discantus duet (18 breves) = 4 lines	Discantus duet (17 breves) = 1 line
4vv. (23 breves) = 5 lines	4vv. (45 breves) = 7 lines	4vv. (32 breves) = 1 line

Precisely this textural scheme governs Brassart's motet *Fortis cum quevis actio* for St. John the Evangelist.[11] Despite the anonymity of *Lamberte vir*, several scholars—notably Charles Hamm, Keith Mixter, and Peter Wright—have endorsed Brassart's authorship of both motets.[12] That the two works tell similar stories about the same saint's life supports this view.[13]

---

[11] The recurring duet sections of Brassart's equal discantus motets may have been inspired by English practice. Julie Cumming observes that while extended discantus duets are not found in the Italian and devotional double-discantus pieces contained in I-Bc Q 15, they are characteristic of contemporaneous English music of all genres, which may have inspired Brassart's approach to texture. See Cumming, *The Motet*, 229-30. My search through the repertory in the Old Hall Manuscript as well as the motets of Leonel Power and John Dunstable, has not, however, yielded an exact match to the textural scheme shared by *Christi nutu, Lamberte vir*, and *Fortis cum quevis actio*. For a recent study of the *liégeois* context of *Fortis cum quevis actio*, see Saucier, 'Johannes Brassart's Civic Motet: Voicing the Biblical Topography of Medieval Liège', in *Acta Musicologica* 85 (2013), 1-20.

[12] See Charles Hamm, 'Manuscript Structure in the Dufay Era', in *Acta Musicologica* 34 (1962), 166-84 at 170-71. Wright endorses Hamm's attribution in 'A New Attribution to Brassart?', 24 and 27 n. 13. Both motets are published in Brassart's *Opera Omnia*, ed. Keith Mixter, 2 vols., Corpus mensurabilis musicae 35 (Rome, 1971), vol. 2, 15-18 (*Christi nutu*) and 39-43 (*Lamberte vir*, under *opera dubia*). The music examples in this article are from this edition, and are reproduced with permission.

[13] Extant biographical evidence favours Brassart's authorship of both motets. Not only did this priest-musician cultivate life-long ecclesiastical ties with the city of Liège, he held a securely documented musical position (as succentor, 1428-31) at the cathedral dedicated to St. Lambert. See Keith Mixter, 'Johannes Brassart: A Biographical and Bibliographical Study', in *Musica Disciplina* 18 (1964), 37-62; and Pamela Starr, 'Letter to the Editors', in *Plainsong and Medieval Music* 1 (1992), 215-16. Brassart also made two trips to Italy—visiting the court of Pope Martin V in 1424-25 and singing alongside Guillaume Du Fay in the chapel of Pope Eugenius IV in 1431—where he would undoubtedly have encountered other examples of the 'Italianate' double-discantus motet genre. See Mixter, 'Johannes Brassart: A Biographical and Bibliographical Study', 40-44; and Margaret Bent, 'Early Papal Motets', in *Papal Music and Musicians in Late Medieval and Renaissance Rome*, ed. Richard Sherr (Oxford-New York, 1993), 5-43 at 34-36. Yet we cannot rule out the possibility that *Lamberte vir* was composed by one of Brassart's contemporaries. In this case, the most likely candidate is Johannes de Sarto (fl. c. 1430-40), Brassart's compatriot at the imperial chapel during the 1430s and a remarkable emulator of his musical style. See Wright, 'Johannes Brassart and Johannes de Sarto', in *Plainsong and Medieval Music* 1 (1992),

By scrutinizing the hagiographic narratives vocalized in *Christi nutu* and *Lamberte vir* we gain greater insight into the meaning, origin, function, and performance context of the two motets. To familiarize ourselves with the life and legends of St. Lambert, we begin by identifying the hagiographic sources of the narratives common to both works. These anonymous poems combine older and newer tales in keeping with the narrative conventions found in the saint's late-medieval *vitae* and liturgical music.[14] As we will subsequently note, the periodic reduction of the texture to two voices allows for greater textual clarity at key moments in the narrative. Yet the motets do not tell an identical story, and hagiographic differences underscore their complementary function. Identifying the hagiographic roots of *Christi nutu* and *Lamberte vir* strengthens the possibility that these motets were written and sung in fifteenth-century Liège. Decoding their meaning illuminates the extent to which freely composed votive polyphony draws from and enhances hagiographic narrative.

St. Lambert's Life and the Legend of his Martyrdom

St. Lambert belongs to a group of sixth- and seventh-century Frankish bishops murdered by political rivals and sainted in increasing numbers as the Church spread into new areas of the Merovingian realm.[15] We can infer from the eight-century *Vita prima*,[16] several episodes of which are echoed in *Christi nutu*, that Lambert was born into a noble Christian family (as implied in lines 4-5 of the motet, see Appendix 1) and received his education under episcopal supervision at the Merovingian royal court. Following the assassination of Bishop Theodard, Lambert was promoted to the episcopal seat of Tongeren-Maastricht-Liège (referenced in line 13), but was soon deposed and exiled at the Abbey of Stavelot for seven years while an impostor ruled the cathedral. Lambert's exemplary conduct at Stavelot is illustrated by his willingness to stand barefoot in the freezing night at the abbey's cross (in lines 17-18) as punishment for having disturbed the monks by dropping his shoe. Once restored on the episcopal throne through the intervention of King Pippin II (in lines 19-20), Bishop Lambert embarked on a mission to convert pagans in the surrounding countryside.

Brassart and other *liégeois* clerics would have performed the earliest surviving musical account of these hagiographic events in the versified office compiled by Bishop Stephen of Liège in the early tenth century and sung throughout the diocese well into

---

41-61; and idem, 'Sarto, Johannes de', in *Grove Music Online*, <http://www.oxfordmusiconline.com> (accessed 20 January 2014). We can thus envision two equally possible compositional scenarios: that both motets are the product of a single composer, or that these works reflect a 'house style' cultivated by Brassart and his *liégeois* contemporaries. How Brassart and other *liégeois* composers were exposed to the double-discantus genre merits further research, especially in light of the recent questions on the issue of 'French' vs. 'Italian' raised by Karl Kügle in 'Glorious Sounds for a Holy Warrior: New Light on Codex Turin J.II.9', in *Journal of the American Musicological Society* 65 (2012), 637-90 at 679-80.

[14] The poetic texts of the two motets clearly emanate from an individual or institution intimately familiar with St. Lambert's multi-layered late-medieval profile—in all likelihood a cleric from the city or diocese of Liège who was in some way affiliated with a church where the saint's cult was strong, such as the cathedral marking the site of Lambert's martyrdom. It is entirely possible that the composer(s) Brassart (and his *liégeois* contemporary?) wrote the motet texts.

[15] The following discussion of Lambert's life and legend draws upon my book, *A Paradise of Priests: Singing the Civic and Episcopal Hagiography of Medieval Liège* (University of Rochester Press, forthcoming).

[16] *Vita prima sancti Lamberti*, in *Acta Sanctorum* (hereafter AASS), ed. Joannus Bollandus and others, 69 vols. (Antwerp, 1643-1940), September vol. 5, <http://acta.chadwyck.com> (accessed 20 January 2014).

the early modern era.[17] The lections and responsories for matins, based on Bishop Stephen's own *Vita secunda* for St. Lambert, narrate the principal events of the saint's life, from his birth and childhood perfectionism, to his episcopal promotion and exile at Stavelot, to the heavenly reception following his demise. Subsequently, the five antiphons for lauds detail the event of Lambert's martyrdom.[18]

The circumstances of Lambert's death, however, were problematic. The *Vita prima* portrays Lambert as the victim of a private power struggle between two families competing for territorial control—a situation that is hardly Christ-like. Lambert's family had apparently come into conflict with relatives of the king's most powerful administrator, known as Dodo, who had harassed the bishop by intruding on his land and seizing his goods. When Lambert's relatives retaliated by killing two of Dodo's men, the vengeful administrator mounted a small private army to attack and slay Lambert at his residence.[19] Because Lambert's family had committed the first mortal crime, the events leading to the bishop's death *prima facie* do little to promote his candidacy for sainthood. As depicted in the *Vita prima*, Lambert's martyrial status is entirely dependent on his final acts in the face of death itself—his decision to drop the sword he had seized for self-defense and to prostrate himself in prayer.

Not surprisingly, Lambert's first *vita* was soon embellished with a supplementary legend, implicating the Merovingian royalty in his murder. As depicted in a tenth-century hagiographic poem, the *Carmen de sancto Landberto*, Lambert pales at the illicit relations between Dodo's sister and the king, who, 'scorning the laws of chastity' (*proculcans iura pudoris*) had taken her as his mistress.[20] While the king remains nameless, this additional narrative substantially revises the cause of Lambert's martyrdom, shifting the source of enmity between Lambert and Dodo from the exclusive domain of inter-familial violence to the realm of royal immorality.

The legend adopted a decidedly anti-Carolingian stance in the early eleventh century by identifying the immoral king as Pippin II of Herstal, great-grandfather to Charlemagne.[21] Having repudiated his first wife, Plectrude, Pippin is known to have fathered Charles Martel with his bigamous wife, Alpaïda, while Plectrude was still living.[22] Subsequent versions of this legend—penned by clerics with connections to the cathedral chapter in the mid eleventh to mid twelfth centuries—cast Pippin's mistress in an increasingly unflattering role. The most influential of these later *vitae* is that by the

[17] Research on the office of St. Lambert includes the following: Antoine Auda, *Etienne de Liége* (Brussels, 1923); Ritva Jonsson, *Historia: Etudes sur la genèse des offices versifiés* (Stockholm, 1968); Gunilla Björkvall and Andreas Haug, 'Performing Latin Verse: Text and Music in Early Medieval Versified Offices', in *The Divine Office in the Latin Middle Ages: Methodology and Source Studies, Regional Developments, Hagiography*, ed. Margot Fassler and Rebecca Baltzer (New York, 2000), 278-99; and Saucier, 'The Sweet Sound of Sanctity: Sensing Saint Lambert', in *The Senses and Society* 5 (2010), 10-27.

[18] Jonsson, *Historia*, 154-64, 218-21.

[19] *Vita prima sancti Lamberti*, 577E-78B.

[20] Paul von Winterfeld (ed.), *Carmen de sancto Landberto*, Monumenta Germaniae Historica [hereafter MGH] Poetae Latini Aevi Carolini (Berlin, 1899), vol. 4, 151-52.

[21] Georg Waitz (ed.), *Annales Lobienses*, MGH Scriptores (Hannover, 1881), vol. 13, 227. See also Jean-Louis Kupper, 'Saint Lambert: De l'histoire à la légende', in *Revue d'histoire ecclésiastique* 79 (1984), 5-49, esp. 35-37.

[22] For a recent study of Alpaïda, see Gustav Adolf Beckmann, 'Les deux Alpais et les toponymes épiques (Avroy-) Auridon-Oridon-Dordon(e)', in *Le Moyen Age* 114 (2008), 55-65.

cathedral canon Nicholas of Liège (d. c. 1146), who, unlike previous hagiographers, attributes the cause of Lambert's death solely to Pippin's affair (see Table 3).[23]

Table 3. Principal medieval narratives of St. Lambert's martyrdom

Hagiographic source	Cause of Lambert's death
Vita prima sancti Lamberti (mid 8th cent.)	Interfamilial violence
Stephen of Liège, *Vita secunda sancti Lamberti* (early 10th cent.)	Interfamilial violence
Carmen de sancto Landberto (early 10th cent.)	Interfamilial violence; Lambert condemns 'the king' for adultery
Anselm of Liège, *Gesta pontificum Trajectensium et Leodiensium* (mid 11th cent.)	Interfamilial violence; Lambert condemns King Pippin II for adultery
Sigebert of Gembloux, *Vita prior sancti Lamberti* and *Vita altera sancti Lamberti* (late 11th cent.)	Interfamilial violence; Lambert condemns King Pippin II for adultery
Nicholas of Liège, *Vita quarta sancti Lamberti* (mid 12th cent.)	Lambert condemns King Pippin II for adultery
Giles of Orval, *Gesta pontificum Leodiensium* (mid 13th cent.)	Lambert condemns King Pippin II for adultery

While Bishop Stephen's tenth-century office conspicuously avoids this legendary cause of Lambert's death, later liturgical texts and music embrace it. *Liégeois* clerics in the later Middle Ages would have heard this tale in the six lections for the first and second nocturns at matins read on the Octave of Lambert's Martyrdom, which narrate this dramatic story in language inspired by Canon Nicholas.[24] They would also have sung the hymns and sequences referencing this legend transmitted in service books from the fourteenth century onwards.[25] The hymn *Hymnum cantemus gratiae*, sung at vespers and lauds on the feast of Lambert's Martyrdom in the cathedral and collegiate churches of Liège,[26] relies exclusively on the legendary account of the saint's death (as given in the fourth stanza):

Crimen Pipini prohibens
Curam solerter adhibens
Incestas damnat nuptias

Prohibiting Pippin's crime,
offering care diligently,
he condemns the incestuous nuptials,

---

[23] Nicholas of Liège, *Vita quarta sancti Lamberti*, AASS, September vol. 5. For more details on the development of this legend and the influence of Canon Nicholas, see chapter two of my book, *A Paradise of Priests* (forthcoming).

[24] These lections are prescribed in two copies of the cathedral breviary: Chicago, Newberry Library, Inc. 9344.5 [US-Cn Inc. 9344.5], fol. 118v (dated 1484); and Liège, Bibliothèque de l'Université, Res 1310 A [B-Lu Res 1310 A] (dated 1509-11). See also Joseph Daris, 'La liturgie dans l'ancien diocèse de Liège', in *Notices historiques sur les églises du diocèse de Liège* 15 (1894), 1-276 at 103-4.

[25] The lack of extant liturgical sources between the tenth and early fourteenth centuries complicates the dating of this repertory, which likely emerged between the late eleventh and mid-twelfth centuries or later.

[26] This hymn is assigned consistently to the feast of Lambert's Martyrdom in service books destined for institutions across the diocese dating from the fourteenth to sixteenth centuries, including the cathedral breviary dated c. 1320: Darmstadt, Universitäts- und Landesbibliothek, 394 [D-DS 394], vol. 2, fol. 231r (present foliation). The edition most faithful to the *liégeois* service books is that by Daris, 'La liturgie', 66. See also Guido Maria Dreves and others (eds.), *Analecta hymnica medii aevi* [hereafter AH], 55 vols. (Leipzig, 1886-1922), vol. 4, n. 324, <http://webserver.erwin-rauner.de.ezproxy1.lib.asu.edu/crophius/ah_ado_full.asp> (accessed 20 January 2014).

Verae saluti noxias.[27]   detriments for true salvation.

We find a direct textual echo of this scene in the eighth tercet of *Christi nutu* (see Appendix 1, lines 22-24). Likewise, the Sequence *Letabunda laus beato*, sung at the cathedral on the Octave of Lambert's Martyrdom and at the weekly votive mass,[28] depicts the martyrial consequences of the bishop's moral judgement (in the fourth versicle):

Detestans adulterium,	Detesting adultery,
Presul subit martyrium	the prelate suffered martyrdom
Orans in ecclesia;	as he prayed in the church.
Sic ad aram immolatur,	Thus he is sacrificed at the altar,
Sic cruore consecratur	thus his beloved Liège
Grata sibi Legia.[29]	is consecrated by his blood.[30]

That Lambert is murdered while praying before the altar emphasizes the sacrificial and Eucharistic aspects of his death introduced by Canon Nicholas.[31] We find similar imagery in the motet *Lamberte vir*, in which the bishop dies in the act of officiating (see Appendix 2, lines 22-28). Both the sequence and motet conflate Lambert's sacramental actions with his sacrificial death.

Yet what was the significance of this legend, and why did it continue to be embellished? In denouncing adultery, Lambert emulates one of the most popular, and highest ranking, martyrs of the medieval church—St. John the Baptist.[32] Having condemned as sinful Herod's adulterous and incestuous marriage to Herodias (Herod's niece and wife of his half-brother), John was imprisoned at the adulteress's insistence and later beheaded at her daughter Salome's behest, as recounted in the Gospel of Matthew (14:3-8). By modeling Lambert's disapproval of the adulterous couple on this well-known biblical scene, hagiographers intimate Lambert's candidacy for martyrdom prior to his murder—a prime example of the power of prolepsis in hagiographic narrative.[33] These embellishments transform the victim of a private power struggle into a genuine martyr, according to the biblical model, whose potential claim to this lofty title—suggested by his condemnation of adultery—is fulfilled through his Christ-like sacrifice.

We are now in a position to interpret the initially puzzling allusions to the king's sinful and unchaste conduct in lines 22-24 of the two motets. Like the hymns and

---

[27] Daris, 'La liturgie', 66 (with *prohihens* instead of *prohibens* given in *liégeois* service books).
[28] *Letabunda laus* enjoyed particular popularity at the cathedral, where it was also sung on the feasts of the Translation and Triumph of St. Lambert's relics, as documented in the cathedral missal printed in 1509: Liège, Bibliothèque de l'Université, Res 143 A [B-Lu Res 143 A]. See Daris, 'La liturgie', 181-82; and AH, vol. 40 n. 267.
[29] Daris, 'La liturgie', 181-82 (with *sihi* instead of *sibi* given in *liégeois* service books).
[30] Translated by Barbara Newman.
[31] The Eucharistic undertones of another sequence, *Christi laudem predicemus* for the feast of Lambert's Martyrdom, are even more pronounced. See Saucier, 'Sacrament and Sacrifice: Conflating Corpus Christi and Martyrdom in Medieval Liège', in *Speculum* 87 (2012), 682-723.
[32] Lambert was not the only bishop to benefit by this comparison. John the Baptist also figures in the *Vita Albini* by Venantius Fortunatus, as a model for Bishop Albinus of Angers who had punished a couple guilty of an incestuous marriage with excommunication. See Simon Coates, 'Venantius Fortunatus and the Image of Episcopal Authority in Late Antique and Early Merovingian Gaul', in *English Historical Review* 115 (2000), 1109-37 at 1127.
[33] Prolepsis (i.e., the prefiguring or foreshadowing of a future event) helped readers to understand time in hagiographic narrative not as historical, but rather as salvational. See Hahn, 'Picturing the Text', 3.

sequences sung on the feast of Lambert's Martyrdom, *Christi nutu* and *Lamberte vir* attribute the cause of Lambert's death solely to this legend. This hagiographic similarity is enhanced by the polyphonic setting. In both works, the singers disclose the king's adulterous affair in a four-voice texture that leads to the third, and last, duet. As we shall see by examining these four-voice passages (shown in Examples 1 and 2), moments of textual clarity highlight Lambert's opposition to the king's immorality.

In *Christi nutu* (see Example 1), the upper voices utter the word 'adultrina' syllabically on a repeated pitch (*a'*) in strict imitation followed by a return in the top voice to this same pitch for the first syllable of the word 'spernens', thereby audibly emphasizing Lambert's scorn for adultery. Following a more obscure reference to the king, Brassart reduces the texture to two voices synchronized by homorhythm on the word 'probra' (unchastity) and coordinated by a brief rest after 'dampnando' (condemning) before the singers summon Lambert as Christ's champion.

Example 1. *Christi nutu sublimato*, bb. 69-80

The comparable passage in *Lamberte vir* is far less subtle (see Example 2). Lambert openly spurns the king's sin as the upper voices jointly declaim the words 'spernens regis peccatum' in clear homorhythm. After brief syncopation on the word 'blasphemasti' and a melisma in the top voice on 'nupcias', the motet dwells on the martyrial consequences of Lambert's reproval of these sinful nuptials in a carefully coordinated duet (discussed later, in conjunction with Example 5) that facilitates aural comprehension of the lines recounting his death at the altar. Through imitation, homorhythm, and the manipulation of texture, both motets highlight the legendary cause of Lambert's death legitimizing his martyrial status.

Example 2. *Lamberte vir inclite*, bb. 105-17

St. Lambert's Childhood Miracles

St. Lambert's scorn for adultery, however, is not the only legend these motets share. A comparison of the second duet of *Christi nutu* (see Appendix 1, lines 7-12) to the corresponding passage in *Lamberte vir* (see Appendix 2, lines 10-17) reveals shared references to Lambert's unburned garment and to the fountain that satiates foreigners. While one might initially interpret the 'fire' Lambert carries simply as a metaphor for the fervor of the saint's faith burning within him and the 'fount' he causes to spring forth as an allusion to the baptismal font,[34] the motets do, in fact, allude to two specific late-medieval miracles that served to predict Lambert's sanctity from childhood. These miracles gained credibility through parallels to stories from the Old and New Testament.[35] As we shall presently observe, the biblical allusions lend additional authority to Lambert's hybrid status, as both a martyr and a bishop.

A closer look at the second duet in *Christi nutu* gives us greater insight into these miracles. Brassart at once sets these tercets in a sparser duet texture and deliberately coordinates the two voices to give extra clarity to each word (see Example 3). The discantus voices synchronize in strict homorhythm for the phrases most essential to these miracles (see Appendix 1, lines 7, 9, and 10), followed by a brief passage of rhythmic imitation (in line 11). Not only are the rhyming line-ends of the poetry punctuated by cadences and rests, but the consistency with which the two voices join on a unison or double at the octave highlights their unity.[36]

---

[34] See, for example, Weller's notes in *The St Emmeram Codex*, 34.

[35] Parallels to the Old and New Testament were crucial to the acceptance of a miracle, as noted by Hahn in *Portrayed on the Heart*, 14.

[36] In a brief analysis of this passage, Thomas Schmidt-Beste notes the textual clarity of line 7 (*A Landwáldo póst instrúctus*) resulting from the alternation of stressed and unstressed syllables. More generally, he associates Brassart's approach

Example 3. *Christi nutu sublimato*, bb. 26-50

The opening homorhythmic reference to Landoald is telling, for it was during Lambert's studies with this fictitious bishop that both miracles supposedly occurred.[37] These stories were first introduced into St. Lambert's life by the Benedictine monk Sigebert of Gembloux in his *Vita altera* commissioned by the cathedral dignitary Henry

to text setting with the tradition of Johannes Ciconia. See Schmidt-Beste, *Textdeklamation in der Motette*, 224-25.

[37] These miracles took place at Landoald's villa in Wintershoven, located between Tongeren and Maastricht. In 980, St. Landoald's relics were translated to the abbey of St. Bavo in Ghent, where Landoald was subsequently venerated with a proper office. See Barbara Haggh, 'Musique et rituel à l'abbaye Saint-Bavon: Structure et dévelopement du rituel, le chant, les livres du rite et les imprimés', in *La cathédrale Saint-Bavon de Gand: Du Moyen Age au Baroque*, ed. Bruno Bouckaert (Paris, 2000), 46-85 at 55-57.

of Montaigu around 1080.[38] Sigebert borrowed from the tenth-century *Vita Landoaldi* attributed to Heriger of Lobbes to embellish his portrayal of Lambert's childhood perfectionism with an account of two miracles: the glowing embers that Lambert carries voluntarily to Landoald in the folds of his own garment without burning himself; and the water satiating thirsty masons that Lambert and Landoald, invoking the name of Christ or the Holy Trinity, cause to gush forth from a clear spring, the location of which they had marked in a Cross with their staff. Canon Nicholas subsequently quoted and paraphrased Sigebert in his influential *Vita quarta* for St. Lambert,[39] and the miracles would continue to circulate in *gesta*, chronicles, and sequences from the thirteenth century onwards.[40] Brassart and his clerical companions would have also heard these stories in the lections read on the Sunday during the Octave of Lambert's Martyrdom.[41]

Both miracles are inspired by biblical events. The fire that Lambert carries in his unburned garment, specified in both motets with the word 'veste' from *vestis*, recalls the story of the three Hebrew children or young men cast into the fiery furnace by King Nebuchadnezzar but unharmed by its flames,[42] as told in the prophecy of Daniel (3:21, 94):

> And immediately these men were bound and were cast into the furnace of burning fire, with their coats and their caps and their shoes and their garments.

> And the nobles and the magistrates and the judges and the great men of the king being gathered together considered these men, that the fire had no power on their bodies and that not a hair of their head had been singed nor their garments altered.

This Old Testament story would have been especially familiar to clergymen, since the voices of the Three Children praising God resound in the *Benedicite*, the lesser canticle sung at lauds on Sundays and feastdays. Referencing this canticle, Amalarius of Metz (c. 775-c. 850) compared the Hebrew children to the saints in his *Liber de ordine antiphonarii*: 'The three children cast into the furnace…displayed patience in tribulation…In their perseverance, they anticipated the perseverance of the saints who, in the time of Antichrist, will not give in to his traps or threats but will persevere in the catholic faith.'[43] The steadfast perseverance of the Hebrew children could thus be understood as analogous to the patient suffering of the saints. As a test of the three men's faith in God through their willingness to sacrifice their lives rather than worship idols, this story was equally invoked in medieval rituals for the judicial trial by fire, in which the accused was burned

[38] Sigebert of Gembloux, *Vita altera sancti Lamberti*, in *Patrologia cursus completus, series Latina* [hereafter PL], ed. Jacques-Paul Migne, 221 vols. (Paris, 1844-65), vol. 160, 783C-784A, <http://pld.chadwyck.com.ezproxy1.lib.asu.edu/> (accessed 20 January 2014).

[39] This hagiographic borrowing is identified by Renaud Adam in 'La *Vita Landiberti Leodiensis* (c. 1144-45) du chanoine Nicolas de Liège: Etude sur l'écriture hagiographique à Liège au XIIᵉ siècle', in *Le Moyen Age* 111 (2005), 503-28 at 513 n. 63.

[40] See Giles of Orval, *Gesta pontificum Leodiensium*, ed. Johann Heller, MGH Scriptores (Hannover, 1880), vol. 25, 39; and Mathias de Lewis, *Chronicon Leodiense*, ed. Stanislas Bormans (Liège, 1865), 25. These miracles are also referenced in two sequences: *Martyris egregia* (AH, vol. 42 n. 267), and *Christo laudes dans applaude* (AH, vol. 9 n. 275).

[41] US-Cn Inc. 9344.5, fol. 114v; B-Lu Res 1310 A; and Daris, 'La liturgie', 100-1.

[42] Tino Licht, *Untersuchungen zum biographischen Werk Sigeberts von Gembloux* (Heidelberg, 2005), 158.

[43] Amalarius of Metz, *Liber de ordine antiphonarii*, ed. Jean Michel Hanssens, *Amalarii episcopi opera liturgica omnia*, 3 vols. (Rome, 1948-1950; repr. 1967), vol. 3, 22-23. Translated by Roger Evans, 'Amalarius of Metz and the Singing of the Carolingian Offices' (Ph.D. diss., City University of New York, 1977), 92.

by a hot iron or boiling water to determine their innocence.[44] It was also cited in the ritual application of fire to saintly relics, wrapped in linen, to verify their authenticity.[45] In each case, bodily resistance to the destructive force of fire frees the individual from the suspicion of evil and proves the truth of their actions or status. Since it was believed that the bodies of the damned or of sinners requiring justification would burn on Judgement Day, only the bodies of the elect would enter heaven intact.[46] In *Lamberte vir*, the miracle of fire—set musically in a brief duet that culminates with a homophonic allusion, replete with coronas, to the presence of Christ—can be seen to prefigure the patient suffering Lambert endures at the end of his life (see Appendix 2, lines 29-30). Thus, this miracle suggested that, even from childhood, Lambert was destined for sainthood—specifically martyrdom—through the sincerity of his faith and the purity of his body.[47]

The story of the spring, meanwhile, resembles the miracle in Exodus (17:6) and Numbers (20:1-11) in which Moses and Aaron satisfy the thirsting Israelites by striking a rock with the rod by which Moses had parted the Red Sea, causing water to spring forth so that the people could drink.[48] The Apostle Paul infused this miracle with sacramental symbolism in 1 Corinthians (10:4) by identifying the rock as Christ. Because Moses had passed unharmed through the destructive waters of the Red Sea and had satiated the Israelites with the salvific water of the rock, these miracles subsequently became associated with the purifying water of the baptismal font.[49] Yet the miracle of the rock also belongs to the medieval typology of the Cross, since the wound in the side of the crucified Christ was understood as a source for the fountain of salvation and the rivers of life.[50] Appropriately, *Lamberte vir* identifies Lambert's spring specifically as a 'living fount' (*fons vivus*), recalling the 'fountain of life' in the Books of Psalms (35:10) and Proverbs (13:14; 14:27; 16:22; 18:4), the 'well of living waters' that flow from Lebanon in the Song of Songs (4:15), and the fountain or river of the 'water of life' that emanates from the throne of God in Revelation (21:6 and 22:1). In an influential and widely circulating commentary on the Song of Songs (4:15), Honorius Augustodunensis (fl. c. 1098-c. 1133) associated this living fount both with Christ and with the Church:

> This spring is Christ, who is the spring of life, from whom there flow streams of 'living water' (John 4:10, 14)…He washes away the filthy deeds of sinners, he quenches the thirst of those who 'thirst for righteousness' (Matt. 5:6) with the fullness of the vision of himself, and he restores to souls the image of God they have lost…But the Church herself is also a spring; for she overflows with grace and wisdom, from which their flow streams full of teaching with which she waters the plants in her garden.[51]

[44] Robert Bartlett, *Trial by Fire and Water: The Medieval Judicial Ordeal* (Oxford-New York, 1986), 21-22.

[45] Thomas Head, 'Saints, Heretics, and Fire: Finding Meaning through Ordeal', in *Monks and Nuns, Saints and Outcasts: Religion in Medieval Society. Essays in Honor of Lester K. Little*, ed. Sharon Farmer and Barbara H. Rosenwein (Ithaca NY, 2000), 220-38 at 222-29.

[46] As explained by St. Augustine in *The City of God* and discussed by Head, 'Saints', 228-29.

[47] Burning is the third most common form of torture in martyrs' passions, as discussed by Hahn in *Portrayed on the Heart*, 70.

[48] Licht, *Untersuchungen*, 154. The miracle of the rock is also referenced in Psalm 77:15-16.

[49] Gertrud Schiller, *Iconography of Christian Art*, trans. Janet Seligman, 2 vols. (Greenwich, 1971-72), vol. 1, 130.

[50] Schiller, *Iconography*, vol. 2, 125.

[51] Honorius Augustodunensis, *Expositio in Cantica Canticorum*, PL 172, 423C-26D. Translated by Richard Norris, *The Song of Songs Interpreted by Early Christian and Medieval Commentators* (Grand Rapids, 2003), 184.

Honorius thus interprets the living water from two perspectives: as a symbol of baptism, and as a source of spiritual wisdom and teaching (found in Proverbs). This double meaning mirrors the ideal of the episcopal mission, characterized by the paired activities of preaching and baptism.[52] In the *vitae* and motets, the evangelical association of these aquatic references predicts the missionary work that Lambert would undertake as a bishop.

The childhood miracles in *Christi nutu* and *Lamberte vir* infuse St. Lambert's legend with extra prophetic and biblical resonance. On first hearing, these stories might be understood to merely embellish the beginning of Lambert's life by predicting his episcopal undertakings and saintly merits. Yet when we listen for the underlying biblical imagery and symbolism, the two motets gain a richer meaning: Lambert impersonates his illustrious precursors. Not only does Lambert act on the morals of John the Baptist, he embodies the purity and perseverance of the Hebrew children, the life-saving guidance of Moses, and the life-giving wounds of Christ. These biblical attributes directly benefit the singing supplicants, for as a more worthy saint, Lambert becomes a better advocate on their behalf.

Indeed, the symbolic connection between Lambert's childhood miracles and his martyrdom is underscored by the musical texture, specifically the periodic reduction to two voices. Both in *Christi nutu* and *Lamberte vir*, the second duet exposes the miracle of Lambert's unburned garment while the third highlights the legendary circumstances of Lambert's death, resulting from his condemnation of adultery. At this decisive moment in Lambert's life, the two motets adopt the same strategy, contrasting the full four-voice setting of Lambert's scorn for the king's illicit affair with a sparser two-voice reference to Lambert's martyrdom.[53] Through the manipulation of texture, both works emphasize the hagiographic link between the initial and final tests of Lambert's faith.

St. Lambert's Birth and Death

Despite the multitude of their thematic similarities, the two motets are not hagiographically identical. Unlike the four-voice sections of *Christi nutu*, which reference details pertaining to Lambert's family and episcopate found in the saint's earliest *vitae* and in Bishop Stephen's tenth-century office, *Lamberte vir* recounts exclusively newer legends introduced in the twelfth and thirteenth centuries. These tales enhance Lambert's saintly profile with Christ-like imagery, apparent most prominently in the depiction of Lambert's birth and death, and illuminate the complementary function of the two motets.

A comparison of the first four-voice passage of each motet reveals their most substantial hagiographic difference. Where *Christi nutu* lauds Lambert's noble heritage (see Appendix 1, lines 4-6),[54] *Lamberte vir* references a miracle from Lambert's infancy

---

[52] Hahn notes the consistency with which preaching and baptism appear in bishops' lives. These paired activities epitomize the episcopal mission. See Hahn, *Portrayed on the Heart*, 131, 141, 147-53.

[53] The third duet of *Christi nutu* does not describe Lambert's death explicitly, but alludes to his martyrdom by invoking Lambert as 'Christ's champion' immediately following his condemnation of 'unchaste conduct'.

[54] Nobility can be read as a hagiographic *topos* signaling Lambert's potential for sanctity. As it applies to St. Remigius, see Marie-Céline Isaïa, *Rémi de Reims: Mémoire d'un saint, histoire d'une église* (Paris, 2010), 57.

(see Appendix 2, lines 4-6). The brief allusion to his suckling from divine breasts recalls the story of Lambert's virgin nurse, Lina, who, heeding an angelic prediction, cured her own blindness by rubbing her eyes with the virginal milk by which she suckled Lambert. This tale was documented in the 1250s in the *Gesta pontificum Leodiensium* by the Cistercian monk Giles of Orval, who compared Lambert's nursing miracle to that of Bishop-Saint Remigius of Reims (c. 437-c. 533), venerated as the Apostle of the Franks for having baptized King Clovis.[55] In truth, Hincmar of Reims had introduced into his late ninth-century *Vita Remigii* the story of the miraculous cure of the blind monk Montanus. Having prophesied the birth of Remigius as told to him by a celestial voice, Montanus announced this news to the saint's mother, Celinia, and predicted that she would restore his sight by anointing his eyes with the milk by which she nursed Remigius. Subsequently, after his birth, the infant did indeed cure the monk's blindness with his mother's milk.[56]

The curative effect of the milk in the nursing miracles of Remigius and Lambert identifies the saintly infant as a source of faith and salvation. From biblical times throughout the later Middle Ages, milk and nursing were widely used as metaphors with which to emphasize the beneficial effects of instruction in the Christian faith. This association is explicit in 1 Peter 2:2-3: 'As newborn babes, desire the rational milk without guile, that thereby you may grow unto salvation, if so be you have tasted that the Lord is sweet.'[57] The Church itself might be compared to a mother suckling Christians with the milk of doctrine,[58] while the newly baptized, who had been reborn into the faith, were seen as infants thirsting for spiritual nourishment. Early Christian writers and late medieval commentators alike imagined Christ or the apostles as nursing mothers and visualized spiritual instruction as a form of milk given to individuals who had not yet reached full maturity.[59] Inspired by Paul's words to the infant-like Corinthians: 'I gave you milk to drink, not meat, for you were not able as yet' (1 Corinthians 3:2),[60] the second-century theologian St. Irenaeus of Lyon explained the sacramental consequences of this spiritual nursing in vivid terms: 'That we as sucklings having been nourished from the breast of His flesh and having by such a milkfeeding become accustomed to eat and drink the Word of God, may be able also to contain in ourselves the Bread of

---

[55] Giles of Orval, *Gesta*, 38-39. This story continued to circulate in local chronicles closer to Brassart's time. See Mathias de Lewis, *Chronicon*, 25. Comparing one saintly bishop to another is a common stategy in confessors' lives, as discussed by Hahn in *Portrayed on the Heart*, 131-32. Through this comparison, Lambert's hagiographers demonstrate his conformity to the episcopal type.

[56] Hincmar of Reims, *Vita Remigii*, MGH Scriptores rerum Merovingicarum (Hannover, 1896), vol. 3, 260-61. St. Remigius was venerated with a feast of nine lessons at the cathedral of Liège where relics of his teeth could be found in the treasury. While the office of St. Remigius sung in Reims references the nursing miracle in the responsory *Ablactatus igitur sanctus puer Remigius* (quoting from Hincmar), this chant is not found in the *liégeois* office of St. Remigius transmitted in the cathedral breviary of c. 1320, D-DS 394, fols. 138r-42r. None of the chants or lections in the *liégeois* office recount this miracle. For a detailed analysis of the office of St. Remigius sung in Reims, see Jean-François Goudesenne, *Les offices historiques ou Historiae composés pour les fêtes des saints dans la province ecclésiastique de Reims (775-1030)*, 2 vols. (Turnhout, 2002), vol. 2, 72-90.

[57] See Gail Paterson Corrington, 'The Milk of Salvation: Redemption by the Mother in Late Antiquity and Early Christianity', in *The Harvard Theological Review* 82 (1989), 393-420 at 407.

[58] Annewies Van de Bunt, 'Milk and Honey in the Theology of Clement of Alexandria', in *Fides sacramenti, sacramentum fidei: Studies in Honour of Pieter Smulders*, ed. Hans Jörg auf der Maur et al. (Assen, 1981), 27-39 at 33; and Corrington, 'Milk of Salvation', 412.

[59] Caroline Walker Bynum, *Jesus as Mother: Studies in the Spirituality of the High Middle Ages* (Berkeley, 1982), 125-26; and Bynum, *Holy Feast and Holy Fast: The Religious Significance of Food to Medieval Women* (Berkeley, 1987), 150.

[60] See also Hebrews 5:12-13.

Immortality, which is the Spirit of the Father.'[61] Imbibing the Word of God through the milk suckled from Christ's breast thus prepares believers for the Eucharistic bread and, ultimately, for the promise of everlasting life. These associations likely reflect the Early Christian practice of giving a mixture of milk and honey—the pure, unprocessed substances symbolizing new life, wisdom, paradise, and the afterlife that had sustained the Messiah of the Old Testament—to neophytes with their first Eucharist.[62] Similar maternal imagery, however, might also apply to the pastoral authority of prelates, idealized by later writers such as Hincmar of Reims and Bernard of Clairvaux as 'nourishers' of their flock.[63] Urging superiors to nurture their communities lovingly, rather than rule tyrannically, Bernard exhorted: 'Learn that you must be mothers to those in your care, not masters…Be gentle, avoid harshness, do not resort to blows, expose your breasts: let your bosoms expand with milk, not swell with passion.'[64] Thus, the milk suckled by Remigius and Lambert—both future bishops—might be understood to symbolize at once the saintly child's Christian nourishment and their episcopal care. With the milk of their own faith, both infants open the eyes of the blind to the Christian life and to the hope of redemption.[65]

Yet the explicit references to Lambert nursing from 'divine' breasts (in the motet) and to his nourishment from 'virginal' milk (in the chronicles), equate the saintly infant more specifically with the Christ child nursing from the Virgin Mary.[66] Not until the thirteenth century did images of *Maria lactans* become widespread in Western Europe.[67] In Liège, however, a sculpture of the seated Virgin with the baby Jesus grasping her uncovered breast was displayed as early as 1149-58 at the Benedictine abbey of Saint-Laurent.[68] Just prior to this time, Rupert of Deutz (a native of Liège who was raised and educated at the Abbey of Saint-Laurent, where he resided for close to forty years) praised the breasts 'filled with virginal milk from heaven' that had suckled God.[69] Rupert used this and other vivid nursing images in his Marian interpretation of the Song of Songs (completed by 1126) to portray Mary both as a vehicle of the Incarnation and as a

---

[61] Quoted in Van de Bunt, 'Milk and Honey', 31.

[62] Van de Bunt, 'Milk and Honey', 27-28; and Robin Jensen, *Living Water: Images, Symbols, and Settings of Early Christian Baptism* (Leiden-Boston, 2011), 148-49. The association of milk and honey with eternity can be traced back to the ancient Romans, who attributed the origins of the Milky Way to the milk Juno sprayed across the sky while she suckled Hercules. See Maria Warner, *Alone of All Her Sex: The Myth and the Cult of the Virgin Mary* (New York, 1976), 194-96.

[63] Bynum, *Jesus*, 115-18, 127, 146-66. Hincmar identifies the bishop as a *nutritor* in *Opusculum LV Capitulorum adversus Hincmarum Laudunensem*, PL 126, 488.

[64] Bernard of Clairvaux, *On the Song of Songs*, trans. Kilian Walsh, 4 vols. (Kalamazoo, 1971-80), vol. 2, 27.

[65] Healing the blind is a common miracle in bishops' lives, as noted by Hahn in *Portrayed on the Heart*, 153-54.

[66] St. Lambert and the Virgin shared a special connection in Liège as the joint titular patrons of the cathedral, represented architecturally by the church's double-choir form (with the western choir dedicated to Lambert and eastern choir to the Virgin). See Matthieu Piavaux, 'La cathédrale Notre-Dame-et-Saint-Lambert, cathédrale d'Empire', in *Notger et Liège: L'an mil au cœur de l'Europe*, ed. Jean-Pierre Delville, Jean-Louis Kupper, and Marylène Laffineur-Crépin (Liège, 2008), 51-64 at 54-55. The *liégeois* chronicler and cathedral canon John of Hocsem (1279-1348) documents the dedication of the high altar (in the eastern choir) to Mary and Lambert in 1250. See *La chronique de Jean de Hocsem*, ed. Godefroid Kurth (Brussels, 1927), 7-8. Not surprisingly, the Virgin with Child appears alongside St. Lambert in cathedral seals dating from the 1250s and later. See Joseph Philippe, *La cathédrale Saint-Lambert de Liège: Gloire de l'occident et de l'art mosan* (Liège, 1979), 132; and Philippe George, *Saint Lambert: Culte et iconographie: Exposition organisée dans le cadre des manifestations du Millenaire de la principauté de Liège* (Liège, 1980), 67-68.

[67] Schiller, *Iconography*, vol. 1, 74 and 122.

[68] Jacques Stiennon, 'La vièrge de dom Rupert', in *Saint-Laurent de Liège, église, abbaye et hôpital militaire: Mille ans d'histoire*, ed. Rita Lejeune (Liège, 1968), 81-92 at 83.

[69] Rupert of Deutz, *Commentaria in Canticum Canticorum*, Book 1, ed. Hrabanus Haacke, CCCM 26 (Turnhout, 1974), 17. For Rupert's life and works, see John Van Engen, *Rupert of Deutz* (Berkeley, 1983).

prophetess who would teach the apostles.[70] As Mary holds the Christ child between her breasts, she prophesies his death, saying: 'On the outside he was bound to these breasts and nursed by the same, and at the same time inside between these breasts in a heart foreknowing the future it was always clear what sort of death he was to die. But yet I knew that he would rise again.'[71] Mary's breasts, as imagined by Rupert, at once nourish her infant son and harbour her foresight of his resurrection. Moreover, the growing visual emphasis on Mary's breasts, as a symbol of the Virgin's nurturing love for all Christians, was not limited to scenes of Christ's birth and infancy. Mary might also offer her breast as she intercedes for mankind in images of the Last Judgement.[72] By the thirteenth and fourteenth centuries, breast milk had become equated with the Eucharistic blood, and images of Christ exposing his wounds might include the Virgin Mary bearing her breast in what was understood as a double intercession.[73] Thus, by suckling the 'divine breasts' of his virgin nurse, St. Lambert emulates Christ, not only in his infancy, but in the salvific effects of his future martyrdom.

In the motet *Lamberte vir*, Lambert's nursing tale is not an isolated miracle. This event is just one of three involving a drinking vessel. Lambert suckles divine breasts (see Appendix 2, line 6), pilgrims drink from the living fount that sustains them (lines 13-17), and the singing petitioners seek new life from cups of death (lines 32-35). By implication, each receptacle contains a salvific substance: the milk suckled by the infant, the water sustaining the foreigner, and the Eucharistic wine, representing the blood of Christ and his martyrs, that redeems the supplicant. In the medieval mind, these fluids were understood as interchangeable. Early Christian writers such as Zeno of Verona (died c. 371) had equated milk with the water of the baptismal font,[74] while Bernard of Clairvaux likened the endless supply of a mother's breast milk to the ever flowing fountain of life: 'For when these [breasts] have been drained dry they are replenished again from the maternal fount within, and offered to all who will drink…Out of her heart shall flow rivers of water, there will be a spring inside her, welling up to eternal life.'[75] Thus, the nursing bride of the Song of Songs is perceived to draw her milk from an interior source of life-giving water. Both water and milk were similarly equated with wine and blood. Just as Christ had turned water into wine at the wedding feast at Cana (John 2:1-11), the martyr's blood might transform into milk, as exemplified most famously by St. Catherine of Alexandria, whose severed head reportedly spurted milk instead of blood, thereby emphasizing the nourishing consequence of her sacrifice for the Christian community.[76] The receptacles for these vital fluids are thus related by the interchangeability of their contents—a similarity that is reinforced musically in *Lamberte vir*. Each section of the motet features one salvific vessel—the breasts in the first section (in *tempus perfectum*

---

[70] Van Engen, *Rupert*, 291-98; and Rachel Fulton, 'Mimetic Devotion, Marian Exegesis, and the Historical Sense of the Song of Songs', in *Viator* 27 (1996), 85-116 at 93-94 and 103.

[71] Translated in Fulton, 'Mimetic Devotion', 109.

[72] Marilyn Yalom, *A History of the Breast* (New York, 1997), 36; and Miri Rubin, *Mother of God: A History of the Virgin Mary* (New Haven, 2009), 211.

[73] Bynum, *Holy Feast*, 270-72. The association of milk with blood can be traced back to Antiquity, especially to Aristotle's belief that menstrual blood nourishing the fetus transformed into milk after childbirth. See Bynum, *Jesus*, 132-33.

[74] Jensen, *Living Water*, 251.

[75] Bernard of Clairvaux, *Song of Songs*, vol. 1, 60.

[76] Joyce Salisbury, *The Blood of Martyrs: Unintended Consequences of Ancient Violence* (New York, 2004), 124-25. See Jacobus de Voragine, *The Golden Legend: Readings on the Saints*, trans. William Granger Ryan, 2 vols. (Princeton, 1993), vol. 2, 339.

diminutum), the fount in the second highlighted by a mensuration change (to *tempus perfectum*), and the cups in the third (with a return to *tempus perfectum diminutum*)—evoked in each case in a full, four-voice texture. These sections are unified melodically by a recurring six-note motive in the first discantus voice,[77] consisting of the sequential treatment of a descending second followed by a descending third in a melisma after the word 'ubera' in line 6, on the words 'non moritur' following the reference to the living fount in line 13, and in a melisma on the word 'piacula' in line 34 explaining the beneficial effects of the cups of death (see Example 4).

Example 4. *Lamberte vir inclite*
a. bb. 40-43

b. bb. 74-77

c. bb. 164-69

---

[77] This motive is identified by Wright in 'A New Attribution to Brassart?', 30-31 (Figure B). As documented by Wright, it is found in roughly half of Brassart's works and appears a total of eight times in *Lamberte vir*.

The recurrence of symbol (the vessel), texture (four voices), and motive subtly underscores the ubiquity of Lambert's salvific powers.

Of the two motets, *Lamberte vir* gives greater verbal and musical attention to the event and consequences of Lambert's martyrdom. Where *Christi nutu* merely implies that the saint's moral rectitude—demonstrated by his condemnation of adultery—will spare the supplicants from danger and cleanse them from sin, *Lamberte vir* identifies the moment of Lambert's death, specifically in the act of officiating. This previously mentioned hagiographic detail, invented by Canon Nicholas of Liège in the mid twelfth century, receives special musical emphasis through a prolonged duet in which the upper two voices synchronize in exact homorhythm for the words 'celebrans occideris' (see Example 5). After a pronounced pause of a full breve rest at the end of this duet, the singers meditate on the beneficial effects of Lambert's patient suffering, invoking the rejuvenating effects of the cups of death.

Example 5. *Lamberte vir inclite*, bb. 111-39

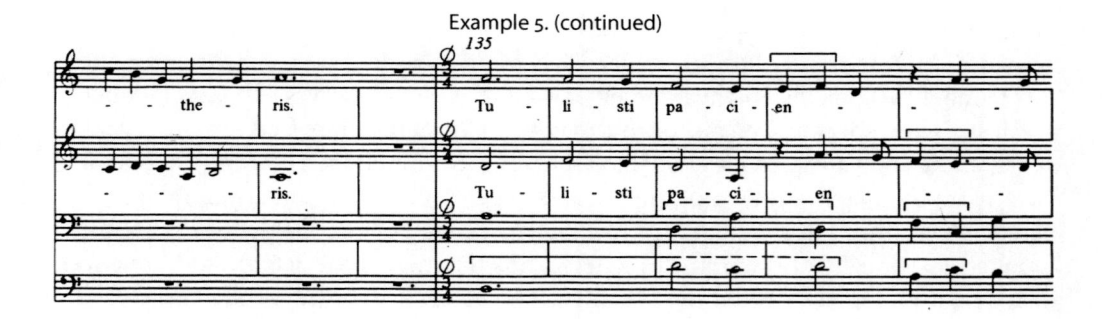

Example 5. (continued)

In its varied biblical contexts, the image of the cup or drink of death (*calix* or *poculum mortis*) has both a positive and negative association.[78] The bitter cup is filled with God's wrath, symbolizing eternal damnation (see especially Isaiah 51:17-23 and Revelation 14:10), and even Christ identifies the chalice as a sign of the terrible suffering he is bound to endure (Matthew 26:39). Conversely, the redeeming cup filled with the Eucharistic wine (1 Corinthians 10:16) represents Christ's life-giving death and eternal salvation. Christ's question to the sons of Zebedee, James and John, 'Can you drink of the chalice that I shall drink?' (Matthew 20:22) infuses the symbolism of the redeeming cup of his Passion with yet another meaning—the cup of martyrdom, from which Christ's followers willingly drink. Commentators found support for this association by linking Christ's chalice in Matthew 20:22 to the chalice of salvation in Psalm 115:13-15 representing the death of God's saints.[79] At the cathedral of Liège, as elsewhere, the words 'mortis pocula' harmonized in the final four-voice section of the motet would have been chanted monophonically in the widely-known Marian hymn *Fit porta Christi pervia* on Christmas Eve and Mary's annual feasts, as well as at the weekly commemorative office of the Virgin.[80] The third stanza of this hymn links Christ's physical death, represented by the cups of his passion, to salvation:

Honor matris et gaudium	[His] mother's honour and joy,
Immensa spes credentium	infinite hope of all the faithful;
Per atra mortis pocula	with black cups of death
Resolvit nostra crimina.[81]	he dissolves our sin.

Hymn and motet alike invoke the salvific benefits of the 'cups of death' with which Christ literally 'dissolves' the sins of believers (in the hymn) and Lambert medicates his sinful supplicants (in the motet). Thus, by spilling his blood at the altar and patiently enduring a violent death, the Christ-like Lambert drinks the cup of martyrdom—thereby guaranteeing his own salvation and that of his devotees.

The hagiographic differences between *Christi nutu* and *Lamberte vir* are symptomatic of the contrasting rhetoric and goal of each motet. In sequence-like tercets paired by rhyme and syllable count (a8-a8-b7 + c8-c8-b7), *Christi nutu* summons the

---

[78] Hugh Magennis, 'The Cup as Symbol and Metaphor in Old English Literature', in *Speculum* 60 (1985), 517-36.

[79] Magennis, 'Cup', 520-22. See commentaries on Matthew and the Psalms by St. Jerome, Cassiodorus, and St. Augustine. Psalm 115 is quoted frequently in martyrs' passions, as noted by Hahn in *Portrayed on the Heart*, 75-76.

[80] D-DS 394; and B-Lu Res 1310 A. See Daris, 'La liturgie', 35.

[81] Daris, 'La liturgie', 35.

group of singing faithful to praise the life of Lambert, described in the third person (see Appendix 1). As a result of the exemplary deeds and miracles that recur throughout his life, Lambert becomes a worthy intercessor. *Christi nutu* thus serves to justify Lambert's merit as a saint, specifically a bishop-martyr. By contrast, the more freely rhymed seven-syllable lines of *Lamberte vir* read like a prayer (see Appendix 2). From the opening vocative acclamation, the singing supplicants appeal to Lambert directly, imploring his benevolence. Through a series of tributes in the second person, the petitioners remind Lambert specifically of the miracles and legends that herald the salvific consequences of his death—the very event by which they hope to be reborn. While these works conclude with the same plea for salvation, the two motets provide alternative, and complementary, ways of achieving this goal.

Festal and Votive Performance Possibilities

The specificity of the hagiographic narratives shared by *Christi nutu* and *Lamberte vir* invites us to speculate on suitable contexts for the performance of this newly composed polyphony. Where, when, and by whom could the two motets have been sung? For a local saint, Lambert was venerated widely. From as early as the eighth century, the cult had already surpassed the diocesan border, and would subsequently spread throughout the area of present-day Belgium, Holland, and Luxembourg, into the regions of the Middle Rhine, Bavaria, Saxony, Austria, and France (as far as Brittany and the Loire valley).[82] Considering both the diffusion of Lambert's cult in the Germanic lands and the transmission of the two motets alongside Brassart's motet for Frederick III, a performance at the imperial court during the years of Brassart's service as *rector cappelle* and *rector principalis* (1434-43) seems possible, perhaps on the feast of Lambert's Martyrdom or as part of a votive service.[83] In this context, however, the motets would probably have been heard from a more conventionalized perspective, as mere tributes to Lambert's sanctity. Within the city of Liège, however, the hagiographic subtleties of their texts would surely have been recognized.

The cathedral of Liège, built over the very soil sanctified by the titular patron's martyrial blood, marked the epicentre of St. Lambert's cult.[84] Consequently, Lambert held a distinctive rank in the *liégeois* rite. Of the thirteen local bishops featured in the annual cycle of saints' feasts, only Lambert and his predecessor, Theodard, were venerated as martyrs. Through his martyrial status, Lambert thus outshone the most distinguished early bishops of the diocese—Maternus (the diocesan 'founder' and first bishop of

[82] George, *Saint Lambert*, 26-27.
[83] During Brassart's service at the court of Frederick III, the chapel was resident in Graz, capital of the province of Styria. St. Lambert's cult was ubdoubtedly strong in this region, as attested by the location of the Benedictine Abbey of Sankt-Lambrecht (founded c. 1076) in the diocese. Indeed, a fourteenth-century missal from this monastery (Graz, Universitätsbibliothek, Ms. 395) ranks the feast of St. Lambert's Martyrdom (17 September) among the highest of the liturgical year and assigns to it the proper sequence *Alme festa lucis* (AH vol. 10 n. 301). This missal also includes the feast of St. Lambert's Translation (celebrated locally on 22 June).
[84] A legend prevalent throughout the Middle Ages—largely corroborated by archaeological findings—places the actual site of Lambert's martyrdom in close proximity to the saint's crypt beneath the western choir of the cathedral. The most recent archaeological excavations of this site are reported in Marcell Otte (ed.), *Les fouilles de la place Saint-Lambert à Liège*, 4 vols. (Liège, 1984-92); and Denis Henrard, Pierre Van der Sloot, and Jean-Marc Léotard, 'La *villa* de la place Saint-Lambert à Liège (Belgique): Nouvel état des connaissances', in *Revue du Nord* 90 (2008), 159-74.

Tongeren) and Servatius (first bishop of Maastricht)—commemorated as mere confessors. Not surprisingly, Lambert was venerated at the cathedral with the most pomp and splendour of any saint in the *sanctorale*.[85] Not only did the feast of Lambert's Martyrdom (17 September) receive the highest rank of *totum duplex*, but the Octave of this feast was given duplex rank, and memorials—called the *hore de sancto Lamberto*— were celebrated therein. St. Lambert's relics were also venerated at the cathedral twice annually on the feast of his Translation (28 April) and military Triumph (13 October), both celebrated at *totum duplex*. These solemnities commemorated the enduring presence of the saint's corporal remains sheltered in the crypt of the western choir marking the location of Lambert's martyrdom, and, from the early fourteenth century onwards, visible atop the jubé at the entrance to the eastern choir.[86]

By the first decades of the fifteenth century, at least one of these annual ceremonies could have featured a polyphonic performance. The feast of Lambert's Martyrdom was enlivened by the joint participation of the clergy of the cathedral and the city's seven collegiate churches, accompanied by the full choir of each institution at mass and the choirboys from the churches of Saint-Martin, Saint-Paul, Sainte-Croix, Saint-Jean, and Saint-Barthélemy at first and second vespers.[87] Every one of these institutions supported a choral establishment, averaging four to eight choirboys overseen by a succentor and one or more assistants.[88] The cathedral boasted the most impressive musical forces, with two chapters of minor canons, the succentor and his two assistants, and eight or nine choirboys documented annually between 1428 and the mid 1440s. While no extant source prescribes polyphony for St. Lambert's feasts, singers at the cathedral and collegiate churches performed counterpoint, polyphonic masses, motets, and *alternatim* settings of the *Salve regina* antiphon on other occasions, as attested by foundations and payments from 1388 (at Saint-Jean), 1448/9 and 1475 (at Saint-Denis), 1457 (at the cathedral), 1476/7 (at Saint-Barthélemy), and 1483 (at Saint-Paul).[89] In keeping with the performing forces documented in a foundation from 1475 at the collegiate church of Saint-Denis, the motets would likely have been sung by four choirboys (two each for the discantus parts) and two adult singers including the succentor.[90] The presence of extra singers on the feast of Lambert's Martyrdom would have allowed for the selection of the best voices to ensure a truly harmonious performance of polyphony lauding the saint germane to the city's founding and to the identity of its clerical community.

Lambert's protective oversight was publicly beseeched in Liège at precisely this time. As documented by the fifteenth-century chronicler John of Stavelot, the cathedral chapter hosted a special mass on 10 July 1430 in the presence of 'all the clergy and the

---

[85] D-DS 394; US-Cn Inc. 9344.5; B-Lu Res 1310 A; and B-Lu Res 143 A.

[86] The location of St. Lambert's reliquary is documented in the crypt beneath the western choir until 1319, when it was moved to a more visually prominent location on the jubé. See Schoolmeesters, 'La fierte de Saint-Lambert en 1365', in *Leodium* 7 (1908), 3-7 at 4; and Piavaux, 'La cathédrale', 55-56.

[87] AEL Sainte-Croix 5 fol. 214r; Stanislas Bormans and Emile Schoolmeesters (ed.), *Le liber officiorum ecclesie Leodiensis* (Brussels, 1896), 63-65; and Saucier, 'Sacred Music and Musicians at the Cathedral and Collegiate Churches of Liège, 1330-1500' (Ph.D. diss., University of Chicago, 2005), 227-29, 232-33, 277.

[88] For a comparative study of the size and structure of the choral establishment at the cathedral and seven collegiate churches of Liège, see Saucier, 'Sacred Music and Musicians', 278-372.

[89] Saucier, 'Sacred Music and Musicians', 195-96, 308-9, 325, 328-29, 346, 350.

[90] The foundation by cantor Antonius Kerss de Blisia specifies similar forces (four of the best choirboys and three competent adult singers) for the performance of a motet: AEL Saint-Denis 27, fols. 30v-31r. These forces, as well as the ranges of the discantus parts (c'-e'' in *Christi nutu* and a-c'' in *Lamberte vir*), are consistent with Nosow's findings in *Ritual Meanings*, 120-21 and 192.

people' specifically to invoke the protection of 'God and St. Lambert.'[91] Did this ceremony inspire the composition of the two motets? While such a question must remain speculative, we can assert with certainty that on this occasion the participating clergy and musicians (including Brassart) would have witnessed first-hand the ongoing importance of Lambert's saintly life and oversight for the welfare of their church and city.[92]

In addition to these annual and extraordinary ceremonies, the cathedral chapter sponsored smaller-scale votive observances at the altars endowed by individual canons. By the 1430s, the cathedral housed at least seven altars dedicated to Lambert in side chapels surrounding the nave.[93] On the south side, Lambert was venerated with other saints in three chapels: at the altar founded by canon John of Hollogne (d. 1318) in the chapel of St. Eligius; at the altars founded by dean John of Cambiis (d. 1303) and canon Libert of Langdries (in 1340) in the third chapel; and finally at the altar founded by canon John Bachelaer (d. 1433) in the fourth. The corresponding third and fourth chapels on the north side featured two more foundations for St. Lambert, at altars founded by canon Rigald of Fexhe (d. 1413) and canon Gerard of Oxhem dictus Chabot (in 1348). Lastly, the imperial altar located on the right side of the jubé was also dedicated to Lambert.

Devotional observances held at these altars and in the choir would have been equally suitable occasions for a polyphonic performance. Although lacking provisions for polyphony, a motet might have been sung at the votive mass founded by canon Gerard of Chabot, celebrated every Tuesday in the aforementioned fourth chapel on the north side of the nave where he wished to be buried.[94] A motet might possibly have also concluded the votive office and mass, called the *Commemoratio beati lamberti* in late fifteenth-century service books, sung every Thursday in the choir.[95] That the cathedral cantor Henry of Palude would later found, in his will dated 1515, a polyphonic mass for St. Lambert to be sung every Tuesday in the cathedral's 'old' (or western) choir built over the site of Lambert's martyrdom testifies to the local votive context for polyphonic performances honouring the cathedral's titular patron.[96]

The complementary function of these annual and weekly observances matches the previously noted differences between the two motets. The 'melodies of harmonious accord' with which the singers of *Christi nutu* recount in sequence-like form the saint's exemplary life would have been especially appropriate for the annual celebration of the feast of Lambert's Martyrdom or within its Octave. In this scenario, the motet would most likely have been sung in one of three places: during the procession preceding mass; at the conclusion of mass in place of the *Deo gratias* or immediately thereafter; or at the

---

[91] John of Stavelot, *Chronique*, ed. Adolphe Borgnet (Brussels, 1861), 249. John of Stavelot (c. 1388/90-1449) resided at the Abbey of Saint-Laurent in Liège and is considered a reliable witness to the events he reported in his historical writings.

[92] In 1430, Brassart received payments for anniversaries (AEL Cathédrale CA 84) and for a 'gratia facta' at the cathedral (AEL Cathédrale CG 29), in addition to another 'gratia facta' on the feast of St. Denis (9 October) at the collegiate church of Saint-Denis (AEL Saint-Denis 199). For an explanation of the form of Brassart's name (Johannes de le Wegge) given in this previously unstudied document, see Saucier, 'Sacred Music and Musicians', 321.

[93] AEL Cathédrale S 234-236; and Emile Schoolmeesters, 'Liste des autels de la cathédrale de Saint-Lambert', in *Leodium* 8 (1909), 87-93.

[94] AEL Cathédrale C 688, and LC 2, 466; and Stanislas Bormans and Emile Schoolmeesters (ed.), *Cartulaire de l'Eglise Saint-Lambert*, 4 vols. (Brussels, 1893), vol. 4, 86.

[95] US-Cn Inc. 9344.5, fol. 48v; B-Lu Res 1310 A, fol. 78v; and B-Lu Res 143 A, fol. 22r.

[96] AEL Cathédrale S 266, fol. 61v.

end of first or second vespers in place of the *Benedicamus domino*.[97] In keeping with the widespread and local practice of singing motets before an image, object, or space associated with the saintly subject, we can imagine the singers leaving the choir to sing *Christi nutu* in the vicinity of the jubé surmounted by Lambert's reliquary, beneath the great chandelier (called the *corona sancti Lamberti*) in the middle of the nave, or in the western choir marking the site of Lambert's martyrdom.[98] Conversely, the prayer-like appeals for benevolence and salvation voiced directly to St. Lambert in *Lamberte vir* may have been better suited to weekly devotions, such as the mass founded by Gerard of Chabot in his chapel or even the votive office and mass sung in the choir. In this more meditative context, the motet would likely have been paired with a collect beseeching St. Lambert's intercession and might have constituted a musical response to this short prayer in prose.[99] When we consider that both *Christi nutu* and *Lamberte vir* conclude by invoking Lambert's intercessory powers, there can be little doubt that the singers' prayers would have had the highest chance of a favourable heavenly reception when voiced in Liège. As commonly believed, only at the site purified by the martyr's blood and blessed by the enduring presence of their body were supplicants guaranteed a spiritual reward.[100]

Hagiographic Polyphony

For the clergy and musicians of late-medieval Liège, St. Lambert was unavoidable. As attested by the proliferation of new miracles, hymns and sequences, artwork, and altar dedications long after the completion of the saint's last *vita* (in the mid twelfth century), the martyr whose blood had originally consecrated the site of the city's cathedral elicited the ongoing attention of chroniclers, singers, artists, and donors seeking to invoke the saint's continued intercessory presence with the most contemporary media at their disposal. Given the ubiquity of Lambert's saintly profile both in the cathedral rite and its votive spaces, we can hardly be surprised that local composers likewise enhanced the cult of their martyred patron with newly composed polyphony.

Thus, *Christi nutu* and *Lamberte vir* are saturated with the imagery of St. Lambert's *liégeois* legend. When read from this localized perspective, the two motets function as a pair by projecting similar, but not identical, profiles of their shared saintly subject. Both works reference the biblically inspired stories of Lambert's childhood miracles and the legendary cause of his death, yet they differ by contrasting earlier accounts of Lambert's episcopate (in *Christi nutu*) with newer tales of Lambert's infancy and the salvific effects of his Christ-like sacrifice (in *Lamberte vir*). With the diffusion of Lambert's cult and the transmission of these motets beyond the diocese, the possibility

---

[97] Nosow documents these customs in France and the Low Countries. See *Ritual Meanings*, 116-17, 122-23, 128, 174-75, 233. In a foundation of 1475, the cantor of the collegiate church of Saint-Denis in Liège specified the performance of a motet or the *Benedicamus domino* at the end of Compline. AEL Saint-Denis 27, fols. 30v-31r; and Saucier, 'Sacred Music and Musicians', 329.

[98] Special rituals for St. Lambert are documented at all of these locations, as discussed in my book, *A Paradise of Priests* (forthcoming).

[99] Nosow, *Ritual Meanings*, 144, 147, 151.

[100] This widespread belief is especially prominent in the *Peristephanon* by the influential poet and martyrologist Aurelius Clemens Prudentius (348-after 405) and persisted for centuries thereafter.

remains that this music could have been performed elsewhere. Yet unquestionably, these polyphonic appeals would have had the greatest spiritual and cultural resonance in the cathedral marking the site of Lambert's passion.

Hagiographic motets are more than a polyphonic amplification of the saint's *vita*. By setting familiar tales to new music, composers 'updated' the saint's legend in the latest style much the way artists reclothed that saint in contemporary garb as they decorated spaces conducive to a polyphonic performance. If the initial goal of hagiographic narrative was to invite believers to renew their faith through the saint's example, hagiographic motets and artwork urged believers to recognize both the relevance of that example for the present and the enduring benefits of the saint's intercessory powers. On the surface, these anachronous narratives resist comprehension. It is in the study of literary and pictorial hagiography that we find the tools with which to excavate the multiple layers generated by successive multi-media retellings of a saint's life.[101] Only with a discerning eye and a mind attuned to the conventions of hagiographic narrative can we probe the inner workings of the hagiographic motet, to grasp the underlying meaning of this music and better understand how it was heard.

---

[101] Hahn equates the succession of textual and pictorial updates to a saint's *vita* with archaeological layering, as discussed in *Portrayed on the Heart*, 5.

Appendix 1. Text and translation of *Christi nutu sublimato*[a]

1	Christi nutu sublimato	Let us offer melodies of harmonious accord
2	Lamberto demus beato	to blessed Lambert,
3	Simphonie modulos;	exalted by the will of Christ.
4	Celsi qui fuit generis	He who, gathering the first flowers [i.e. bishops],
5	Traiectensibus ab heris	was of high birth,
6	Primos carpens flosculos.	from Maastricht sovereigns.

7	A Landwaldo post instructus,	Instructed later by Landoald,
8	Sancto flamine conductus	led by the Holy Spirit,
9	Ignem lini fert veste;	[Lambert] carries a fire in his linen garment.

10	Per hunc fons scaturizavit,	Because of him, the spring gushed;
11	Extros et non suos pavit,	it nurtured foreigners and not his own [people]
12	Sed hic fluit hijs meste.	but flows sadly for them [i.e. so as to make them sad].

13	Cathedralem post honorem	Later in life, he rose to the honour of the episcopate
14	Vite scandit ob decorem,	on account of propriety;
15	Ast pro fide pugnavit,	moreover, he fought for the faith,
16	Quo privatur abs vicio;	whereby it is deprived of vice.
17	Admiratur religio	Admirable was his religious observance
18	Pre cruce dum se stravit.	when he strew himself before the cross.
19	Ex hinc ipse restitutus	Restored from here,
20	Sede mansit sua tutus	he remained secure on his see,
21	Pro reprobis precando;	by praying for the damned,

22	Adultrina multum spernens	spurning greatly adulterous [acts],
23	Ac salutem regis cernens	and seeing to the welfare of the king
24	Eius probra dampnando.	by condemning his unchaste conduct.

25	Precemur Christi athletam	Let us beseech the champion of Christ
26	Ut non ducat nos ad metam	that the enemies' impulse
27	Iniquorum incursus;	not lead us to the [final] end.
28	Sed cum sumus in peccatis	But when/since we are in the midst of sin,[b]
29	Collocando cum beatis	may the Lord wash [us] anew
30	Dominus lavet rursus.	by placing [us] together with the blessed.

[a]   The Latin text follows Brassart, *Opera Omnia*, ed. Mixter, vol. 2, 15-18, with changes to punctuation and the spelling of 'Christi'. For an alternate translation by Philip Weller, see *The St Emmeram Codex*, Stimmwerck (CD, Aeolus, AE-10023, 2008), 24. My thanks to Peter Wright for bringing this recording to my attention.
[b]   While the words cum sumus ('when we are') appear clearly in I-TRmp 87-1, fol. 76v, a slight variant cum simus ('since we are') is found in D-Mbs 14274, fol. 117v. My thanks to Leofranc Holford-Strevens for his insight into these grammatical differences.

Appendix 2. Text and translation of *Lamberte vir inclite*[a]

1	Lamberte vir inclite,	O Lambert, illustrious man,
2	Bonitati solite	make us equal to
3	Tue nos equipera.	your habitual goodness.
4	In etate tenera	You warded off afflictions
5	Propulisti scelera	at a tender age,
6	Diva sugens ubera;	sucking divine breasts.
7	Fide vixisti vera,	You lived by true faith,
8	Gesti ministerio	by the ministry of [your] deeds
9	Ut patris imperio;	as by the command of the Father.
10	Veste nec comburitur,	He is not burned by the garment,
11	Votis tuis flectitur,	[the Father] is swayed by your prayers,
12	Christus quibus oritur.	by which Christ appears.
13	Fons vivus non moritur,	The living fount does not die:
14	Peregrinis colitur,	it is cherished by pilgrims,
15	Incolis est abditus	it is hidden to the inhabitants,
16	Illis raro bibitus	by them it is rarely drunk from,
17	Exterus hoc alitur.	[yet] the foreigner is sustained by it.
18	Fixus in certamine	You have been made firm in strife,
19	Fuisti ne famine	not by hearsay.
20	Volgi in cantamine,	In the incantation of the people,
21	Rex manetur nomine.	the king is preserved in name.
22	Spernens regis peccatum	Spurning the sin of the king,
23	Captaret ne reatum	lest he seek fault,
24	Blasphemasti nupcias;	you reproved the nuptials;
25	Hinc presul invideris	Hence, prelate, you are begrudged,
26	Et per servos sceleris	and by servants of sin
27	Celebrans occideris,	you are murdered while officiating,
28	Spiritum dans etheris.	giving up [your] spirit to the heavens.
29	Tulisti pacienter	You have born patiently
30	Bilatum violenter	the wrath violently,
31	Volgus ut delicias.	so that the populace [might have] comforts.
32	Sint hec mortis pocula	May these cups of death
33	Nostre vite fercula	be the means for our life,
34	Peccatis piacula,	the atonements for sins,
35	Medicando singula.	by healing one at a time.

---

[a]   The Latin text follows Brassart, *Opera Omnia*, ed. Mixter, vol. 2, 39-43, with changes to punctuation and the spelling of 'Christus'.

Abstract

Two fifteenth-century motets, *Christi nutu sublimato* ascribed to Johannes Brassart and the anonymous *Lamberte vir inclite*, are assumed to originate from the city of Liège on account of their common addressee, the diocesan patron St. Lambert. This resemblance is matched by notable similarities in manuscript transmission and musical style. Copied adjacently in two sources, I-AO 15 and I-TRmp 87-1, these works share distinct melodic motives and similar patterns of textural variety. Yet what do the texts of the two motets reveal about their shared saintly subject?

A comparative reading of *Christi nutu sublimato* and *Lamberte vir inclite* uncovers previously unidentified hagiographic parallels originating from late-medieval accretions to St. Lambert's life, strengthening the possibility that this music was written and sung in fifteenth-century Liège. We find the tools with which to interpret enigmatic references to legends and miracles related to Lambert's youth, episcopate, and death in studies of literary and pictorial hagiography. By analyzing the symbolism and complementary function of these equal discantus motets, we recognize how freely composed votive polyphony draws from and enhances hagiographic narrative.

Time Travel and its Discontents: Historical Performance, Historical Reconstruction, and Culture Tourism[*]

■

JOSHUA RIFKIN

I

On a visit to Antwerp in 2009, a year before I wrote this paper, I took part in an event of a sort that we have come to take for granted but should perhaps subject to a bit of scrutiny. An invitation from Bart Demuyt and the Festival Laus Polyphoniae gave me the opportunity to join forces with the singers of Cappella Pratensis in a concert of music from the court of Pope Leo X. The programme consisted of eight motets by composers including Josquin Desprez, Jean Mouton, and Adrian Willaert. The performance took place in AMUZ, a decommissioned Baroque church beautifully restored as a site for music (see Figure 1). What with the wonderful acoustics, not to mention the beautiful Rubens altar paintings—copies, admittedly, but old ones nevertheless—one could hardly imagine a more felicitous match between music and surroundings.

Beautifully as the elements all seemed to coalesce, however, it takes only a moment's reflection to see that some very disparate things had got jumbled together here. These begin with the design of the programme itself. Although we know very little about the actual circumstances under which people sang, and heard, motets in the Renaissance, and although most of our pieces came from a single manuscript, I think it safe to say that no-one in the early sixteenth century would ever have encountered all eight of them on the same occasion, especially in a manner of presentation like ours: one after the other, straight through from the first to the eighth, with little more than a moment's pause between items—much as one would experience them on a CD. Yet if the image of the CD allows us better to appreciate one chronologically jarring note in the cohesive and comforting picture of 'old music' that the concert appeared to offer, other rifts in the canvas can more easily escape notice.

Consider, for example, the performance space. We somehow find old churches a more satisfactory environment for early music than modern concert halls, especially those since the Second World War. But why, apart from the indeed often better acoustics, do we think so? Yes, the repertory sung by Cappella Pratensis fell mostly on the sacred side of the sacred-secular divide; but the same festival saw performances of Italian

---

[*] I wrote this paper on invitation from the organizers of the festival and conference *Sounds of the City 18* (Antwerp 11-14 March 2010) as the keynote address for a session of performance practice; David Burn and Stratton Bull kindly arranged for its publication here after the organizers decided not to include anything from that session in the conference proceedings. In revising the text—minimally—for this forum, I have decided to leave it without footnotes or any other form of reference; readers may thus consider everything in it a statement of personal conviction rather than historical fact.

10.1484/J.JAF.1.103839

Figure 1. Sint-Augustinuskerk, Antwerp (AMUZ - Flanders Festival Antwerp)

madrigals in the same space, and no one, so far as I know, felt any greater sense of cognitive dissonance than they would have with motets or masses. As already intimated, moreover, even the most dedicated lover of music in Josquin's time, or Bach's for that matter, never, or hardly ever, heard sacred music performed 'in concert' at all, whatever the location—barring such occasional exceptions as the evening *Salve* in the Low Countries or the *Abendmusik* in Lübeck, the music belonged to the liturgy or, in some instances, to devotions at the banquet table. Our performance basically represented a tradition of more recent pedigree the nineteenth-century church concert. These concerts owed their existence to the efforts at reintroducing great sacred music of the past—Palestrina, Lassus, Bach, or still others—into a living musical repertory. Bach proves especially revealing here. Let us recall that Felix Mendelssohn's revival of the *St. Matthew Passion* took place in what we would essentially consider a concert hall, although one admittedly not without certain numinous, if not specifically Christian, references: the Singakademie in Berlin, whose architecture unmistakably evoked the Greek temple. No less to the point, Mendelssohn's performance, notwithstanding its advance characterization by Adolf Bernhard Marx in the *Berliner Allgemeine Musikalische Zeitung* as a 'high religious ceremony' rather than a mere 'artistic celebration', removed the music from its original liturgical framework; and despite sporadic efforts over the years, the music has never made its way back into the liturgy. The church concert, in effect, sought to square the circle, returning the music to its native architectural habitat, even if this now functioned in effect as a stage set for a modern, secular ritual.

With an edifice like AMUZ, dare I say, the circle turns yet again: a functionally secular space but one whose history, architecture, and decoration still give it a sacred 'feel'—a modern colloquialism that I use here advisedly. We find AMUZ appropriate, even reassuring. For despite the best efforts of scholars and, especially, performers to keep us aware of the secular—sometimes very secular—products of composers from the Baroque era and earlier, the heritage of the Caecilian movement or the Bach revival still leaves us with at least a residual sense of something inherently religious about early music: we may have no objective reason to consider a fugue from the *Well-Tempered Clavier* 'sacred', but more than a few do so nonetheless. Of course, reflection provides some justification for their instinct: sacred music, like sacred history painting, long occupied the highest rungs on the hierarchy of its particular art, and by the early sixteenth century, elaborate imitative polyphony not so far removed from that of the *Well-Tempered Clavier* formed the bedrock of sacred composition. But the link remains tenuous at best; and in any event, none of us thinks about these things when attending a concert of early music in a church: we simply like it there. Our unarticulated belief in some sort of innate connection between music and architecture would thus seem to represent merely a trace element of historical conditions long vanished and accessible to us as little more than nostalgia.

Yet the argument has one more twist. Whatever kinds of space Josquin, Bach, or even Mozart could have had in mind when composing their music, and whatever the spaces in which their contemporaries heard that music, the range of possibilities obviously did not include the concert hall as we know it: even leaving aside questions of liturgical versus 'concert' presentation, Bach, say, could no more have conceived of a building like the Amsterdam Concertgebouw than he could have anticipated the Steinway piano. This clearly separates 'early music' from most of the repertory that makes up modern concert fare: we hear the orchestral works of Mendelssohn, Mahler, Stravinsky, and so forth for the most part in precisely the acoustic and architectural environment for which its composers intended it, or at the very least in linear descendants of such environments. Seen from this perspective, AMUZ, even the functioning church of the right age, becomes something less than an exercise in nostalgia after all. The sacred penumbra might not matter, might even foster an element of self-deception. But measured against most concert halls, structures closer in time to the music, or at least closer in design and style to structures from the time of the music, may well provide a more suitable fit.

This fit, however, may not extend to the kind of programme Cappella Pratensis and I put together. Not a few scholars, critics, and musicians have decried the habit of presenting 'early music', especially sacred compositions from the Middle Ages to the seventeenth or eighteenth century, in a format that allegedly deprives them of all meaningful context—which, from this point of view, amounts to all meaning *tout court*. Indeed, with regard to the fifteenth and sixteenth centuries, some scholars have even chided other scholars for focusing so much energy on the sort of music we chose to perform. The exquisitely sophisticated art of a Josquin or a Mouton, they remind us, represents only the tiniest, most atypical sliver of medieval musical life, not least in the church. If we wish to get back to music as it really existed in, say, the churches of the southern Netherlands in the fifteenth century, we should worry less about refined polyphony and more about late plainchant and *cantus planus binatim*, the modest holdover of the Notre Dame conductus. Similarly, if not so extreme, we have seen the rise of performances that seek somehow not just to recreate 'the notes' of a given work or body of works but to re-embed those notes in a thicker web of reclaimed cultural experience—sometimes, indeed, to the point where 'works' and composers themselves fade into the background or disappear entirely. Whole-scale, perhaps even wholesale, 'reconstructions' of events in fact more imagined than documented have become something of an order of the day. We can hear Palestrina's *Missa Papae Marcelli* as arranged in early seventeenth-century Rome as part of a quasi-service replete with generous helpings of *falsobordone*—although lacking a sermon or any other verbal matter. Less radically but more frequently, we do not merely sing and play our way through the various items of what we habitually call 'Monteverdi's Vespers of 1610' but seek to restore them to their supposed liturgical place, with Monteverdi's concerted pieces garnished with the chant and perhaps instrumental items that we presume went with them in the composer's time. We do not, of course, attend an actual church service. Indeed, the 'Monteverdi Vespers'—and, for that matter, the *St. Matthew Passion*—could not really find a home in such a service today: both the Catholic and the Lutheran church have moved too far from earlier centuries to accommodate this music any more. So the 'liturgically correct' Vespers becomes, in the end, another concert, its avowedly historical trappings more a kind of cultural tourism than a means to a true immersion in a temporally distant world. Not surprisingly, such renderings of the Vespers as often as not find their ultimate home on CDs.

II

But if 'reconstruction' and 'concert' represent not so much opposite ends of the spectrum as two sides of the same, contemporary coin, they nevertheless seem to reflect different motives. I think we might find these motives worth some contemplation—both in themselves and in how they play out in our performances. The motives of the concert prove easier to discern, if only because they have had such a long tradition with us. When, as with Cappella Pratensis at AMUZ, we isolate a group of Renaissance motets from whatever framework they occupied in the era of their creation and present them essentially as autonomous musical objects, we align them, at least implicitly, with the repertory that has formed the backbone of 'serious' musical culture since the nineteenth century: with 'masterpieces', defined as works of transcendent artistic value that retain their aesthetic power in context or out. Naturally, we understand that 'transcendent artistic value' in fact depends on a number of things—not least political and religious ideology—that go unaccounted for in the canons of 'absolute' musical criticism. The revival of the *St. Matthew Passion*, to return to an earlier example, could hardly have taken place unless carried along by broader currents then moving German society as a whole. Yet whatever considerations go into shaping aesthetic judgment, aesthetic judgment still has an identity and force of its own; and Mendelssohn, who surely knew a well-composed and effective piece when he saw one, must have responded to the *Passion* in the first instance with no conscious awareness beyond that of musician and composer. Similarly, although many in the audience at the Singakademie on 11 March 1829 had presumably come primed for an epoch-making event by Marx's articles in the *Berliner Allgemeine Musikalische Zeitung*, their response surely cannot have fulfilled his prophecies as it did unless they felt that Bach's music—which for them, of course, meant words as well as notes—spoke to them on a very profound level. No amount of aesthetic propaganda will have much effect if the work itself cannot deliver the goods: let us not forget how 'many people of all ranks', at the Medici wedding festivities of 1600 who, as Emilio de' Cavalieri observed, found Caccini's lavishly produced *Rapimento di Cefalo* 'tedious...like the chanting of the Passion'. Bach had to do something right for Berliners in 1829 to find *his* 'chanting of the Passion'—which in fact dominated Mendelssohn's performance, as many of the arias, ariosos, and chorales fell victim to cuts—so compelling.

At first sight, what we might mischievously call the aesthetics of the reconstructionist event stand in complete opposition to those of the modern concert. The attempt not merely to sing or play music but to set it in a multi-dimensional recaptured past clearly takes us away from 'masterpieces'—if not always from the objects themselves, then certainly from the aura of aesthetic autonomy that surrounds them—to give us something 'more than music'. Yet reconstructions, for all their historicist justification, still tend to remain more than a little under the sway of aesthetic judgments and traditions not necessarily close to those of the lost times in search of which we have embarked. We have seen how the evening of Palestrina and *falsobordone* stopped short of bringing the speaking clergy onto the scene. Clearly, this represented an artistic choice: to recapture something of the sensation of hearing the music in its seventeenth-century context but not overstepping the bounds of a purely musical event—a concert, in other words. By the same token, I suspect that an evening of *cantus planus binatim* and chant, the sole adornment of the liturgy in many places right through the fifteenth and even later centuries, would not cause the heart of even the most ardent contextualist to beat faster—or at least would not have done so before the rise of minimalism. Indeed, if we think of it, minimalism and the cultural shift it represents could well have set the stage for the revival of simple polyphony or extended medieval monodies in the first place. But whatever the case, aesthetics, not the historical past—and certainly not liturgy, let alone the belief system on which it rested—proves decisive.

Indeed, I would argue that aesthetic judgment plays an even greater role in the reconstructionist project than the foregoing examples suggest. For such judgment lies at the root of the decisions we make as to what we present as 'autonomous music', what as part of a 'reconstruction', in the first place. If we wish to restore *cantus planus binatim* or *falsobordone* to a place in our musical consciousness comparable to that which they held in the consciousness of earlier days, we hardly have a chance to do so except as part of a more embracing context in which these items become just one of several elements, not all of them necessarily musical. In such a situation, 'more than music' means 'more than *just* music', with that slightly dismissive 'just' understood as applying less to all and any music than to the particular music at hand. To put it simply, we fear dullness. No such worries, however, attend a presentation of the *St. Matthew Passion* or, for that matter, Josquin's *Miserere*—dull as some performances of both may become. Longstanding critical and scholarly acclaim has conditioned us to regard these pieces as music that can stand on its own, divorced from its original context—which again, especially in the case of the *Miserere*, we can determine only very imperfectly at best anyway. But as with Mendelssohn and his Berlin audience in 1829, we find enough within the notes and words left us by the composer to bridge the yawning distances that could otherwise seem to make this music inaccessible to us.

III

As others before me have pointed out, a concert performance of the *St. Matthew Passion* or the *Miserere* in effect turns such music into the equivalent of paintings in a museum or, if you will, animals in a zoo. I shall not get into the charged question of whether the snow leopard at the Antwerp Zoo looks less noble and fearsome than it would far from our gaze in its native habitat—assuming, in counter-Heisenbergian fashion, that we could not only get to see it there but that our presence would leave its essence completely untouched. But I should like to pursue the matter of paintings a bit further. More Rubens altarpieces now adorn the walls of museums than the altars of churches—and we do not necessarily think ourselves, or them, poorer for that. The *Coup de lance* may well speak to us differently at the Royal Museum of Fine Arts than it might have at the Church of the Récollets. Yet the difference, I suspect, has less to do with the change in setting than with the changes in our consciousness wrought by almost four hundred years of history; and in any event, I also suspect that any difference amounts more to one of degree than one of kind—how much more searing an impression can the painting make whatever the circumstances? Of course, we all feel grateful that the *Descent from the Cross* remains in Antwerp cathedral. But although not a few viewers in Rubens's time doubtless marvelled at the painting 'in and of itself', and indeed could well have crossed the threshold of the cathedral expressly for the purpose of seeing it, the totality of painting and context still had a very different meaning for them—and a meaning that we cannot recover, not least because we do not in fact know just where in the cathedral the *Descent from the Cross* originally stood. Not only that: although we today unquestionably find our experience of the painting enriched by seeing it in the cathedral, I hope no-one will accuse me of blasphemy if I suggest that most of us, on reflection, would regard the setting as in effect the icing on the cake. The painting gains from its surroundings; but its power over us does not depend on them. From that perspective, Antwerp cathedral functions in relation to the *Descent from the Cross* in much the same way as, if on a much greater scale than, the stylistically appropriate frames or wall hangings with which curators seek to enhance our response to works in their museums.

Still, whether or not the de-contextualization through which we continue to experience most of the art, music, and exotic animals we come across diminishes the objects it puts on display, some viewers or listeners certainly feel diminished by it—and not just in connection with what we might regard as 'lesser' musical products. Yet this sense of diminishment, and the concomitant urge to re-contextualize, may themselves grow out of much the same aesthetic impulses, and not least the same aesthetic fears, as I have already touched on. The 'Monteverdi Vespers' provides a case in point no less timely now than when I first wrote these words, 400 years after its contents first appeared in print. The assumption that the Psalm settings and concertos sent to the press by Monteverdi in 1610 require a liturgically appropriate completion today implies that the music as left us by the composer somehow remains incomplete, even inadequate, in a fashion that no-one would suggest with the *St. Matthew Passion*. This anxiety itself, moreover, depends to no small extent on the presupposition of a 'complete', 'unitary', fundamentally continuous major work—a presupposition shaped not least by pieces such as the *St. Matthew Passion*.

I shall leave aside the question of how appropriately the concept of the unitary work applies to the 'Monteverdi Vespers' except insofar as I always surround those two words with scare quotes. But the question of incompleteness demands some further consideration. As commonly rendered in the last few decades, Monteverdi's succession of Psalm settings and sacred concertos has become rich fare indeed, with choral and solo vocal forces alternating in often kaleidoscopic fashion and a lavish continuo group shifting colours at a no less quicksilver pace. It almost seems as if we need the more ascetic chants to cleanse our palettes; at the same time, however, those chants in turn seem almost to make such an extravagantly coloured rendering of the Psalms and concertos all the more necessary as a counterbalance.

In practice, in other words, the 'Monteverdi Vespers', while certainly an acknowledged 'masterpiece', winds up occupying an uneasy middle ground between what we comfortably—perhaps too comfortably—regard as self-sufficient pinnacles of art complete in themselves and those cultural productions so beholden to their original context as to lose stature in its absence. No less than with the more obvious instances considered earlier, I sense anxiety here. What would happen if, say, we returned to Monteverdi's publication and took it at its word? Especially if we look at the original partbooks rather than a modern score, we can recognize clearly that Monteverdi nowhere distinguishes between 'choral' and 'solo' voices, and that his Bassus generalis nowhere signals the presence of any instrument beyond the organ. Conversely, if we trace the modern performance history of, and commentary on, the Vespers back to its start in the 1940s, we can recognize the extent to which the conviction that Monteverdi's few indications of vocal and continuo scoring point not to the simple default position of one to ten singers accompanied by organ throughout but to a glittering submerged iceberg reflects not so much genuine evidence from contemporary sources as a kind of circular logic dictated in the end by the fear that we would find the music insufficiently interesting without the sort of intervention I have described. Perhaps we would. Once we get past the fanfares of the opening respond and the ritornellos of the 'Dixit Dominus', after all, we face a long drought of instrumental colour until the final three items—which come rather late to save the day, or rather, the evening. If we encountered all this as believing Christians in a real Vespers service in a real church, things might have seemed considerably better: there, the music, however much we may admire and respond to its own internal qualities, serves in the final analysis as the intensifier and capstone to an experience whose essence lies elsewhere. To a certain degree, I might add, this experience amounts to the opposite of seeing Rubens in church: there, we can focus on the work virtually to the exclusion of its surroundings should we choose to do so; here, the passage of time itself forces our attention away from the original items of Monteverdi's music.

But if the Vespers proves so wanting in a presentation lacking the inducements of so many performances today, why perform it in the first place? If we accept that Beethoven's Op. 131 doesn't need the kind of recomposition that modern tradition has accustomed us to take for granted as obligatory with Monteverdi, does this mean that we implicitly place the Vespers on a lower footing? Even if we change the footing—Beethoven represents 'absolute' music, Monteverdi more recognizably forms part of a liturgical or cultural fabric—the problem remains. Of course, Monteverdi never meant the Vespers to aspire to the same kind of status as 'work' that we take for granted with Beethoven, or with Bach. Yet beneath all our efforts at contextualization, the goal of our performances seems in the end to make good what we somehow regard as Monteverdi's deficiency. We doubt the efficacy of Monteverdi's music at the very same time we claim to affirm its value.

Despite what may have seemed like so much critical comment, I should like to close on a positive note or two. For starters, recent developments have already encouraged the conviction that we can do Monteverdi differently, and better: we have many wonderful singers nowadays, and we can place greater trust in them to carry Monteverdi's message without the crutches that might have seemed necessary only a couple of decades ago. Looking beyond this one example, moreover, I do not mean my exploration of what 'concerts' and 'reconstructions' hold in common with one another to draw invidious comparisons between them, and especially not to favour one over the other. I would even go further. If I have hinted that 'reconstruction' will inevitably wind up as a form of theatre rather than an 'authentic' cultural recovery, I do not mean this either as condemnation. For if we think about it, concerts, too, belong to the realm of theatre—as indeed does all communally shared spectacle. But whatever the context in which we present music—and the 'standard' concert programme, if less obviously 'contextual' than reconstructions, no less obviously constitutes a context of its own—our decisions about what music to engage with, and where and how to perform it, will embody a complex mixture of motives, many if not most of them submerged from daily view, and some of them perhaps at odds with the motives we consciously profess. I hardly intend to derogate any of these motives. Especially in the world of early music, however, we do well to subject ourselves to self-examination from time to time.

Abstract

Mediating between the past and the present has always presented a challenge to practitioners of early music. If they no longer face the charges of historical escapism, or even fetishism, that once burdened their existence, the recognition of how much they reflect predilections very much of our own time brings its new questions and problems. To what extent do we seek to 'recreate history'; to what extent do we choose to ignore it? Does our interest focus on contexts or on works—or does it do so differently under different circumstances, and if so, why? Consideration of this last dichotomy in particular suggests that, in practice at least, some currently favoured trends in presentation reflect criteria at odds with the motives that supposedly underlie them.

Contributors to this Issue

■

Aaron James is a doctoral student at the Eastman School of Music, University of Rochester, completing a dual-degree program (Ph.D./DMA) in musicology and organ performance. His previous studies were at the University of Western Ontario. His research focuses on issues of genre, theology, and devotional culture in the sixteenth-century motet.

Honey Meconi is on the faculty of the University of Rochester, where she is Susan B. Anthony Professor of Gender and Women's Studies, Professor of Music in the College Music Department, and Professor of Musicology at the Eastman School of Music. Her publications include *Pierre de la Rue and Musical Life at the Habsburg-Burgundian Court* (Oxford, 2003), *Early Musical Borrowing* (ed.; New York and London, 2004), and *Fortuna desperata: Thirty-Six Settings of an Italian Song* (ed.; Middleton WI, 2001), as well as other volumes and numerous shorter essays. She is currently writing a book on Hildegard of Bingen.

Hannah Mowrey Clarke recently completed her Ph.D. at the Eastman School of Music. Her dissertation examines intersections of music, art, and theology in the Habsburg-Burgundian manuscripts owned by Frederick the Wise, elector of Saxony. Clarke has presented her research at a number of conferences, including national and local meetings of the American Musicological Society. She currently serves as Director for the Center for Worship and Music at Redeemer Theological Seminary in Dallas, Texas.

Joshua Rifkin has performed and recorded extensively as conductor of ensembles ranging from the Renaissance vocal group Cappella Pratensis to major symphony orchestras, and especially with The Bach Ensemble, which he founded in 1978. He has also written scholarly studies on topics including Josquin Desprez and Johann Sebastian Bach.

Catherine Saucier is assistant professor of music history at Arizona State University. Her research focuses on late-medieval sacred music and clerical culture in the Belgian city of Liège, where she has conducted extensive archival and liturgical research. She has published articles in *Early Music History*, *The Senses and Society*, *Speculum*, and *Acta Musicologica*. Her monograph, *A Paradise of Priests: Singing the Civic and Episcopal Hagiography of Medieval Liège*, will be published by The University of Rochester Press in 2014.

Zoe Saunders is currently a postdoctoral fellow of the Research Foundation - Flanders (FWO) at the KU Leuven, where she is also associated with the Alamire Foundation. She received her Ph.D. in 2010 from the University of Maryland, College Park under the guidance of Barbara Haggh-Huglo. Her dissertation, *'Anonymous Masses in the Alamire Manuscripts: Toward a New Understanding of a Repertoire, an Atelier, and a Renaissance Court'*, provides editions and analyses of eight anonymous masses preserved in the Alamire manuscripts, as well as discussion of numerous codicological and paleographic elements in the entire Alamire complex. Her current research interests include the musical style and historical context of anonymous masses, performance practice, and the intricate relationships between patron, composer, and scribe. She has taught musicology at The Peabody Institute and Johns Hopkins University, the University of Delaware, and the University of Maryland, College Park.

Plates

Plate 1. Jena, Thüringer Universitäts-und Landesbibliothek, Ms. 22, fol. 102v. Virgin and Child with *Missa Sicut spina rosam* (Jacob Obrecht). Acquisition. Reproduced by permission